Ghouls and Gambits

K. Malady

To deadlines, for keeping us honest, and to loopholes, for keeping us entertained.

(From both Emily and the author—who can confirm neither of us is getting enough sleep.)

And just for posterity: as ever, this is not real law or lawyering. Except for the stubbornness and insomnia. And now add stress.

Also By

THE HARMONY CHRONICLES
NA paranormal romance/contemporary fantasy

THE ASCEND TRIALS
YA fantasy romance adventure

WELCOME TO THE TROPE-ICS
Sweet and spicy standalone romantasy novellas in an
interconnected world

THREADS OF FATE
NA/Adult romantic fantasy retellings

KNEELING KINGDOMS
Adult interconnected standalone romantasy

Gambit (n.)— a move in which something is risked, often sacrificed, to gain a greater advantage.

Chapter 1

I fan my cards like a stage-magician short on rabbits, trying to look casual while sitting in the heart of the northern vampire coven's game room—a retrofitted Victorian parlor that smells faintly of old velvet, candle wax, and something coppery I'd rather not identify. A battered poker table squats between brocade sofas, its green felt pocked with decades of fang marks where over-excited players forgot to retract.

Across from me, Stardust lounges sideways on a Louis-the-something chaise, all glittering cheekbones and glam-rock hair—dressed like he got lost on his way to a masquerade ball in the '80s and decided to conquer the city instead—shuffling his own deck at warp speed just to show off. Think *Labyrinth*-era Bowie—if Bowie had fangs, opinions on antique upholstery, and a habit of mocking vampires twice his age. He doesn't walk into rooms so much as *materialize*, in velvet, glitter, and judgment.

On the floor beside him, Ray rests his chin on Stardust's knee and hums a Zeppelin riff under his breath. He's human—emphatically so—with a warm tan, a relaxed smile, and a wardrobe that suggests he's either very chill or very late to laundry day. Ray is loyal, kind, and a little chaotic in a "forgot to charge his phone but will absolutely remember your birthday" kind of way. Newly moved in together and still radiating *honeymoon phase* sparkles, those two are basically an ad for mutual adoration—if that ad also involved blood bags and beaded curtains.

This is my job now: hustling potential clients over cards. Since I walked away from Johnson & Marcus and went independent, my office is either the sagging couch in my apartment or the back booth at Moonlit Haven. But each time I spread my binders across Severin's table, he looks like I'm staining a priceless rug. So I'm not sure how long that sticky pleather seat is going to welcome me.

And no matter how *famous* I became clearing Lucian's name, becoming *infamous* after blurting out Sara Harper's witch lineage in front of the entire Chicago coven council means some covens still treat me like a walking subpoena. Stardust volunteered to play plus-one slash bodyguard since the potential client is a friend of his.

I clear my throat, and let the cards snap together. "Go fish, gentlemen... and gentle-immortals?"

"The gender-neutral term is 'fangsters,' darling," Stardust purrs.

The vampire I'm actually here to court—Armand Aldana, elegant to the point of ossification—raises a snowy brow. He's got the vaguely translucent look of someone who's been dead long enough to forget how sunlight works, with a jawline that probably turned heads back when gentlemen wore gloves and women couldn't vote.

We're only ten blocks north of Lucian's coven, but it feels like a thousand miles: heavier drapes, darker humor, zero tolerance for strangers who once outed a secret witch by accident. Armand's problem—and my potential payday—is estate planning. He keeps swearing he'll draft a will before moving to New Orleans "once my last human cousin toddles off this mortal coil," but the *execution* part of 'executing a will' gives him analysis paralysis.

"I'm simply unsure," Armand says, folding his hands over the lapel of his midnight-black suit. "My eighth cousin is the only living relative I care about, and once he's gone, I plan to leave the city. But what does one *do* with a collection of antique snuff boxes and seven Louis XIV chairs?"

"Burn them," Stardust suggests, examining a ruby cufflink he definitely did *not* arrive wearing.

"Donate them," Ray says, elbowing him. "Someone handcrafted those gargoyles."

"They carved them drunk," Stardust murmurs.

I swallow a grin and lean forward. "You *do* need a will, Armand. Not because you plan on getting staked next week, but because eternity is unpredictable. I'm not just trying to cover next month's rent when I say this: everyone could use one. It's cheap insurance for your interests."

Armand taps the edge of his cards, then lays them down with a sigh. "Two pair."

"Gauche to beat the guest," Stardust drawls, folding what looks suspiciously like a full house. He glitters when the lamplight hits him, so *of course* he'd cheat beautifully too.

Armand snorts. But elegantly. Like someone who's been mildly amused by a lesser being and a reaction isn't worth the wrinkle. "Perhaps I'll leave *you* my favorite snuff box, Richard. As a conciliation."

"Hear that, love?" Stardust tells Ray, nose only slightly wrinkling at the mention of his original name. "Pick something out and we can pawn it for something pretty."

"You need a will," Ray chimes in, brushing Stardust's wrist as he pours more tea. They're inseparable post-cohabitation. I've never seen Stardust look more smug about anything in his life.

"Like rock and roll—I'm immortal," Stardust says, dealing us each a fresh hand.

"Couldn't hurt," I say. "If you... passed on... where would Ray be?"

"Devastated," they chorus, dissolving into mutual goo-eyes. I focus on shuffling.

"You can revise a will anytime," I remind Armand. "This isn't a contract in blood."

"Oh, well, then." Armand visibly relaxes. "Some of those supernatural deals give me nightmares."

"If you slept," Stardust says, now that he and Ray have left their own orbit.

I ignore him, focused more on my meal ticket for the next week. "Drafting a will is vanilla law, I promise."

Armand steeples his fingers. "The recent disappearances *do* help your sales pitch. I simply don't know..."

"Disappearances?" I ask.

Stardust waves a jeweled hand. "Fledgling season. January is amateur hour—fresh turns, old egos, too much champagne. Half the 'missing' are napping in linen closets learning not to drink the cat."

Ray's mouth tilts. "But a couple still haven't checked in."

Armand's nostrils flare. "What form of payment do you accept, Ms. Lane—blood, jewels, or paper?"

"Cash is king if 'paper' means dollars," I quip. "My account could use the workout."

The only thing keeping me from dipping into my savings is Montgomery and the few one-off cases like Armand's. With the mayoral race postponed, Montgomery hasn't sent me to a late-night fundraiser in a while, but he still has me talk up his interests at city council assemblies and zoning board meetings. He also tosses me the occasional small claims dispute or contract scuffle like breadcrumbs to a very tired, very cynical legal pigeon. It's not glamorous, but it keeps the lights on and my name in his books for the few 'big' things that come up.

Armand's face creases in horror. "You have... an *account*?" His eyes cut to Stardust. "Richard—"

"Human bank," Stardust answers for me. "Honestly, Armand, you need the will so it's cleaner when I eventually murder you for irritating me."

"What other kinds of accounts are there?" I ask.

"You don't want to know," Stardust and Ray say in perfect sync.

Even now I'm peeking through a window into a world I'll never fully enter. But that's the gig.

I slide a business card across the felt—white, simple: *E. Lane & Associates* (the plural is aspirational). "Shall we make this official?"

Armand studies it, then folds his hand and his indecision simultaneously. "Draft it. Everything—not counting sentimental bric-a-brac—is to be liquidated and placed in a trust for my eventual relocation. If I change my mind after the move, I shall... amend."

"Music to my rent check," I say, jotting notes on my phone.

Stardust claps once, delighted. "Splendid. Now can we *please* switch to euchre?"

"After what happened with that last trick in 1992?" Armand raises white brows. Or, raises them as much as his face allows. "Not on your unlife."

"I grew up with Spite and Malice," Ray says.

"I've never heard of it," Armand says, suspicion curling his voice.

"We called it Cat and Mouse," Stardust adds. You can practically hear the silent *idiot* tacked on the end.

"It's like solitaire, but meaner," Ray explains, eyes glinting. "You go head-to-head, racing to empty their decks onto shared piles. You can block each other, sabotage moves. All spite. All malice."

"Like law school in card form," I deadpan.

"Sure," Ray says, grinning.

Stardust flicks a queen of hearts into the discard like he's bored with humanity. "We'll save your vendettas for another evening, darling. Poker is brutal enough."

"Poker it is," I decide, dealing a fresh hand while rain taps the stained-glass windows.

The game moves on. Cards are dealt. Choices are made. I tell myself that's all this is: 52 chances reshuffled until something clicks. Deal enough hands, eventually you win one.

I just hope I'm still at the table when the stakes go up.

Chapter 2

Morning finds me at E. Lane & Associates' downtown head-quarters, a.k.a. my living room. Dirty laundry and empty takeout containers provided gratis.

The cursor blinks accusingly at me from the middle of the page, right between *"Trust Beneficiary Designation"* and *"Executor's Discretionary Authority."* I've read that sentence five times, and I'm still not sure if I'm drafting a supernatural estate plan or an ancient curse.

I toss the laptop aside, stretch out on my secondhand couch, and groan up at the ceiling. "This is fine. This is totally fine. I'm a very real lawyer with very real clients. One of whom sleeps in a crypt and wants to leave his fortune to… an airboat rental business in Biloxi. Who cares that I've never created a trust before?"

I eye the walls, hoping for a ripple of shadow or the clink of my still-missing silverware. Something, *anything*, to confirm Herle, the allegedly real wall-dwelling hobgoblin, is actually listening. Hobgoblins nest in old buildings. While mine is old like "may contain asbestos," not old like "brimming with charm," I've been told he's there. But hobgoblins only come out at their leisure. Or when someone knows the magic words to summon them. It certainly isn't *please*, as my own wall-dweller refuses to appear.

Which is rude, considering I've decided to make him the "Associates" part of *E. Lane & Associates*.

"You know," I say aloud, adjusting my laptop, "if you're going to keep living here without paying rent, the least you could do is help with client intake. I'm not picky—you don't even need a JD. I've been winging it half the time myself lately."

No response, only the soft hum of the radiator and the smell of slightly scorched espresso.

I start typing Armand's full name into the trust template. Even this feels a little fake, like I'm playing dress-up with actual contracts. I'm a litigator by trade—more comfortable tearing contracts apart than writing them. But, hey. This is the life I chose. Legally adjacent, morally flexible, and supernaturally weird. All to bring options to those left out of human law.

And, *fine*, to keep the lights on.

The mail slot clanks, a happy interruption from my drafting work. I peel myself off the couch and shuffle over to the door. The mail's the same as always—ads, coupons, bills with my name sharp in print. At least it's my name, right? Growing up, I never got to count on that. My parents didn't exactly make a hobby out of remembering me, not even when a card or a phone call would've been the easy part.

It makes you itch to put things on paper, official, undeniable—because once it's filed, someone has to admit you existed.

And then, something catches my eye. An envelope. Cream cardstock, embossed return address. *Mrs. Abigail Jennings, Prairie First Trust.* My recent acquaintance, who was quite useful in the Baxter mess. She collects exclusivity like some people collect action figures, and just so happens to be married into local banking royalty.

I tear it open with the confidence of someone who used to have an assistant for this sort of thing and skim the crisp pages. My heart does a little skip at the contents.

It took weeks of backdoor negotiations, three tea sessions *and* an enchanted brooch for Mrs. Jennings, and an impromptu dinner party with the Abernathys. An astronomical amount of effort for something most small businesses take for granted.

It's not technically a legal victory, but it's a win. Paperwork filed. Barrier breached. A supernatural business owner with no official identity is about to get a bank account. It's small, but real. A crack in the system. And *I* helped make it happen.

Severin will probably pretend not to care. Probably accuse me of smuggling in marketing materials disguised as federal banking forms. But this is a chance to get him—maybe others—on the books. Quietly. Legally.

It's a step. It's why I went out on my own. Cookie-jar accounting is just one way the supernatural stay sidelined from the human world, how they're othered. A bank account isn't only convenience; it's a paper spine: proof you exist in systems that only believe what they can reconcile.

I press the letter flat against the table, hoping the wood will absorb the validation and radiate it back to me later.

That's when my phone buzzes.

"Lunch. Today. Fifteen minutes. Election finally rescheduled." A text from Frances Montgomery.

I stare at the screen as if it's insulted me personally.

Because this is how it always goes with Montgomery, always old money and new problems. Around him, you're never sure if you've been recruited or indentured—only that you're suddenly playing in a league with higher stakes and better catering. He says "lunch," and what he means is "I need you to smile vaguely while city council members say things they shouldn't in front of you."

He likes having me at these meetings because I'm outspoken, moderately clever, and I don't scare easily. This is where the 'legal adjacent' part of my career started, going to fundraisers to be seen and ask questions. My lingering notoriety from outing the mayor as a murderer has turned me into Montgomery's favorite conversation piece. I'm a little scandalous, a little useful, and very, very available—for the right price.

I'd read about the new election date on a blinking sign on the back of a bus yesterday. They'd finally rescheduled the mayoral race for a few months from now. After the incumbent murdered his lead opponent in a stunning display of hubris and bloodlust, most viable challengers dropped out, leaving the city in limbo until things quieted down. I don't even know who the current candidates are.

Montgomery must smell policy opportunity, and apparently I'm the bait, clearly convinced I can charm whichever candidate survives the political arena into passing his preferred reforms.

But I'm *not* a lobbyist, I'm a lawyer who's hustling for "real" clients, even if today's matter happens to be a trust for a centuries-old vampire with a baroque-coffin collection and enough money to make a du Pont blush.

"Can't. Busy lawyering." I type, then hesitate. Last week's groceries were courtesy of setting up a Super PAC, the Solstice Foundation, for one of Montgomery's associates. Despite the fact that he's got big mob boss energy and an ac-

cent that only appears when he's trying to intimidate someone—Montgomery (and the friends he throws my way) *is* the only reason I was able to go out on my own.

"But feel free to send the details on whatever you need and I'll get started." I add a smiley face emoji for good measure.

"The car's already on its way. Wear something nice."

I mutter something unprintable and drag myself toward the bedroom. I throw on a blazer, pull my long hair back into its usual ponytail, pretend I'm not three seconds from feral, and make a mental list of questions *not* to ask during whatever this is.

Montgomery picked the restaurant, obviously. It's the kind of place with tablecloths thicker than my comforter and menu prices discreetly omitted, on the assumption that if you have to ask, you should be dining somewhere else.

He's already seated—corner booth, high-backed chairs, optimal view of every entrance. He looks immaculate, as always: tailored suit, silk pocket square, watch worth more than my car, glossy shoes I could check my mascara in if I wore any. Golden-brown skin, neatly trimmed beard, hazel eyes that clock exits and weaknesses in the same glance. He's sipping espresso and eyeing the room like he's conducting surveillance. Everything about him says investment with teeth, with a vibe that's half velvet glove, half brass knuckles, and manners that make servers teleport. Honestly, if a violinist appeared from behind the curtain playing something moody and dark for his personal soundtrack, I wouldn't blink.

"Emily," he greets warmly, waving me into the chair across from him. "Glad you could tear yourself away."

"I live to serve," I say dryly, unfolding the pristine napkin onto my lap. "What do you need?"

"Need?" He feigns surprise. "I simply enjoy your company."

"And I enjoy root canals," I reply. "But we both know why we're here. Let's skip to the part where you pretend I'm the plucky young lawyer you bring to make yourself more 'relatable' with the common man, and I pretend I'm here because you need someone who can quote statutes while holding a glass of cabernet, instead of the *real* reasons."

His smile doesn't quite reach his eyes. "You wound me."

"Only emotionally."

He takes a slow sip of his espresso, glancing toward the maître d' like he's checking for backup. "There's a dinner next week. Private residence. A few donors, one council member, possibly a judge. The kind of thing where it helps to have someone at the table who can deflect questions with charm and minor legal threats."

I suppress a groan. "Montgomery. I'm a lawyer."

"And I pay handsomely," he reminds me, not missing a beat.

I eye him over the rim of my water glass. "You know I'm not a lobbyist, right?"

He shrugs. "You're adjacent. And let's be honest—you're far more effective than most people who actually wear the label."

I can't argue with that, which is irritating. Damn my mouth.

The server appears, somehow managing not to sneer at my off-the-rack blazer, and takes our order. I point to the chef's special because the last time I asked for a price somewhere Montgomery took me, the server offered me a separate menu with fewer adjectives and smaller words.

Once she's gone, I lean in. "Who's the target this time?"

He chuckles softly. "Target's a strong word."

"Uh huh."

"It's about relationships," he says. "Strategic ones. This mayoral race is unstable, and no one's sure which way the wind is blowing. Everyone's trying to position themselves behind a frontrunner who might actually survive the election. One of them, I'm interested in."

I tilt my head. "Someone sensitive to your needs?"

The specifics of which even *I'm* still guessing about. Something supernaturally friendly, sure. But other than that? He's playing twelve-dimensional chess, and I'm the pawn he sometimes turns into a queen.

"We'll find out. There are at least two who might understand... nuance." He says it lightly, but there's weight under the word. "Politics are unpredictable. Every dinner counts. Every room we're in matters. And you, Emily, are memorable."

"Infamous, you mean."

He smiles faintly. "Same thing these days."

There's a beat of silence as our drinks arrive. I stir mine idly, watching the shimmer of something herbal and expensive swirl in the glass.

"I'm not your fixer," I say, so I can have it on record I said it. "Or your pet lawyer with a punchy soundbite."

"No," Montgomery agrees easily, "you're something rarer. The supernatural-human line is fraying. To make sure that line doesn't snap somewhere inconvenient, I need someone with credibility in both worlds. Human enough to be trusted. Supernatural-adjacent enough to be useful. And reckless enough to say what everyone else is too careful to admit."

I snort. "So I'm your chaos goblin with a law degree."

He smiles, as if I've proven his point. "Exactly."

A month ago, I might have asked who sent him to me. And how they knew I'd be willing to play his game. How they knew I'd end up here, solo and supernatural-focused. But now I just take a sip and try not to grimace at how good it is. "You're lucky I like expensive appetizers and having my rent paid."

"Luck has nothing to do with it," he replies, leaning back. "I chose you for a reason. And I keep my people close, Emily."

That's when the conversation shifts—softly, like a pressure change in the room.

"If you ever find yourself in need," he says, gaze steady, voice deceptively casual, "I can help. Not just dinners and campaign donations. Bigger things. Favors. Introductions. The sort of assistance that doesn't require a paper trail."

I pause mid-sip. Not because I'm shocked—Montgomery has always given off 'mob consigliere with excellent skincare' vibes—but because of the way he says it. Calm. Measured. Like he slid a live grenade across the table and was waiting to see if I'd pull the pin.

"I'm good," I say finally. "But I'll keep that in mind."

He clinks his glass lightly against mine. "To the future."

I smile back. But my stomach twists just a little. Because I don't know if that was a promise, a warning—or both.

CHAPTER 3

The booth at Moonlit Haven rocks slightly when I drop my bag onto the cracked vinyl. It's a wobble that says "well-loved" if you're generous and "on the verge of collapse" if you're honest. Luckily, I'm both.

I slide a manila envelope onto the table, the reason for my impromptu visit. It's addressed to Severin, in my neatest handwriting... mostly so he can't find another reason to be irritated with my presence.

He appears the way he always does: silently, and with the judgmental energy of a librarian who's caught you dog-ear-ing pages. He looks like someone Photoshopped a magazine ad onto a Prohibition mugshot, all golden hair, chiseled features, and eyes that don't miss a damn thing. He doesn't smile unless he means it, and he doesn't serve you unless you're supposed to be here. His bar caters to supernaturals, supernatural-adjacent, and humans too enchanted or obliv-ious to know which side they're on—and Severin keeps them all in line with a raised eyebrow and a bottle of something potent.

Lately, he tolerates me the way you tolerate a grackle that's moved into your window box—annoyed I'm still here, re-signed I'm not leaving.

"Ms. Lane," he says, setting down a glass of water and a black coffee. No matter how whimsical Moonlit Haven's nightlife can be, Severin's always all business.

"You've got mail," I say, nudging the envelope toward him.

"I wouldn't let that Fulton character put up campaign flyers, I won't let you—"

"It's a bank application," I interrupt, swallowing my eye roll. *He is letting me take up an entire booth for hours at a time*, I remind myself. "Prairie First Trust. Mrs. Jennings is on the board, and Ethel Abernathy's husband runs risk compliance. They've quietly opened a supernatural program. Pilot only, for now."

He doesn't sit. Just eyes the envelope like it might sprout teeth.

"Why?" he finally asks.

"Because having to keep your tips in a jar behind the bourbon isn't exactly dignified," I say. "And because you deserve better than under-the-table, off-the-books, and one step from hexing your accountant."

He peels the envelope open with deliberate fingers. He doesn't look at the paperwork inside, just stares at the flap like it insulted his bloodline.

"They'll let me open an account?"

I smile. "Limited ID, limited precedent, limited risk. But yes, real routing number and everything."

He gives a skeptical nod and slides the envelope into his back pocket. "You could do better than this booth for an office." It's Severin's version of a thank you.

"You could let me put advertisements in your front window," I reply.

His lip twitches, which for Severin is basically a belly laugh. "No."

"Didn't think so." I drain my water, slide my bag over my shoulder, and take my coffee to go. I've got two more errands and a rapidly approaching electric bill deadline.

As I reach the door, a man steps in and holds it open for me.

He's standing just inside the door, framed by the golden lamplight, and for a second, I wonder if my brain hired a casting director and hired a brooding actor from a black-and-white rerun. He's tall, with the kind of build that suggests tailored suits and quiet threats—broad shoulders, slim waist, long legs, the whole Cary Grant starter pack, if Cary Grant had a nervous texting habit and less patience for streetlights. His overcoat is gray and perfectly fitted, just brushing his knees, with gloves still on like he's either just come in from the cold or just doesn't trust the room.

His hair is dark, slicked back as if it were styled to imply recklessness without ever actually achieving it. His jaw could've been cut from marble, and his mouth—God help me—looks like it's been practicing half-smirks since the 1920s.

But here's the kicker: he looks twenty. *Maybe* twenty-one if he's trying to impress a bartender.

"Ms. Lane?" His voice is smooth the way vinyl records are—nice enough until the needle scratches.

I pause, coffee halfway to my mouth. "Yes?"

He offers a gloved hand like he expects me to kiss it. "Victor Little. I was told you're the sort of lawyer who doesn't flinch when things get... complicated."

I don't take his hand. But I don't step back either. "Depends on who's telling you. And what kind of complicated."

Behind me, Severin is polishing a glass that definitely doesn't need polishing, eyes tracking the newcomer with the faint interest a hawk gives a rabbit. At least I know if this guy tries anything, he'll be removed with the efficiency of a man who organizes his sock drawer by tone. It's a welcome change from when Sev used to be removing me from *allegedly* bothering his coven members.

Victor's other hand emerges, phone clutched tight. Screen dark, but he checks it anyway, a nervous tic that tells me this is serious.

He manages a smile that never reaches those ice-blue eyes. "The kind that involves contracts. Old ones."

I get a quick flash of tiny wings and glittery hair—my last 'contract case'—and suppress a wince. "Legal or magical?"

"A bit of both." He flinches when the neon beer sign outside sputters—tiny pop of electricity, tiny jerk of his shoulders. "Can we chat outside?"

He's charming. Generally polished. Clearly rich or pretending very well. If I didn't know better, I'd think he was a trust-fund rich kid with a vintage wardrobe addiction.

There's also something about him that hums—an energy, a presence. The way people who win too often move. Casual. Controlled. A little smug. Like he already knows the ending, and he's waiting for you to catch up.

No one that young carries themselves like that—like a man used to people folding under pressure, like he's already calculated how this conversation ends and has change for the toll.

Behind those barely hidden nerves, his eyes—cool, blue, and sharp. The kind that make you want to check your wallet and your pulse. And when he smiles, it's not young at all.

It's... tired. Like he's seen more than his face admits.

I follow anyway.

January slaps me in the face with a wind sharp enough to file teeth. Sidewalks gleam from the recent sleet, reflecting streetlamps like scattered coins. Victor sets a pace brisk enough to pass for casual, but his knuckles are white on the phone.

Finally, he cuts a sidelong glance at me, his breath visible in the chill. "I've heard you have experience with… unconventional contracts."

"You heard right," I say. "So, no need to be coy."

The phone again—still no alerts, still that brief, desperate glance. Whatever façade he's wearing, panic is leaking through the seams. When he speaks, it's still tentative. "I made a deal some time ago. A supernatural one."

"Magic isn't usually my wheelhouse," I say cautiously. "At least not directly."

He smiles faintly, as if I'd made a private joke. "It was more of a wager. A game of chance."

I raise a brow. "Cards or something more like yeti racing?

"Dice." He stops near a streetlamp, the yellow glow casting sharp shadows across his youthful features. "A century ago—give or take—I gambled with the House."

I stare at him blankly. "You're going to have to clarify."

"A supernatural casino, one of the House's enterprises," he says, his voice low, nearly a whisper, as though afraid someone—or something—is listening. "I won against it back when I was younger and luckier."

I eye him again. The eyes are the giveaway: something worn and experienced swims behind the panic there. Strip that out, and he could pass for one of the snot-nosed college interns trying to decide if being a lawyer is their life's passion. I'd never peg him as a centenarian. "I'm assuming your prize wasn't a brand-new car."

"I won time," he says. "Two human lifetimes' worth, to be exact. But there's a catch."

"There always is," I mutter.

He chuckles humorlessly. "When the contract was drawn confirming my prize, it defined a human lifetime as roughly sixty years. That's how long we were living back then. Two lifetimes meant around one hundred and twenty years. The House didn't account for advancements in medicine, improved standards of living... modern lifespans upping the average. Sixty years is outdated. We live closer to eighty now."

I nod slowly, the edges of the picture becoming clearer. "And?"

"With the terms... ambiguous." Another glance at the phone. "I need the contract negotiated."

"You want me to renegotiate immortality?" I can't keep the skepticism out of my voice. "With something called the House? Seriously?"

His answering smile is too quick, too brittle. "I hear you have experience navigating tricky situations."

"Yeah, tricky like zoning permits and werewolf family feuds," I say, frowning, suppressing how the latter left a jagged scar on my calf. "Not eternal life insurance policies."

"But you read fine print—both human and otherwise," he insists, tugging at a cuff that's already straight. "And you have connections. The House respects rules and traditions, Ms. Lane. It thrives on fairness—its version, anyway."

"And let me guess—you're not just hiring me to *review* paperwork. You want me to walk right into the lion's den and play negotiator."

His nod is rapid, almost frantic. "Is that a problem?"

I look away, sighing into the crisp night. It's always the pretty ones with the impossible requests. "That depends."

"On?"

"On how much you're paying," I say, "and how likely I am to survive this."

"Generously—very," he rattles off, voice cracking on the second word. "Respectively."

I rub my temples, already feeling a headache starting. "And you think walking in with a lawyer—particularly a human lawyer—will change their minds?"

"Not necessarily," he says, looking away from me. "But I believe it'll at least get me an audience I can't manage on my own. A chance to make my case."

I study him. "Your case?"

A swallow bobs in his throat. "My... circumstances have changed since the original agreement."

"In what way?"

He shifts his gaze back, jaw tightening minutely. "Personal ways. It doesn't matter. What matters is getting in front of them. Convincing them to reconsider."

"It'll matter if it impacts your case," I say slowly, carefully.

"It won't," he says too fast, too flat. "Trust me."

"I'd rather verify." I sip the coffee again, buying time. "Look, if you want me to argue contract terms with supernatural loan sharks, fine. But I don't like surprises. If there's something you're not telling me—"

"There isn't." He looks me squarely in the eye, perfectly controlled. "At least, nothing that affects your ability to negotiate."

I hold his gaze, not believing him for a second. But he's right: his secrets aren't my concern unless they become my problem.

"Fine," I relent. "What exactly do you need from me?"

"First," he says, relief creeping subtly into his voice, "I need you to review my original contract. Then, I need you to help me arrange a meeting with whoever runs the House. A chance to talk terms directly. Immediately."

"How long do we have until they try to collect?" I ask.

He checks his phone again—third time in one sentence—then shoves it away like it's a live grenade. "Time is of the essence. Every day adds to he—my risk."

I sigh quietly, more for effect than anything else. "I won't make any promises. Especially if they're as dangerous as they sound."

Victor's lips quirk up slightly, tired and sharp. "They are."

"Okay." I drop the empty coffee cup into a nearby trash bin. "Bring me everything tomorrow—six p.m. sharp—and we'll start there."

He winces, fingers tightening around his phone. "Could we meet sooner? Morning, maybe? Noon at the latest?"

I arch a brow. "My calendar's already stacked like Jenga, and the next piece that moves brings the whole tower down. Six is non-negotiable."

A flicker of frustration crosses his face. "This is... time-sensitive."

"Everything in life is time-sensitive," I say, folding my arms. "Unless someone's bleeding out, six stands. Use the day to gather every scrap of paperwork you've got. If you show up half-prepared, we're dead in the water anyway."

He exhales through his nose—half a sigh, half a surrender. "Six, then."

"Good." I turn toward the street, finding my clunker of a car by the curb. Before climbing in, I glance back. Victor hasn't moved, framed in the glow of the streetlamp, jaw set, phone clenched like a lifeline.

Whatever clock he's racing, it's ticking loud enough for both of us.

CHAPTER 4

I settle back into my usual booth at Moonlit Haven, tapping a pen restlessly against the chipped wood.

In the corner, Rebecca—my favorite succubus, onetime client, and occasional drinking buddy—has already selected tonight's entertainment. Her latest—early thirties, glasses, three undone buttons and the lost expression of a man whose soul is in escrow—laughs nervously as she twirls a lock of white hair around her finger. I raise a brow, and she catches my eye, grinning like the cat that's about to charm the canary into giving her his credit card and sexual energy.

"Busy night?" I call.

"Research," she purrs, voice like warm honey and mild threats. "You know how it is."

"I'm a lawyer, Rebecca." As rare as my real legal work may be these days. "Not a biologist."

She winks, showcasing the kaleidoscope colors in her eyes. "You're missing out."

Before I can volley back, Victor tumbles into the opposite seat.

He looks tired tonight, the crisp edges of his charm softened—but still like he's five minutes from a 1930s cologne shot. His gloves are off, tucked into his coat pocket, and when he reaches into the inside lining, I expect a folder.

Instead, he slaps down a single, yellowed flyer printed in bold Art deco lettering—the gesture a fraction too hard, like his control slipped. I glance at it, then at him, brows raised.

"This isn't a contract," I say slowly, picking up the flyer. "This looks like an invitation to a Gatsby-themed speakeasy."

THE HOUSE OF CHANCE
Presents an Evening of
DECKS • DICE • DESTINY
Friday, February 13th, 1925
Underground Location Provided
—by Invitation Only—
Dick Fritz will find you
Step Through Our Doors and Stake a Life

The last line makes my stomach do a slow roll, tempered by the name of the so-called finder. Beneath the tagline, a stylized ace of spades with a "C" in the center, a logo I don't recognize and already hate.

"It's from the casino," Victor says quietly. "From Prohibition. Back when they advertised openly, at least to the right clientele."

"Lovely." My tone is flat. "But where's the actual paperwork? You know, the fine print we were going to read together?"

He reaches into his coat again and sets something on the table with the gravity of a man offering a sacred relic.

A tiny brass key.

I stare at it. Then at him. "That is *also* not a contract."

"No," he agrees, solemn. "I don't have it with me."

"You don't have it." I repeat the words slowly, hoping clarity will appear if I emphasize each syllable. "Victor, you're asking me to negotiate immortality terms without giving me the actual immortality contract?"

"I *will*," he says, uncharacteristically defensive. "Hence the key. It's to a storage unit in River North. The contract's in there."

My brow twitches. "You were supposed to *bring* me everything."

"I promised everything you *need*." His tone stays level—only the quick flick of his eyes toward the bar's entrance betrays unease. "The key and location are that."

"Victor."

"It's all in the unit. You'll just need to dig through it."

I blink. "How much is in there?"

"A hundred years' worth of paper. Receipts, letters, betting slips." A ghost of a smile scurries across his youthful features. "I was thorough."

"Of course you were," I mutter. "Dig through a century of historical clutter, Emily. It's in there. Somewhere. Like saying, 'Sure, the gold's in the landfill—bring a shovel.'"

What *is* it with supernatural contracts? People don't keep scans? At least this time, I'm digging through a dusty storage unit instead of stealing the document out from under a pixie with an undisclosed penchant for revenge. I still flinch around winged creatures. I haven't been to the Butterfly House since.

"Fine," I say, already resigning myself to an irritating chore. "I've got time to search tonight. What else would I be doing on a Friday? Spa night? Hot date? Actual legal work?"

I pluck the key off the table and hold it like it might bite me.

"We'll set up the meeting for the end of next week," I add, already mentally rearranging my calendar-slash-chaos board. "That should give me enough time to find the thing, strategize loopholes, and figure out how to contact the signatory."

Surely one of my supernatural friends will recognize the name. The House can't be *that* secretive...right?

"That's the second complication." He leans in; I catch the faint smell of cold sweat under expensive cologne. "You can't *find* the casino unless it wants you to or you're invited."

"You're joking." I stare at him, incredulous. "So, we can't even get a meeting, because we can't even find the damn place?" I toss the key back onto the table, letting it skid atop the flyer as I start rethinking all my life choices. "You know what? Just run." I'm only slightly kidding. "You're pretty, you're charming, and you clearly have experience staying a step ahead of anyone discovering your secret. The House can't chase you forever, right?"

Victor's expression darkens. "Yes, Emily, it absolutely can."

I frown. "Come again?"

He lowers his voice further, leaning in so closely I can see the faintest trace of stress lines around his youthful features. "The House has ghouls. They're... enforcers, of a sort. Debt collectors. If you gamble with your life, they ensure payment. *They* don't care about fairness, ethics, or loopholes, just the rules and their job. And they're frighteningly efficient at collecting debts."

"Ghouls," I echo flatly. I remember the first time I saw one in the flesh—at the joint coven meeting. She'd looked like someone had sculpted her out of ash and regret—cheekbones sharp enough to cut glass, skin the color of damp cement stretched too thin over her bones. Her hair had hung limp and black, like old mop strings, and her eyes glowed faintly orange, the kind of glow that said the fire was almost out. When she talked, her voice sounded like dried leaves scraping pavement.

Word was that ghouls had been the reason supernaturals were outed in the first place. When the first supernaturals were uncovered in prohibition times and the U.S. government caught wind of a creature eating people, they panicked hard enough to crack open the whole hidden world. The ghouls ratted out the rest of the supernaturals to avoid ending up in some black site containment unit, which... fair.

All that to say, it doesn't surprise me that they're working for something called the House. It's just another way to keep their claws bloody since the government restricted them from the real thing.

Victor's voice cuts back in. "They don't sleep, they don't relent, and they collect payment directly," he says grimly. "Life force, memories, years—whatever debt is owed, they'll extract it. So no, running isn't an option."

I exhale slowly, staring down at the battered flyer again, trying to ignore how thoroughly my night—and possibly my entire career trajectory—has just been ruined. "Okay. No running. So, our only hope is that the casino decides it wants a meeting?"

"Essentially," Victor says, frustration coloring his voice. "Unless we find them first."

I glance at him. "But... if the House wants their debt paid, and they send the ghouls—why not let them come to *you*? Let them drag you back and then I come with you. Or I follow. Or I negotiate *while* they're dragging you in. I've talked my way through worse." If I can argue with a county clerk about lost filings and live to tell the tale, I can manage a life debt collection.

"No," he says firmly. Too firmly. "That won't work."

I tilt my head. "Why not? If you're so collectible, then—"

"It's not that simple." His voice is calm, but there's a tension under it now, tightly leashed. "Once they dispatch collection, talks are over. We must go to them."

"Meaning we need an invitation." I drum the pen. "Any way to nudge them?"

"Recovering the original contract is a start." He exhales through his nose—controlled, but the micro-sigh tells me he's not sleeping well. "Are you still in?"

I eye the key on the table. Then the flyer. Then him. "I'm already holding the damn key, aren't I?" I snatch it up and drop it into my bag. "At this point, I should put 'supernatural retrieval expert' on my business cards."

Then, the air in the bar shifts. Subtle, but unmistakable. Like the moment before a storm breaks.

Lucian Belmont walks in. My erstwhile makeout buddy and recent friend. We've agreed—out loud, even—to be just that: friends. At least, that was the theory.

In practice? My pulse still stutters when he walks into a room. He looks the same: tall, tailored, all cool grace and quiet gravity. And for half a second, his gaze finds mine and holds.

Lucian is weaponized elegance. Always in cufflinks and a tailored coat that looks custom even when it isn't, he walks like he owns the ground under his feet—and maybe he does, metaphorically if not magically. Dark hair, sharp cheekbones, and eyes that could slice through pretense faster than I can cite case law. He hardly ever raises his voice, except against me, never breaks a sweat, and somehow manages to be intimidating without ever being impolite. He also has the unsettling ability to make you feel like the only person in the room—and like he's already weighed your soul and found it interesting, if not necessarily trustworthy.

That might just be a 'me' problem though.

Victor follows my gaze, and something flickers in his eyes—maybe tension, or something more complicated. He stands quickly, gathering the flyer and folding it with neat precision. "We should go."

As we hit the sidewalk, Victor hails a cab like it's still 1940.

I glance back—just once—and catch Lucian still watching from inside. His expression is unreadable, all calm control and quiet calculation, but when our eyes meet again, he lifts his glass in a faint toast.

I raise my eyebrows in return, because I don't do cryptic toasts without context, and make a quick little 'call me' gesture with my hand. Not that it'll help. He's one of the few supernaturals who still treats modern technology like it might bite—so unless he's planning to send a carrier raven, I'm not holding my breath.

Victor clears his throat, and gestures to the open cab door. I linger for a moment, wind tugging at my coat, staring at the brass key.

"I'm charging extra for this," I say.

"I expected nothing less," he replies.

As I climb in the cab, brass key cold in my palm, I decide his calm-under-pressure act is holding—barely—but that's good. Total panic never pays retainers on time.

And I bill hazard rates for storage-unit archaeology.

The River North self-storage complex doesn't look like a place that harbors century-old supernatural IOUs. It looks like the sort of place where overworked consultants stash kayaks they'll never use. Stacked shipping-container chic, security cameras on every corner, keypad gates. Totally normal.

Victor and I stop at the entrance. Steam ghosts from our breaths while he works the keypad: six digits, pause, eight digits, pause, then a third string. His hand is steady, but I catch the faintest hitch on the second code—like a pianist hitting a sour note no one else notices. Finally, the gate groans open with the enthusiasm of a cat dragged to bath time.

"Triple-layer password?" I arch a brow. "That paranoid?"

"Cautious," he corrects, giving half a smile that seems only slightly sincere. "Fake name too. You're speaking with Marcel Valentine."

"Subtle. Very Clark Kent."

"I get by."

I eye him and the outfit that costs more than the entire contents of my apartment. "Speaking of which—how do you actually *get by*? You look like old money, but if the bank statements in that unit turn out to be Monopoly cash, I'd like advance warning."

"Diversified investments, periodic art sales, a dash of good timing." He says it like a rehearsed line, but the cadence is smooth enough to pass inspection.

My brows raise. "In your own name or does Mr. Valentine do a little business on the side too?"

Victor gives a one-shouldered shrug. "Little's common enough. Never needed anything else official. Valentine's just for—" here his lips twitch into a frown—"security."

Supernaturals can't have bank accounts or own property without subterfuge (or weird legal loopholes that I'm currently exploiting). Victor's technically human, but someone pushing 130 years old would set off alarms at every financial institution. "Please tell me that isn't code for laundering."

"Nothing illegal." Beat. "Nothing *recent*."

I snort and follow him down a row of corrugated-steel doors, our footsteps echoing. He stops at unit 219, finally uses the key I've been clutching, and rolls the door up.

A wall of cardboard boxes stares back. Tall bankers' boxes, cheap plastics, battered leather valises. Some labeled, most not. A century's worth of receipts, betting slips, newspaper clippings, ticket stubs. Whatever his life's been, it weighs a few tons.

I flick on the overhead bulb; it sputters like a cheap horror movie prop. Rhett Baxter would be disappointed in the quality. "Okay, Mr. Valentine. Contract hunt—go," I announce.

Victor stays by the door, shoulders squared, eyes tracking the corridor. "You'll move faster with the paper. I'll handle logistics." His tone is even, but the way he shifts weight between polished shoes says he's measuring every second.

"And the ghouls? Any ETA?"

"Not tonight," he says, but the way his jaw tightens gives me zero comfort.

I kick myself for not bringing nitrile gloves as I slice open the first box. Ledgers. Yellowed invoices. I scan headlines: "Tivoli Club—Speakeasy Raid Netted Six" ... "Lucky Streak Little Cleans Out Back-Room House."

My phone timer dings every thirty minutes; I stretch, take a sip of stale water, and keep scanning. Box after box—roulette odds, cocktail napkin ledgers, letters from names I don't recognize. No contract.

By hour four, my knees ache, my back hates me, and I'm marinating in dust that might predate antibiotics. Victor hasn't complained once, but he also hasn't opened a single box—just shifts stacks as I empty them.

Halfway through box eighteen, I pause at a brittle newsprint sheet mounted on cardboard.

CHICAGO HERALD -18 May 1927- "Midnight Fête Funds Orphans' Library"

A flash-bulb photo shows tuxedoed Victor—hair slicked back, grin reckless—raising champagne with another man. The caption reads:

Mr. Victor Little & Mr. Brian Fulton celebrate the inauguration of the Equinox Educational Foundation at the Aragon Ballroom.

"Look at you, philanthropist." I angle the board his way. "Who's the dashing friend?"

Victor squints, brow furrowing. "Name rings a bell, but... honestly, no idea. Must've been one of a thousand benefactors." He hands the board back, already sliding another lid off a box.

"And what are you doing there?" I narrow my eyes. "You don't exactly scream 'civic booster.'"

He shrugs, casual. "Charity events were good cover for a while. No one asks questions if you're throwing money at schools and hospitals. You smile, you drink, you write a check, and people stop wondering why you've gone five years with the same facial structure."

"Right. Because nothing screams inconspicuous like tuxedos and champagne towers. You ever get tired of hiding in plain sight?"

He doesn't answer, just sets another box between us, the lid half off.

I study the grainy snapshot again. In this city, I guess you can change a haircut and pass for new construction. The skyline mutates, streets get renumbered, and everybody's too busy scrolling to notice a face that never seems to age.

Three more hours of dust inhalation later, a slim black envelope surfaces, sealed in glossy spade-shaped wax and sandwiched between two 1928 tax returns. *Honestly, Victor, the retention requirements are 7 years, not over 70.*

The seal on the envelope is unbroken wax, stamped with a stylized spade. "Victor. I think this is it."

He steps closer, focus sharpening like a camera lens. "Good." He reaches—then snatches his hand back as if the paper is a hot stove.

"You okay?"

"I can't touch it." He flexes his fingers, frown deepening. "Warding. House property can't be handled by the debtor after signing, unless a representative is present."

"And you thought to mention that *when*, exactly?"

"I hoped it wouldn't apply if the contract was dormant."

I give him my best you-have-got-to-be-kidding-me glare and slide the envelope out of its document sleeve. "Just so you know, every secret you've kept from me has doubled my hourly rate."

"Succeed and I'll buy you a new wardrobe."

I snort as I spread out the document on a stack of boxes. "Given my shopping tastes, you're getting the better end of that deal."

The ink shimmers, subtly shifting in the light—probably not normal ink. Possibly bat blood. Or something worse.

Because of course something called the House would use drama ink.

What the contract *doesn't* have is transparency.

"Everything's redacted," I say, gesturing to the blacked-out sections that take up a good two-thirds of the contract. Names, locations, dates—all blotted out in thick, censorship bars. "No party identifiers, no address, no governing jurisdiction. I have dust bunnies with more personality than this."

Victor tilts his head, frowning. "But it's the contract, right?"

"It's *a* contract," I mutter. "Or something like it." I skim the text again, heart sinking further. "This gives me no clue how to find the House, let alone who signed this. I was hoping for at least a map in invisible ink." I keep reading. "This says the Wagered Term expired the first of the month."

Which means our chance to negotiate just got slimmer.

"But the collection clause is in there?" he asks, and there's something too hopeful in his voice.

I flip to the clause near the end and read it aloud. "'In the event the Wagered Term expires without settlement or renegotiation, the debt shall be collected in accordance with standard House procedure, without prejudice or delay. Collection may include, but is not limited to, retrieval of remaining essence, estate reclamation through lineage, or alternate payment per the House's discretion.'"

I pause, reading it again silently. Then a third time, just to be sure.

"That's a blank check," I say slowly. "You said it was years of life. So long, Victor's youth. But this?" I tap the parchment. "This says they can collect however they want and whatever they want."

"I must've misunderstood," he says quietly. "I didn't read the fine print."

"You mean the *actual contract* you signed that's holding your immortality hostage?"

"I didn't go to law school, Emily," he says, hands in his pockets. "I saw years of life and stopped reading. I didn't exactly think I'd need a lawyer a hundred years later."

I sigh and rub my forehead. He has a point. This is the kind of clause that sounds like nonsense to a layperson but rings alarm bells in every legal bone in my body. He probably skimmed for keywords like "immortality" and "no refunds" and called it a day.

"Well," I say, straightening the page carefully, "I'll need to sit with it. Try to reverse-engineer what I can from the structure. See if I can figure out what got redacted or if there's a signature buried somewhere in the binding. But this... isn't going to be fast."

Victor shifts—only a fraction, but I catch the clipped inhale. "We can't spend days on guesswork."

"We're past the Wagered Term. Any chance we had to renegotiate expired at New Years. So, as long as you can continue avoiding the ghouls, there isn't a deadline."

"I—we can't dally."

"It's not *dallying*," I say, rather reasonably, if you consider it is *well* past midnight and I agreed to scrounge through a paperwork hoard for hours. "I have to unredact it. That's the only way to know exactly what we're dealing with and *maybe* discover how to contact the House." I frown as Victor starts to vibrate with tension. "Look, if you've got other ideas, feel free to share. It's not like there's magical bleach that will clear the redactions." As far as I know.

"Just cross-check it with the House Archive," he says, like it's the most obvious next step.

I blink. "The *what* now?"

His expression flickers—there's disbelief, then the mask resets. "The Archive. The official repository. You know—where they keep full copies of the House contracts. Originals, ledger records, adjudication notes. All that."

I just stare at him.

"Emily." He blinks. "You *do* know about the Archive?"

"Victor," I say slowly, "does it look like I know about the Archive?"

He opens his mouth. Closes it like an overly sophisticated fish. "I... figured someone like you would've—"

"Someone like me?" I echo, voice going razor-thin.

"A human with knowledge of supernatural contracts," he clarifies, measured but defensive. "I thought it was common knowledge."

"Victor, I'm a *human* lawyer who's been stumbling through the supernatural world like I missed the orientation packet and no one wants to send me the PDF." I jab a finger toward the contract. "If there's a mystical filing cabinet somewhere with all the answers, maybe lead with that next time."

He winces—an honest, fleeting crumple. "Fair."

"No, *not* fair," I snap. "It's been twenty-four hours and this entire case has been nothing but a scavenger hunt designed by Kafka. And now you drop 'oh by the way, the secret library of magical contracts exists' like it's common knowledge?"

Victor has the grace to look embarrassed. "Anyone in the community knows about it. You learn about the House, then the Archive. I didn't think..."

"Yeah," I mutter. "That's the problem, isn't it? You all assume I know the rules. That I'm *in* this world, not just standing awkwardly on the edge trying to fake my way through the costume party." Rubbing the backs of my hands against my eyes, I stop my etiquette meltdown in its tracks. "I'm sorry. I'm tired and apparently forgetting that you've got bigger things to worry about than whether your lawyer feels looped in. Where can I get into the Archive?"

His steady composure flickers again—this time uncertainty. "I'm... not sure. Debtors aren't granted access. Only House agents and recognized advocates."

I glance again at the contract—so carefully redacted, so aggressively vague—and try not to picture what's still waiting in the dark. "Game plan," I say. "I'll look for a way to get the contract unredacted. *Quickly*, Archive or no Archive. Now, let's get out of here before something with glowing eyes audits us."

Victor doesn't argue. He opens the gate, and we step out into the freezing night.

Behind us, the door to Unit 219 rolls shut with a groan. A century of secrets locked behind it. And one more I'll have to pry loose the hard way.

Chapter 5

I come to at 11:42 a.m. on Saturday with the corrugated imprint of a banker's box pressed into my cheek and enough dust in my lungs to trigger OSHA. Every joint complains when I sit up. Apparently one night in the historical-records cage now qualifies as extreme sports for thirty-something attorneys.

Glamour, thy name is supernatural law.

The cursed-contract folder is exactly where I left it—propping open the fridge so the light would help me read at four in the morning. It made sense at the time. I collect it, shove aside a desiccated banana, and shuffle to the sofa.

I should stretch. Or shower. Or ask Sara to give me a magical version of an ibuprofen, assuming that also exists. Instead, I scowl at the contract like it personally wronged me and resist the urge to throw it in the microwave.

Once upon a time I could pull an all-nighter, testify in court, and still make happy hour. These days my hangovers have a 48-hour recovery window. The only "vices" I've indulged lately are caffeinated drinks and the heavy bag at self-defense class. Healthier, yes. Enjoyable? Jury's still out.

I only drink socially. I don't smoke. And thanks to recent catastrophes, I've officially retired from recreational blood-letting—my questionable stress-management plan during the glory days of "Bill Every Hour Until They Make You Partner." Back when Tina was still... well, undead and kicking. I supplied the O-negative, she supplied the endorphin rush. Very tidy. Very transactional. Until tidy turned into one *actually* dead vampire and a lingering sense of guilt I still haven't shaken. Tina hadn't been a bad person. Or a bad vampire. She'd just... been there. And I'd needed to de-stress.

I thought the blood thing was casual. Turns out, it never is. Apparently, if you start donating regularly, it becomes a whole thing in vampire culture. A connection. A relationship. In vampire etiquette, that's basically "meet the parents" territory. No one told me that until after.

Lesson learned. Once you know the fine print, you don't break out the pen again. Unless you're ready to ante up in hemoglobin and develop a 'serious connection' all over again.

Relationships, therapy, hobbies—all optional. Work? Apparently still my drug of choice, even if I switched dealers when I quit the firm. So I decide to do what I do best: focus on work. With the patchwork contract in front of me, I try rearranging clauses. Sketching out contract structures. Holding it up to the light. I even try the lemon juice trick, because my brain is mush and I watched too many spy movies as a kid.

Nothing.

The only genuine lead is this scuttlebutt about an underground "House Archive."

So, I do what any exhausted counselor does: I text a friend for distraction. But with the contract glaring at me like I missed a filing deadline, I still make it work related. Ish.

"Know anything about secret supernatural archives?"

Matty responds in seconds. *"...are you high?"*

"Not currently." I type back.

"Is this a code for something?" I can imagine him pursing his lips, maybe running his hands through his tousled brown hair, trying to decide how serious I'm being.

"If it was, you failed the test."

There's a pause, three dots starting and stopping. *"Can I call?"*

He calls anyway.

That's Matty Barnes: Assistant District Attorney, serial over-achiever, and the only person I know who can quote both the municipal code *and* the Cubs' batting stats without breaking a sweat. He has this annoyingly magnetic "competent nice-guy" energy that short-circuits my sarcasm every time. He matches my late-night text spirals with deadpan one-liners, remembers how I take my coffee, and somehow makes debating evidentiary rules feel like foreplay. On the surface he's all khaki slacks and the Boy-Scout oath; beneath that taupe exterior is a technicolor brain that cross-examines the world—and lately, me—with the same relentless precision he saves for closing arguments.

"Morning, Counselor," I croak.

"Morning? It's practically lunch," he says, voice teasing, not his usual courtroom polished tone.

I flop back onto the couch. "Quick question: secret supernatural repositories. Got any leads?"

"A little context?" he asks, already tolerant—like this is the most normal Saturday conversation ever. But with me, lately, it is.

"Humor me. Anything come to mind? Supernatural document repository? Mysterious contract vault? Hidden Archive for the House?"

"You're assuming I get invited to the secret vampire librarian club. I barely got into Moonlit Haven for that Christmas party," he deadpans.

"Because you came *not* as a member of our legal justice league," I remind him, "but as yourself. In your work clothes. To a costume contest."

"I was *Corporate America, the Real Monster*."

"Okay," I chuckle. "Put your occult librarian hat on. Do you know anything about it? Something the DA maybe deals with when she's handling the important cases for our formerly murderous mayoral office?"

"Emily," he sighs, half amusement, half worry. "I deal in misdemeanors, not magical archives."

"Figured. Just covering bases." I try to keep it light, but he hears the fatigue.

"You sound wrecked. When was the last time you slept?"

"Does 6am this morning count?"

He chuckles, then softens. "Look, let me bring over real food and fancy coffee. We'll brainstorm the non-glamorous, totally human archive options."

The offer lands like a weighted blanket—comforting, a little dangerous. Matty isn't a fling-level distraction. He's... steady. I'm still learning how to let steady feel safe.

"I'd like that," I admit. "But no interrogations about my life choices until after caffeine."

"Scout's honor. I'll text when I'm outside."

"Thanks, Barnes."

"Anytime, Lane." He hangs up before the moment can get mushy.

I exhale, allow myself half a smile, and turn the contract toward the light again. Backup—caffeinated backup—is en route. That's enough steady for one morning.

A large coffee, three baskets of dumplings, and one well-intentioned Assistant DA later, I can confirm two things:

1. Matty Barnes is excellent Saturday afternoon company.
2. Matty Barnes is utterly useless at analyzing half-redacted supernatural contracts.

Our "strategy session" turned into a pseudo-date. Matty lined our soup dumplings into perfect rows, offered measured commentary on zoning scandals, and politely pretended not to notice me mainlining chili oil. Cute? Absolutely. Productive? Not unless you count the part where he insisted I open my fortune cookie first, and it said "seek knowledge in unlikely places." Thanks, pastry oracle—working on it.

Which is why, as dusk bleeds into Chicago's skyline, I'm swapping sweats for my least-dusty blazer and heading to Moonlit Haven. It's my port in the storm, with the next being the Underground.

But I wasn't joking about being afraid of pixies. So, the bar it is.

The place is rowdy as usual with luminous drink specials, werewolves wagering over darts, a woman in a feather boa crooning Sinatra in a minor key. I tighten my grip on the document sleeve that holds Victor's redacted contract and search for any familiar face that might have intel.

Lucian spots me first—lounging against a support column like he's posing for a menswear ad, midnight suit so sharp it could give papercuts, with an expression only read-able if you've passed Advanced Brooding 101.

The moment our eyes lock, his mouth curves, just a fraction, the kind of half-smile that, on anyone else, would promise either mischief or litigation. "Emily," he says, gaze dipping to the folder I'm clutching. "Still up to trouble?"

"Overtime's lousy, but trouble tips well." I nod toward my usual booth—miraculously empty. "Buy me five minutes of silence and I'll redirect my chaos elsewhere."

"Five minutes," he echoes, straightening—close enough that I catch his natural scent that makes all the live ones (present company included) swoon. "If you behave... perhaps ten."

We slide into the booth; the vinyl sighs under his immaculate posture. Before I can launch into my plea, he breaks the silence.

"Thank you for helping Severin with the bank account." His fingers graze mine as he hands over a crisp creme envelope—accidentally, purposefully, who knows—and the static makes my pulse misfire.

I eye the envelope and I'm almost shaking with how badly I want to rip it open. "Didn't peg you for the gratitude type, Belmont."

"I'm trying new things. One of my resolutions for the new year." A slow sweep of gray eyes—sardonic, but warm at the edges. "Perhaps you'll return the favor and try caution."

"And deprive you of entertainment?" I lean in, voice dropping. "Actually, I came hunting rumors—a House Archive, buried somewhere only the cool immortals know."

His smile withers. "How, precisely, did you tangle yourself with the House?"

I summarize the storage unit fiasco, the redacted contract, and my need for the Archive's control copy. "The client is convinced there's a primary copy in the House Archive," I say. "All I need is a peek. You must have a contact."

His expression shutters. "The House is a private syndicate, Emily. Invitation-only, sealed to outsiders, and fanatically protective of its ledgers. Even most elders aren't accorded that privilege."

"So, you've never been?"

"I make it a point not to be." He angles toward me, the din of the bar blurring into white noise. "The coven is safest when we operate *well* outside the House's reach. Particularly their casino. They trade on essence, favors, memories—anything that keeps the tables spinning. I'd rather my people stay poor in luck than rich in debt."

"Great PSA," I mutter, "but it doesn't solve my redaction problem. I need inside the Archive."

"Emily, you *need* to be careful." He lowers his voice. "The House has powerful backers, entities even I've never encountered. It's older than half the countries on your society's oldest map. It began as a gambling parlor for the gifted and the reckless, then built a bureaucracy to trap both."

"That's poetic. Useless for research, but it'll look great on a throw pillow."

"Poetry is all you're likely to find. I've never known anyone who wasn't working for the House or under their thumb to gain access to the Archive." Lucian leans back. "But if you're determined to dissect the text, enlist someone who can *see* through occult masking. Why not ask Sara? She could likely lift the obscurity on the pages."

"An autopsy on paperwork." I exhale. "That's... actually brilliant." With a pastry from her favorite bakery, maybe I can sweet-talk her into doing some magic. Pun intended.

"I am a good sidekick," he says, that earlier smile slowly reappearing.

"The Samwise to my Frodo," I say glibly. "You can carry me up a mountain anytime."

"I consider myself the Detective Inspector to your Miss Fischer," he says, one brow raised. "The televised version."

My brows follow suit, both rising in shock. "You watch TV?"

He smiles lightly. "Raymond set it up in the drawing room. The latest fledglings seem to appreciate it."

"Let me know when you graduate to texting," I tease, sliding from the booth. But his hand grazes my elbow, stopping me.

"Emily." The single word holds a sigh's worth of resignation. "I know you *will* chase the House."

I attempt innocence. "You don't know that." But it fails instantly.

He arches a brow. "I can easily plot your next moves: 'Step 1—gain unredacted text. Step 2—kick down the House's door.'"

"I don't *kick* doors."

He scrubs a hand over his mouth, halfway between 'kill me now' and 'try not to laugh.' "But you break into basements alongside violent werewolves," he reminds me.

I suppress a shiver at the memory. As far as I know, Rhett Baxter is enjoying the supernatural version of prison, *not* for what he did to me outside that basement, but for his coven interference. The supernatural world has layers I still can't even imagine and desperately want to uncover. Police, fae laws, some dark entity called the House that can barter immortality?

Yeah, Lucian's not wrong about my likely strategy.

"Fair," I admit. "I might be unscrewing hinges to get the doors open."

He gives a low, reluctant laugh. "That is my concern. If you do walk into the House, gamble with nothing you can't bear to lose."

"And what if what I *can't* lose is already on the table?"

Lucian's gaze softens, almost imperceptibly. "Then take allies who will tip the table over."

I tilt my head. "Volunteering, Belmont?"

"Try 'insisting.'" His fingertips drum once on the envelope between us. "You gather enemies the way mortals collect parking tickets. Let them face *me* instead."

Heat crawls up my neck—half annoyance, half something far more dangerous. "Protective streak for a non-coven member?"

"Call it enlightened self-interest. We did agree to be friends, did we not?" he murmurs, eyes like storm clouds over deep water. "Unless you're renegotiating."

The suggestion hits like a card slapped on the table. For a half second, my brain blanks, then I cover it with a laugh that wobbles more than I'd like. *Keep it together, Lane.*

"Flattery," I manage, aiming for breezy and hitting breathless instead. "Cheap tactic."

He notices; of course he does. One corner of his mouth lifts as if he's cataloguing the exact shade my cheeks just turned.

"Cheap," he repeats, low, "yet apparently effective."

The minute fades as he leans in, gaze steady. "Promise me you'll let Sara see the parchment *first*—and that you won't book a one-way ticket to the House without notice."

I mime crossing my heart. "Fine. No solo heists this week." I step away, then glance back. "Oh—and Lucian?"

"Yes?"

"Next time I flip a table, you're covering the damages—dry-cleaning, splinters, the works."

Lucian smiles faintly. "Send me the invoice. Replacing oak is easier than negotiating with the coroner. Especially without counsel present."

The noise of Moonlit Haven swallows me as I weave toward the door, contract tucked safely under my arm—and Lucian's warning echoing like a bass line beneath the music. Allies, tables, futures. I can almost feel the House counting the cards already.

CHAPTER 6

Candles flicker behind Sara Harper's townhouse curtains like it's Halloween in January. Same beige siding as her neighbors, but the glow turns the sidewalk into a Rorschach. Festive or ominous—dealer's choice.

I knock twice. Lavender, iron, and formaldehyde hit me as the door swings open.

Sara's in a black lace dress, platinum hair twisted up with a bone-handled pen she probably borrowed from her day job. Heavy kohl frames hazel eyes that catch every shadow. Behind her, dozens of candles—tapered, stubby, dripping—perch on bookshelves, windowsills, even the radiator. Martha Stewart by way of seance.

"Emily," she says, voice threaded with equal parts fondness and trepidation, like she wasn't sure whether to hug me or throw me out the door. "You look... business-casual possessed."

I step across the threshold into the candlelit hush. The air smells of beeswax, old parchment, and something metallic. "Long story. Got time to revive some paperwork?"

Sara tilts her head, pushing back a loose curl. "Come in and give me the details. Try not to step on Vivvy."

I almost ask who—or *what*—Vivvy is, but a sleek black cat slinks across the threshold, answers the question with a hiss, and disappears beneath a china cabinet.

"Witch with a black cat?" I follow her down the hall into her kitchen. "Bold choice," I tease lightly, trying to keep the tone casual. After outing her as a witch to every coven in Chicago, it feels dangerous to joke too pointedly.

"Vivvy picked me," Sara replies, lighting a stained-glass sconce that bathes the kitchen in bruise-purple light. Copper pots dangle overhead like a mobile of blunt weapons. "She told me all witches need a cat."

"She can talk?"

Sara smirks. "No. But you're an easy mark."

I huff a laugh as we settle at her butcher-block island, the surface scarred with knife indentations and scorch marks. "Before we start," I say, draping my coat over a chair, "is this lawyer-witch privilege? Or is it mortician-client?"

"Document in hand, privilege attached," she deadpans. "Payment is gossip and pastries."

"Done." I drop a maple-bacon donut in a white box tied with a bow on the island. She makes grabby hands, and I slide the box and Victor's envelope across. "Life-wager contract after a big casino win, 1925. Two-thirds redacted with ink. I need the bars stripped."

Sara devours half the donut in one bite before examining the papers. Her fingers ghost over the redactions, forehead creasing. "Magical ink," she murmurs, leaning closer. She inhales sharply. "Iron and... opium."

I shrug. "The roaring twenties."

"And smells like trouble. You sure you want me to dig into this?"

"Need, not want," I say, drumming my fingers nervously. "It's linked to the House."

Sara's gaze sharpens. "The House? Tell me you don't have an account."

A flicker of memory comes over me, chased by glitter and playing cards. "Not me. Strictly business."

"Nothing's ever strictly business with the House," she mutters. She sets the donut aside, brushing crumbs from her fingers. "Alright. Stand back."

She moves the contract carefully to the center of the island, pulling a copper bowl from under the counter and filling it with salt. Four candles—black wax etched with spiky runes—appear from a drawer. With practiced motions, Sara sets them at compass points around the bowl, lighting each with a murmured incantation: first a flame, then a curl of smoke, then a pop of light that has the shadows dancing on the walls.

I've seen a lot in my few months attached to the supernatural world. But never real magic. Rhett Baxter's movie-style magic was smoke and mirrors. Actually, it was magnets and electricity, but who's being specific?

Sara pauses, knife poised above her fingertip. "Before I breach magical security owned by an entity that could scare half the underworld, do you want to give me any last details?"

I shake my head. "If I knew anything else, I wouldn't be wasting your salt."

"Okay then," she murmurs, slicing the blade across her fingertip. Blood wells instantly, crimson drops splashing onto salt crystals. "But if we end up cursed, you owe me a dozen more donuts."

"Two dozen," I whisper.

She nods, satisfied. Her voice drops low, words curling through the room in a language that scrapes against my eardrums. The candles flare, flames stretching tall and blue, casting the kitchen in surreal hues. The copper pots vibrate overhead like tuning forks.

Sara presses her bloodied fingertip to the black bars of ink. A sharp metallic scent floods the air, mingling with something ancient and sickly sweet. The ink bubbles and pulls back, hissing like it's alive and revealing a single line written in delicate handwriting:

Bound and executed by and to the Anchor.

Before I can process that, fresh ink skates across the margin in a jaunty, taunting scrawl:

"Watch what you bargain for, Emily Lane."

My name, on a contract older than my existence. I force my breathing steady, but my pulse refuses to slow. Nothing can be good from being on a supernatural casino's radar.

Sara jerks back her hand like she's been burned, eyes wide. Every candle sputters, the chandelier overhead rattling. Vivvy yowls mournfully from under the china cabinet.

"Hell," she whispers. "It *sees* you."

I swallow hard. "Can it see anything else?"

"Let's hope not." Her voice trembles, but she steadies it quickly, pointing a shaking finger toward the contract's last page. "Look."

ESCROW TO MATURE UPON ANCHOR COMPLETION

"Anchor again?" I say.

Sara exhales, leaning heavily on the butcher-block. "I have no idea. But I guarantee the House doesn't choose words lightly."

I slide the parchment into its sleeve, hands shaking. "Which means I *do* need the Archive—the only place holding the unredacted master."

Sara's mouth twists. "Underground vault, warded beyond imagination, guarded by ghouls. You'll need a death wish or impeccable paperwork."

"Noted." I tuck the contract into my bag, trying for bravado and landing closer to resignation. "At least paperwork's my specialty."

"Promise me you won't end up filed away in their collection," she whispers, half-joking but eyes deadly serious.

"I'll try." I push away from the counter, the air suddenly too heavy to breathe. "Don't tell Lucian."

She makes a face. "Lucian doesn't exactly love surprises."

"That's why I'll tell him later," I say, trying to sound casual. But the fresh ink on that contract feels like it's burned into my skin. "After I've figured out exactly what I'm dealing with."

Sara eyes me warily, fingertips tapping on the table. "Fair enough. But if he finds out I helped you chase trouble..."

"I'll deny everything," I assure her. "This stays strictly lawyer-witch confidential, remember?"

She smiles faintly. "Good. Because he'd lock us both up until the danger passes."

"Hey—dinner soon?" I say as I finish packing up. "My treat. I owe you."

Sara brightens a bit. "I'm free Wednesday?"

"Can't," I grimace. "Client dinner. Political thing, ritzy part of town."

Sara's brows arch in surprise. "Oh, the Fulton fundraiser? I got an invitation too, but tickets are two grand a plate. No way. Not even sure how I made that mailing list."

I shrug. "Knowing the client, I'm surprised it's not ten grand."

"Then, lunch tomorrow?"

"Can't—another appointment. Dinner?"

She shakes her head apologetically. "Coven meeting. Fledglings to initiate."

Which means Lucian and Severin will be tied up too, I think absently.

She sighs, giving me a speculative look. "You're too busy, Em. Remember you're not immortal. You only live once, and all that."

"No kidding," I mutter, reaching for my coat. "Raincheck? I'll text you."

Sara nods slowly. "Be careful."

I glance back at the now-quiet candles, shadows huddling in corners like secrets we've accidentally set loose. "Too late for careful. I'll take lucky."

By the time I stumble into my apartment, it's almost midnight, and I've officially hit that point of exhaustion where even blinking feels like cardio. My place is cold, dark, and quiet. Not even a radiator clank to keep me company.

"Now would be a great time to make an appearance," I say aloud to Herle as I flip on the kitchen lights. "Better you than a ghoul waiting to jump-scare me."

Nothing answers. But nothing leaps out at me either, so I'll call that a win.

I stare blankly at the microwave clock for a minute, then decide sleep is for people who don't have their name showing up uninvited on century-old supernatural contracts. I fill my thrift-store kettle and set it to boil, because tea feels vaguely adult and responsible compared to midnight coffee. A cup of chamomile tea says, "Look, I'm trying."

While the kettle rumbles, I drag my laptop to the kitchen counter and fire up my favorite search engine—the first step in every research project, from obscure zoning ordinances to testing avocado ripeness. The browser cursor blinks impatiently, waiting for keywords I'm barely equipped to provide. Sadly, nobody's written "Supernatural Contracts for Dummies" yet. Trust me—I've checked.

But tonight, I have something more concrete than just "creepy magical casino records" to search, thanks to Sara's magical de-censorship ritual: *anchor bets, escrow maturation*, and whatever "bound and executed by and to the Anchor" means.

The internet coughs up references to nautical terminology, personal finance blogs, and conspiracy forums written by people who live in basements and own too many swords. *I should introduce them to the Baxters*, I think as I keep clicking.

A historical almanac from 17th-century Prague mentions something called the "Dark Anchor Pact." It sounds suitably mysterious, like an ancient agreement to bind an evil creature bent on world domination, but it turns out to be a dull dockworkers' union deal about placing river anchors along the Vltava. Not exactly useful, unless the House secretly moonlights in river transportation infrastructure.

An amateur paranormal site enthusiastically explains "anchor bets" as supernatural gambles that use human lives as collateral. This feels closer—maybe Victor's immortality is tied to another bet, another life? Unfortunately, the site has zero references, so its credibility is hovering around "tipsy uncle after Thanksgiving dinner."

Searching "escrow to mature upon anchor completion" delivers finance pages interspersed with nautical trivia. The House itself is described mostly in vague, bedtime-story language: "exclusive venues," "clandestine betting parlors," or "shadowy casinos" trading in intangible currency like luck, memories, and lifespan. Reddit threads debate its existence passionately but offer only secondhand stories and cryptic warnings. At least I know I'm not hallucinating terms now, so... progress?

But, of course, not one single mention of a magical Archive beneath Chicago's streets. Apparently, the city that invented deep-dish pizza never got around to documenting its supernatural vaults. Shocking.

Then again, maybe I'm the one who forgot. Sleep deprivation will do that. Because Chicago *does* have an Underground—not the subway kind, and definitely not listed on TripAdvisor. The Underground is the supernatural world's best-kept open secret: not a subway but a hidden warren beneath the city, all stone corridors and flickering gas lamps, tucked behind illusions and glamours so thick you need specially warded lenses to spot it. Without them, all you'd spot is wet stone walls and the smell of century-old sewage.

But on the inside? It's part marketplace, part neutral territory, part community hall. Vampires, witches, alchemists, you name it—they all use the Underground. Want enchanted chalk? Blood-bound courier service? A golem-friendly notary? The Underground probably has a booth. It's one of the few places where the supernatural mingle in relative peace, and the kind of place that *might* just hide a secret archive, if you knew where to look—and had the right credentials.

Blinking away sleep, I text Sara. *"You know your way around the Underground better than your average mortician, right?"*

Three dots blink at me for a long, accusing moment.

"Just because I spend half my life with vampires doesn't mean I keep their hours."

"I thought morgues were a 24/7 thing." I quickly send another message, telling my brain to stay on task. *"The Underground. You go more often now, right?"*

"Yes. More often now that everyone knows I'm a witch." She adds a flat-mouthed emoji, which I sincerely hope is her deadpan humor rather than lingering irritation at being outed.

"Right." I quickly push past it. *"You called the Archive an underground vault. Could it be hidden somewhere in the actual Underground?"*

"Maybe?" she replies. *"Honestly, Em, I have no clue. It's a secret archive controlled by a shadowy magical entity whose only legit front business is a casino."*

"Helpful. Thanks. I'll up my donut debt to three dozen."

"And cat treats," she sends back immediately.

I sigh, tossing the phone onto the counter. Quitting Johnson & Marcus was supposed to *lower* my stress. Yet here I am, stalking information about a mythic "House Archive" that might—or might not—keep untampered copies of supernatural IOUs like Victor's with ghouls that might—or might not—try to steal my memories. Some people take pottery classes after quitting; I chase arcane debt-collectors.

I'm clearly thriving.

The kettle clicks off, interrupting my pity party, and I pour the hot water into a mug. I'm halfway through dunking a second tea bag because I'm *not* that far from feral when my eyes land on Lucian's envelope, still sitting untouched on the kitchen table. How I made it several hours without ripping it open is a mystery for the ages.

I snatch it up, break the seal, and unfold thick, creamy stationery. The handwriting is Lucian's, precise and elegant, as if letters still mattered in an age of emails and emojis.

Emily,

I wanted to thank you personally for helping Severin with his financial matters. Yes, I realize this isn't strictly necessary, and yes, I'm aware you'll dismiss this as trivial. But I grew up in a time when written correspondence—and heartfelt thanks—were common.

On a less related, but certainly important note, I worry about you more than I probably should, especially given your extraordinary ability to find trouble without even trying. Stay safe—or at least consider calling me the next time your judgment takes a holiday.

Fondly, Lucian

Warmth blooms in my chest. Lucian Belmont—Mr. Vampire Sophistication himself—has penned a thank-you note. It felt like Lucian was heavily pursuing me throughout the whole fake-cursed-house fiasco, but the moment

I tripped over my mouth and accidentally outed Sara as a witch, he closed off tighter than the Haven's liquor cabinet at dawn. Since then, it's been a dance of sorts. A little awkward, a little strained, all flirting confined to coven game nights and quick exchanges at Moonlit Haven. But maybe his earlier offer to 'renegotiate' our friendship wasn't just our usual give-and-take banter.

I tuck the note carefully back into its envelope and place it gently in a drawer where it won't distract me. Not hiding it, exactly—just postponing my emotional unpacking until I'm better equipped.

My phone buzzes softly on the counter, startling me out of the quiet. I pick it up, screen glowing with Matty's name.

"I know it's late and hopefully this doesn't wake you. I enjoyed the dumplings and company. May I suggest a repeat soon without documents inked in blood and secrets?"

A tiny smile creeps onto my face. Lucian's note still lingers warm in my chest, and now Matty's text layers a comforting softness around it. This is either the nicest night I've had in ages or proof that my standards are on sale. A look at Victor's contract confirms it's probably both.

I type a quick response: *"Agreed. Fewer conspiracies, more dumplings. (No promises, though.)"*

Matty's reply is immediate: *"Your life practically demands conspiracies. I knew that when I signed up."*

I laugh softly and put the phone down. For the first time tonight, the tension in my shoulders eases just a little.

My tea has cooled to lukewarm disappointment, and I down it quickly, hoping the chamomile will dull the paranoia that's still tap-dancing inside my skull. Then I wander to bed, staring up at the ceiling while my mind runs in circles.

Sara and Lucian both warned me away from the House, and now I'm tangled deeper than ever.

But backing off has never been one of my stronger skills, and something about this feels deeply personal. That kind of thing demands answers, or at least a strongly worded complaint.

I pull the covers around me, staring at shadows dancing across the ceiling, but my mind won't settle. It keeps circling back to that elegant, mocking handwriting spelling out my name, as if a century-old contract just threw down a gauntlet.

The House's ink had written me in. It had found me before I'd even begun searching for it. And I don't know what that means.

Yet.

CHAPTER 7

As I turn onto Danielle Greene's street, my eyes catch on a huge, high-res billboard above a boba-shop-slash-massage parlor that's doing God's work for the over-30 set. Glossy, massive, impossible to ignore.

BRIAN FULTON FOR MAYOR

He's in a crisp navy suit. White teeth. Patriotic red tie. The kind of face your grandmother would hand her keys over for. The man whose fundraiser I'm apparently attending as Montgomery's trick pony this week.

And I've seen that face before.

Not at an event. Not in my inbox.

In a society page from 1927, arm slung around Victor. Two philanthropists out on the town. Black-and-white grins, tuxedos, champagne saucers. Brian Fulton looked good in gray scale. He looks good now. Same dimple. Same cheekbones.

I squint, idling at a stop sign a few seconds too long. It could be a family resemblance. I've seen weirder. Ex-Mayor Peterson's looked like an older Lucian and that was just genealogy being cute.

So maybe Fulton's just the great-great-grand-whatever of a bootlegger who once clinked glasses with a man who sold his life to a magical casino. Not weird. Just Chicago.

The billboard's tagline: "Paid for by the Solstice Foundation," the super PAC I created for Montgomery's unnamed associate. Life can just be coincidental, I guess.

By the time Danielle's house comes into view—a forest green two-story with a crooked wind chime and a heart-shaped wreath on the door—I've buried the thought.

The screen door creaks once, and she calls out, "Back door's open!" in a sing-song voice that could advertise organic jam.

I follow the scent of sauteed garlic and something buttery into the most aggressively cozy kitchen I've ever seen. It's like a Pinterest board and a vintage cookbook had a baby and named it "Home." Think: butter-yellow walls, string lights zigzagging across the ceiling, and a mismatched set of mugs hanging above a scratched farmhouse sink. The kind of place where bad days go to get healed by grilled cheese and gentle company. A wolf-shaped potholder dangles from a hook, entirely unironic and a breadcrumb I should have caught before my rose-colored glasses revealed her true form.

Danielle stands at the stove in a polka-dot apron over a cherry red dress, her short curls pinned up with little flower clips like she's a kindergarten teacher who moonlights as a fairy tale character. But when the wolf edges out—eyes bright, jaw set—you remember the moral: be good, or Grandma's bringing cuffs.

"You own a fox teapot," I say, mock-surprised, eyeing the bright orange appliance whistling away on the back burner.

"I own a menagerie," she replies, slicing through a thick loaf of bread like she's cutting through problems. "The pig's my favorite, of course. But this one doesn't leak. Sit."

I collapse into the cushioned bench at her breakfast nook. A wicker basket appears in front of me like magic—overflowing with crusty white bread that is absolutely home baked. A bowl of minestrone soup follows. It's deeply, offensively comforting.

"This is dangerously domestic," I murmur around a mouthful of nostalgia. Not for anything *I* experienced, but what the tv told me was real. "Are you trying to adopt me?"

She arches an eyebrow. "I'm a werewolf, not a golden retriever."

"Close enough," I mutter. "Thanks, Danielle."

Conversation starts light, with Danielle overly apologetic for missing the girl's brunch I organized right after Christmas, trying to marry both parts of my life: the human and supernatural, the legal and... not.

"Tell me what I missed," she says, shoveling bread in her mouth. "Let me feel even worse."

"Don't feel bad," I tell her, trying to avoid inhaling the soup myself. "But... we ordered egg waffles, watched that witchy remake from last summer, played cards, and Megan made us take a fake dating profile quiz."

"Sara got 'mysterious bookstore owner,' didn't she?" Danielle asks.

I snort. "No, that was me, weirdly. She got 'taxidermist with a tragic past.' Megan was 'competitive croquet champion.'"

"I wonder what I'd have gotten," Danielle says around her spoon.

"Friendly forest ranger who makes cinnamon pancakes," I decide.

"Accurate," she says, laughing. "That sounds fun." She smiles at me, like a proud parent. Considering she pushed me to put myself out there more, she's right to take credit. "And it was certainly more fun than the waffle bar *I* ended up going to."

"What happened?"

"Mom ambushed me at brunch with that coven member I told you about. The one who showed up at the meeting ranking us all by 'most likely to survive a siege.'"

I sip my tea. "He did put you in the top ten, right?"

"Yes. As he should," she says with a sniff.

"But..."

"But he wore a full tux to the 'date.' Who wears a tuxedo to a waffle bar?" She groans dramatically, dropping her forehead to the table.

"Maybe he's into syrup-based courtship rituals."

She huffs. "Mom said he's stable. You know what else is stable? Cement."

I laugh until tea threatens to exit through my nose. Danielle sits back, clearly pleased with herself.

By the time we're scraping the last of the soup, she's leaned back with her tea in hand, cheeks pink from the stove. It's like I've stepped into a movie where the stakes are always low and the kitchen always warm.

"So," I say eventually, wiping my fingers on a linen napkin because *obviously* she uses linen napkins, "what's been keeping you busy on the badge side?"

She hesitates, tea halfway to her lips. Her smile fades just a little. "We've got a missing persons case that's starting to wear on me."

I straighten in my seat. "Oh?"

She shrugs. "January's always busy. Welfare checks during the freeze, 'haven't heard from him since New Year's,' and the annual amnesia tour. Transit cops pick up sleepers who ride end-to-end and forget where they boarded. Shelters report wanderers who don't know their own address. None of it hits one neighborhood, it's citywide—like a weather pattern," she finishes, then adds, softer, "but this is a kid. Fifteen."

I set the napkin down. "Go on."

She rises and grabs a folder off the windowsill behind her, returning to the table and flipping it open toward me. "We've had the photo circulating for a week now. Val doesn't have the background to be a runaway, and there are no signs of struggle. She walked from the library to the bus stop—eight minutes of sidewalk—then nothing. It's like she vanished."

I glance at the photo.

It's a girl in a gray cardigan, sitting at a chessboard with an overly worldly smile. Light brown curls. Soft features. Eyes that look just a little too old for fifteen.

My stomach dips. I don't know her. I've never seen her before.

But something about the tilt of her mouth... it rhymes. Not like Brian and Brian, more like Lucian and Peterson.

Same eyes. Same high-bridged nose. The kind of resemblance that might make someone take a second look and mutter knowingly when the connection is finally revealed.

"Any known family history?" I ask, trying to keep my tone light.

"Not much. She lives with her aunt in Hyde Park. Mom's out of the picture. Dad's... older. We're trying to track him down, but the trail's cold."

"Older how?"

"Over one hundred if our records are right. The history's a little unclear. Had the kid late in life, I guess. Some kind of eccentric. Makes Lucian look like a spring break frat boy." She eyes me with a soft smile. "Better age gap than you two would make, at least."

I force down a flush. "Enough of that. But that's terrible. Poor kid."

She smirks but doesn't push, refocusing on the case. "It's been five days and I'm out of leads."

I glance at the photo again, my mind churning. She has a dad, with records that have him too long lived to be reasonable. The resemblance to Victor isn't perfect, but it's there, like a signature passed down in ink instead of DNA.

"You said her name's Val?"

"Short for Valentine," Danielle confirms. "Valentine Little."

"Valentine," I echo. "Pretty name."

Greene nods. "Family name. She was named after her grandmother—Valentine Little, the elder. Married to a Marcel. The records say she died in 1905, he followed in 1919."

I frown. "That's... unusual?"

"Not really." Danielle flips the file closed. "Plenty of families recycle names. Keeps the line alive."

I don't say it out loud, but recycling names is foreign to me. Nobody in my family handed me a legacy, just a birth certificate and good luck.

And yet the name itself is familiar. Too familiar.

Victor Little used the name Marcel Valentine when renting that storage unit. Said it was an alias for security.

Alias, my ass.

"You think it's supernatural?" I ask carefully.

She shrugs, but her expression is all cop. "I don't know. Right now, it's just a human kid who disappeared. Missing persons case until proven otherwise," she says. Her wolf-senses are twitching; her tone is taut. "But my gut says something's off."

"Your gut has fangs," I mutter as my brain flits over the collection clause from Victor's contract.

'Collection may include, but is not limited to, retrieval of remaining essence, estate reclamation through lineage, or alternate payment per the House's discretion.'

My stomach twists as I set the photo down. Of course, Victor didn't mention a kid. Why would he, when he could just drop half-truths like breadcrumbs and let me trip through the woods blindfolded?

Even with my own clients, I'm last to know.

I came into this thinking we were dealing with a contract dispute—something borderline manageable, if morally gray. But this? This isn't paperwork. This is a missing teenager with his name practically written on her cheekbones. And he never said a word. Not one.

I offer the file back, heart hammering like a summons has already been issued.

She places it carefully on the table between us, not taking her eyes off mine. "If you hear anything—even a whisper—we'd appreciate it."

I nod again. I'm already in this.

And somewhere out there, a fifteen-year-old girl with Victor's eyes might be paying off a bet she never made.

Victor's penthouse apartment smells like old leather, and secrets. The good kind of secrets, if you're a car salesperson trying to swindle the buyer of your lemon. The bad kind, if you're trying to convince me you didn't withhold crucial information.

Again.

He opens the door looking rumpled. For Victor, it means the knot in his tie sits a centimeter off center and his pocket square is creased instead of crisp. The silver cufflinks still glint. His smile is still polite. But the edges of him are cracked, and I'm done pretending I don't see them as something more serious than self-preservation.

I don't wait for an invitation. Three sharp steps carry me across polished walnut into the minimalist living room—a symphony of slate, glass, and money—while Danielle Greene closes the door behind us. She's shed the cherry-print dress for black jeans, sturdy boots, and a navy pea-coat lumpy enough to hide a service pistol, extra mags, and a pressure cooker of righteous fury.

"You brought company," he says, nodding once at Danielle.

"She insisted," I reply, dropping my purse on a museum-grade coffee table. *After* I convinced myself that supernatural contracts aren't anything the Illinois Bar was going to regulate, meaning there were no ethical quandaries in revealing Victor's existence to her. That a missing kid is attached made it a no-brainer.

"*She* has a gun," Danielle adds cheerfully, breezing past him into the suite. "And a pot of minestrone justice simmering and nowhere else to serve it."

Victor's eye twitches. "Charming."

I cut in before the banter turns bitey. "We need to talk about *Valentine Little.*"

Victor goes still. The polite façade doesn't fall, but it freezes, and somehow that's worse.

"I was told you don't watch the local news," he mutters.

"She doesn't," Danielle answers for me, revealing her sharp teeth. "Lucky for you, she's got good friends to keep her updated."

Victor sighs, shoulders slumping under the weight of whatever performance he had prepared. "You brought a werewolf."

"I brought a *cop*," I say. "Don't make this a species thing."

He gestures stiffly toward a seating arrangement consisting of one pale-gray sofa and two stunning Barcelona chairs that have never witnessed potato-chip crumbs. "Fine. Sit down. I'll tell you everything."

We stay upright—Danielle against the wall, arms folded; me in the center of the rug like a prosecutor who misplaced her podium. Victor dawdles at the wet bar, as though distance will keep the truth from burning too badly.

"I didn't know they'd invoke the lineage clause," he begins, voice soft. "I'd... forgotten it even existed."

I cross my arms so I don't throttle him. "You *forgot* your kid could be repo'd like a vintage Corvette?"

"I've lived two lifetimes in a single skin." He drags a hand down his face, leaving pale stripes on tanned cheeks. "My dame in 1930? Happily married in '35, widowed in '68. She out-aged me while I stayed twenty. Anyone I thought I could belong with was a non-starter. 'No ties that outlive the lies.' That was my rule." His gaze flickers, haunted. "Sixteen years ago, I broke it. One careless night, and Valentine... happened." His shoulders sag. "One error in a century."

"Easy to say now," I bite out. "When that mistake is out there paying for your sins."

Danielle's brows rise. "Val wasn't the mistake though. The gamble was."

Victor exhales slowly. "Of course she wasn't a mistake. She's what tethers me to this place. My daughter. I have to get her back." He meets my eyes. "If the House wants a soul, it can take mine. I'll swap places—but I need a way in."

"And you didn't tell me about this because?" I ask, arms crossed, feeling oddly vulnerable at his pronouncement. My own dad ditched me for his boyfriend's addiction to blood donation. I didn't even rate above someone *else's* interest.

He meets my eyes. "Because you straddle both worlds. You speak human law and supernatural loophole. I thought if you smelled *kidnapping* instead of *contract breach*, you'd bolt. Emily Lane: newly knee-deep in the weird, but not cultivating roots."

A direct hit. It stings because it's partly true, or it was until Thanksgiving when I went all in.

But adults make bad deals all the time. That's the whole job description of a lawyer: patching over stupid bargains with clever language or convincing the jury it isn't so bad. But a kid? Kids don't belong in ledgers. Val didn't sign anything, didn't shake on it, didn't even get the dignity of screwing herself over. She just... happened to have the wrong last name. That's not a contract, that's theft. If I don't draw the line there—if I let a fifteen-year-old get filed like unpaid taxes—then what the hell am I even doing?

"I'm not bolting," I say. "I'm marching straight into this. Because a teenager is missing, Victor. You don't get to play the noble liar and pretend that makes it better."

"I didn't know who else to go to," he says, and it sounds honest. Exhausted. "The House won't talk to me since they've gotten their collateral. The Archive's sealed. I can't even find either. And I can't walk into the local precinct and say, 'Hello, my missing daughter was taken by an arcane gambling syndicate your records won't show even exist.' And the paranormal police—"

"They won't touch it," Danielle finishes for him. "Because Valentine's human. She's not one of ours."

Victor nods.

I want to scream. I want to throw something. Instead, I squeeze my hands together until they stop trembling.

"Fine. Then we're going to do this my way. No more secrets. No more aliases. No more omission-by-evasion. You tell me every single thing you know, and we start digging."

Greene nods. "And if the House thinks it can collect on debts like this? They're about to meet a whole new kind of enforcement."

Victor offers the faintest smile. "I hope you're right."

I scrub a hand down my face. "I want that contract unsealed, I want access to the Archive, and I want a list of everyone who knew about Valentine's existence. If we're gambling with lives, I need all the chips on the table."

Victor's posture straightens by degrees—like a man fastening armor he thought he'd buried. "Understood."

Standing, I stalk across the room, poking him hard in the chest. "And if you lie to me again, I'll make damn sure you're stuck in your next contract with nothing but your own reflection for company."

Victor nods solemnly. "Of course."

I don't forgive him. But I do sit down. The room shifts, the air growing heavier with something between strategy and reckoning.

Time to work.

CHAPTER 8

We break at dusk, three conspirators acting like b-grade heroes with mismatched skill sets. Danielle has a badge, claws, and supernatural grapevine. Victor has money, charm, and a century's worth of business cards. I have stubbornness, a BAR card, and a talent for ignoring good advice.

Division of labor settled, we scatter to shake our separate trees for intel on the House Archive. Danielle heads for precinct or coven back-channels; Victor for whatever concierge the obscenely wealthy use after business hours. My job is simpler: grab a guide and head downstairs—into the Underground—before the House realizes we're tilting its pinball machine.

Could I go into the Underground myself? Yes. I still have Ray's rose-colored glasses that let me see through the glamours. But am I terrified of a tiny pixie who might still be mad I stole a contract from her? Also, yes. (Look, fear isn't rational. I was terrified of dolphins until the aquarium lifted its no-fish-smell policy. Long story.)

And Lucian is neck-deep in coven politics tonight. Translation: no one to stop me trying to find the Archive. Stardust has the keys (literal and metaphorical) to the tunnels, and—pixie-induced PTSD or not—I'd rather brave the Underground with the glitter prince at my side than dive solo.

The club's neon sign flickers violet against my windshield. I'm halfway out of the car when something shifts at the mouth of the alley across the street—a tall silhouette, shoulders too square, eyes catching light like wet coins.

I lock the car with a beep louder than my pulse, pretend I don't see it, and walk toward the entrance. When I risk a glance back, the street is empty except for steam curling from a grate.

I shake it off and head inside. I find Stardust the second I make it through the doors. Usually pretty easy, but tonight there's a spotlight on him. Literally. Stage left, a single beam hits Stardust—white suit and cape, rhinestone lapels, blond locks bouncing like a shampoo commercial, mismatched eyes brighter than disco balls. He's kneeling.

In front of Ray.

Holding a ring that could finance my student-loan balance twice over.

"In *Metropolis,*"—he gestures theatrically, almost scratching his own cheek from the sharp ring—"the great Fritz Lang reminds us: 'The mediator between head and hands must be the heart.' Ray has been that for me—turning necessity into compassion, donor into partner, vice into... something exquisitely permanent." He turns back to Ray. "Raymond," Stardust croons, "will you bond with me and become an immortal companion of great taste and questionable silence?"

Ray blinks, looking star-struck. No pun intended. "Is this because I let you redecorate the bathroom?"

"Yes," Stardust says solemnly. "And because I love you. And I already booked the officiant for next week."

Ray laughs—bright, incredulous, loud. "Then yes. Obviously."

The room explodes into an impromptu celebration. The house DJ slams on Bowie's "Heroes," and suddenly I'm in the middle of an undead engagement party. Any request that starts with "Hey, congrats—can you risk your immortal hide escorting me past a possibly homicidal pixie?" is officially off the table tonight.

So, I stay for a bit. Because I'm psyching myself up for a solo-Underground run. Also, I may still be new at friendships, but ditching an engagement bash will probably put me on the 'refuse admittance' list for a long while. Possibly an eternity, since we're talking about immortals and their grudges.

I snag something sparkling and questionably alcoholic and watch Ray glow beneath a hail of selfies with all the attendees who can show up on camera.

I get the allure to bask in his glow. Bonding is a big deal. It's the supernatural version of 'til death do us part.' Only... there's no divorce court and the death part is a two-for-one special. A creature hands over a spark of their magic, the human coughs up a shard of their soul, and—boom—they're eternally synced. Great perks: instant VIP access to places like the Underground and a built-in bodyguard who really can't afford to let the human get squished (shared pain and all). Hideous fine print: if Fang-Face catches a cold, the human sneezes; if they lose their head—well, his rolls right beside it.

Tempting, but I prefer relationships where a breakup doesn't require coordinated coffins.

Three toasts later I finally corner the newly betrothed near the stage. They've got their arms around each other, holding court with a handful of celebrants.

"That quote?" someone says. "Only you would use Metropolis to propose."

Stardust lifts a shoulder, unbothered. "Lang's words never go out of style."

"It doesn't hurt that Ziggy himself was inspired by him," another adds, a vampire I vaguely recognize from the northern coven. "Whole reason our boy became Stardust back in '78. After that horrible stint as *Floyd*." He mimes gagging.

"Alas, Bowie's Thin White Duke just didn't have the gravitas I was going for when I decided to rebrand," Stardust says.

"Or personality," Ray adds, smiling. "Not glam enough."

I smother a frown. Also too fascist. Hard pass.

Laughter ripples through the knot of admirers; phones flash, someone starts a chant of *Staaaar-dust, Staaaar-dust.* Ray ducks his head, glowing and mortified, while Stardust soaks it in like a plant under UV.

The chant dissolves into the next Bowie track. Half the crowd peels away toward the bar, the rest swarm the DJ booth with song requests, leaving a sudden pocket of space around the happy couple.

I slip through that gap and lift my glass in salute. "Congratulations, you absolute drama magnet," I say. "When were you going to tell me?"

Stardust beams at me. "Sweetest Emily—tonight was meant to be a surprise for everyone, you included. Forgive me?"

"Forgiven," I say. "To a point. But you two just blew up my schedule."

Ray tilts his head. "Uh-oh. Work-related?"

"Pixie-related," I correct. "I was hoping my favorite glam vampire might walk me past a certain booth that probably has *wanted dead or alive: sticky fingered lawyer* scribbled on it."

Stardust's expression flickers—sympathy, then regret. "Oh, love, I'd do it tomorrow, next week, whenever. But tonight?" He gestures to Ray's hand, where half the room is still trying to photograph the ring. "There's a whole engagement fiesta queued up. Ray's mom is video-calling in twenty minutes, and I promised her I wouldn't vanish into the tunnels smelling of dry ice and moral ambiguity."

Ray squeezes his arm. "Translation: I want him undead and glitter-free for the parental call."

I hold up both palms. "No complaints. You deserve the night. It just means I'll have to improvise. Congratulations again."

Ray's gaze softens. "Come by for game night later this week?"

"Poker?" I suggest, stepping back as another wave of well-wishers crashes over them.

"Spite and Malice," Ray says, grinning.

"Cat and Mouse, darling," Stardust sing-songs, already distracted by someone waving a camera.

"It's a deal," I call after them.

Outside, the party still echoes through the walls, and I lean against my car. No sign of the alley watcher. Either my nerves are inventing creeps or creeps are inventing me. Fantastic.

I slide behind the wheel, pull away from the curb, and aim the headlights south. Tenacity over terror. Archive or bust.

I kill the engine twenty yards away from my favorite—okay, only one I know—Underground access hatch: the sewer. Yanking the trunk open, I paw through the emergency-ish collection that lives back there: gym bag, ratty hoodie, half a roll of duct tape, a busted Halloween wig, and last month's dry-cleaning sack. The last time I went incognito to the Underground, I went flamboyant with a wig, tutu, wild colors. Basically, the works. I'd figured I looked too mundane in my usual getup. But no, the garish just put a neon sign on me labeled 'human trying too hard.' This time, I add a scuffed pleather jacket and gray hoodie (coffee stain artfully tucked under the zipper) to my weekend attire. My hair, still in its signature long pony, gets tucked below a cap pulled low. The finishing touch is the rose-tinted glamour-piercing glasses—hung from my neckline like the world's dorkiest pendant until I need to see the invisible.

The new look screams *dog-walking grad student* more than *vampire groupie*. But since I've been told bonded humans are the only mortals who ever see the Underground without becoming a cautionary tale, it'll have to do.

I thumb a text to Danielle before I can second-guess the alleged suicide mission.

"Escort engaged. Literally. Heading to the Underground."

"Alone?" she responds in a flash.

"Ping if the morgue gets a brunette named Lane," I reply, then shove my phone in my pocket.

The maintenance grate shrieks like I'm prying open a crypt. One tire-iron shimmy later, I'm straddling the hole, reminding myself that terrible ideas still count as ideas. The ladder is slick with century-old condensation and the air hits me in the face, sour and fungal, as if the city's bowels just exhaled. When my boots slap into water colder than an IRS auditor's handshake, I click on a pen-light and settle the rose-tinted glamour specs over my nose.

At first, it's the same sewer my former assistant Liz once called "Chicago's least-visited tourist attraction"—brick walls sweating rust, conduits drooping like dead vines, graffiti layering profanity over lost loves. But thirty yards in, the architecture molts: brick gives way to carved limestone slick with phosphorescent moss, and the ceiling rises until the beam of my flashlight drowns in black. The hush is wrong, too—not city-quiet but *predator-quiet*, the air vibrating with things that smell an unbonded human like sharks smell blood.

Still, the only way out is through, so I clench the light, think relentless, and keep walking while the tunnel's damp breath whispers that I should've updated my will instead of my wardrobe.

The tunnel kinks left, and the air goes from boiler-room muggy to a cool hush that feels... intentional, like the moment a theater's lights dim. My pen-light sputters, dies, and for a breath I'm blind—until something stirs behind the rose lenses.

Color blooms. Neon oranges and impossible violets seep into the stone as if the rock itself has arteries. Archways I'd sworn were solid ripple open into vaulted corridors hung with floating lanterns.

Overflowing stalls of magical wares cover what seconds ago was nothing, shot through with constellations of light. The smell shifts too—no more moldy-basement eau de toilette; it's crushed pine, ozone, roasted coffee, and something sweetly metallic that might be unicorn blood or artisanal beet syrup.

Two goblins haggle over a crate of vintage vinyl; a banshee croons jazz into a gramophone built from bones; sprites zip overhead brandishing tiny sparklers. Everyone seems busy ignoring the human who is very obviously not bonded to anybody.

My death-spiral anxiety eases a notch. Maybe Stardust's specs behave like a VIP pass. Maybe the pixie whose contract I—*cough*—liberated last fall is too busy terrorizing someone else. Maybe Lucian was flexing his big-bad-coven-leader muscles for dramatic effect when he first warned me away.

I allow myself a small, judicious victory grin—which is when it all goes sideways.

A hush ripples through the crowd, like wind across tall grass. Then the grass looks up: half a dozen pixies hover at the far end of the market street, wings flickering humming-bird-fast. Not the cute Disney flavor, or even the jewel-toned pixie I stole from. These wear thorn-black armor stitched from beetle shells atop their colorful skin. Even their short hair looks spiked like knives. One gestures, and every sharp little face swivels toward me.

A hiss—spoon striking crystal—cuts through chatter. "Thief," one trills, voice glass-sharp. "The contract-snatch-er."

I pivot, booking it down a side alley lined with stalls. The pixie swarm follows, shrieking like weaponized toddlers. Pixie war-cries cut the air; glittering bolts—literally *bolts* of ionized shimmer—ricochet off stone. I dodge a table of cursed chess sets, hurdle over a stack of chained-up jack--in-the-boxes, and run straight into a curtained booth that reeks of brimstone and peppermint.

Inside: a horned... something. Eight feet tall, slate-gray skin, tusks roomy enough to rent on Airbnb. It blinks three yellow eyes at me over a cauldron of bubbling violet goo.

"Apologies," I gasp, slamming the curtain shut behind me. "Sales pitch. I represent... premium liability coverage for high-risk retailers. Very exclusive. Need two minutes to discuss deductibles before your foot traffic picks up again."

The creature blinks once, twice, then rumbles, "Kid, I sell nightmares by the ounce. But I respect the hustle. Stay until the winged vermin clear off."

Outside, pixie voices seethe: curses about missing contracts, a rose-gold bounty, something about using human eyelashes for toothpicks. My heartbeat drums in my throat. Eventually their buzz fades into the background roar of the market.

The creature—name tag reads GOLORN, DISTILLER OF DREADS—raises one brow ridge. "You're clean. Out."

"Of course," I say, backing toward the flap. "Pleasure doing almost-business. If you ever need a lawyer, I'm your gal." I press a business card into a massive palm and escape before his generosity wears out.

The thoroughfare is alive again, but no pixies in sight. My pulse finally slows, but my hoodie is damp with sweat and sewer mist, and I'm acutely aware I have zero map, zero escort, and zero clue where the Archive might lurk. I tug the hoodie lower, square my shoulders, and march deeper into the light-soaked maze—utterly bedraggled, utterly alone, and absolutely determined to out-lawyer every monster in the house.

I exit into a quieter stretch lined with half-lit vendor alcoves. A faint cuss—"fungus-kissing fae slime fuckers!"—echoes from a side arch. The voice is gravel wrapped in sandpaper—low, contemptuous, and painfully familiar. I whirl. No one swears quite like a Chicago hobgoblin.

"Wilkin," I say, stepping into view.

Through the rosy tint of the glamour-specs, a shape coalesces: three feet of bark-brown skin etched in faint bronze scales, long neon-green claws tapping an impatient rhythm against bony forearms. Gold flecks jitter in star-bright eyes. Wilkin—the hobgoblin who turned my life into a choose-your-own-misery adventure—turns and smirks at me.

He snaps a claw. "Mother of mold. Thought you'd be pixie chow by now. Disappointin'."

"Nice to see you too, Wilkin," I deadpan, straightening my hoodie. "Still hanging around places humans *aren't* supposed to survive?"

"Humans survive fine if they don't steal shit they don't understand."

A twitch jumps in my left eye. "You told me *to* steal it."

"I said *get* it. *You* heard 'grand larceny.'" Three rows of crooked teeth gleam. "That's your headache, counselor, not mine."

I exhale through clenched teeth. "Look, I'm not here to rehash who tricked whom. But since I've found you: I need someone to take me to the Archive." I try for flattery. "You must know the tunnels better than anyone. Help me."

Wilkin snorts, an impressive spray of sulfur-scented mist. "Archive? The House's? Thought you'd chase kittens before pokin' that bear."

"I poke bears professionally. What do you know?"

He huffs. "Enough to stay clear. And the first thing you gotta swallow, Lane—Archive's *not* part of this market." He raps the stone with a knuckle. "Ain't nailed to Chicago's Underground, never has been."

I frown. "It's underground, but *not* the Underground?"

"Pocket hallway," he says, drawing a door in the air. "House carved it outta the ley-lines centuries back. Slides around like a ferret in ductwork—sometimes a door pops off these tunnels, sometimes off a mineshaft in bloody Tasmania. Only House loyal and invited guests can find it."

I pivot. If Wilkin's a dead end on the Archive, maybe he can find where they're stashing Val. "What about the House itself? Surely the world's largest spy ring," e.g. hobgoblins, "can get intel on it and what it's doing."

Now he preens. "Information's our favorite currency—after barterin'."

"I need information on a girl, a kid. Someone the ghouls took as collateral for a bet."

"Favor economy, counselor." He bares those teeth again. "You know the rate."

"I can pay."

He barks a laugh. "Don't need money. Anything I want, I can pinch before dawn. I go invisible, remember?"

I force myself not to sigh heavily at what I'm about to offer. *Emily Lane, lawyer and fetcher of hobgoblin obsessions.* "There's got to be something you can't get. Imported truffles? Freshly prepared uni?"

He folds arms. "Always wanted to try a *Fudge-Me-Once* bar from that roamin' 'Sweet Cheeses' truck."

Ah. The elusive dessert truck that materializes at 2 a.m. like a sugared mirage, always moving, always mobbed.

I tap a finger to my chin. "Those brownie-cheesecake hybrids with the caramel-brûlée center?"

His eyes flare. *Gotcha.*

"Invisibility's tough inside a sardine can on wheels, isn't it?" I prod. "One elbow nicks a spatula, you're the day's special."

He scowls, which on him looks like a gargoyle contemplating litigation. "Tiny space, hot griddle, too many damned ladles. Bad for business."

"Exactly why you need *me*." I plant my heels. "I get you a *half-dozen* Fudge-Me-Once bars, plus a pint of Meerkat's honey-goat gelato—"

"Make it a *full* dozen," he interrupts, claws drumming a syncopated beat, "and I'll *consider* your information. The House spooks even hobgoblins—rooms move, doors bite. Findin' what they did to that girl won't be easy."

I swallow—the word *bite* conjures teeth-ridden thresholds that I'm betting don't give a relaxing chaser like vampire fangs—but shrug like he didn't just give me the heebie-jeebies. "I'm good for it. You throw in the secret to canceling that pixie bounty and I'll make it two dozen."

He studies me, lantern-light dancing across his scale-mottled skin like constellations. After an eternity he huffs. "I'll *look*. No deal on the pixies—they're sticky as troll boogers. Had to have you fix my problem with them, didn't I?"

"*Fine*," I groan. "Edible bribery only. I can get you the first installment tomorrow."

"Drop the sweets outside my place, by the side door."

I raise a brow. "Is it still a crime scene?"

"Nah." He smiles. It's terrifying. "Got a new tenant now. Nice couple. Even tried to convince my cousin Herle to move in but he's not budging until you cut your hair. Like a hobgoblin's version of a hunger strike."

"Fantastic," I echo, though it comes out sounding more like *kill-me-now*.

Wilkin's claws drum faster. "Green cooler, tomorrow night, side closest to the hydrangeas. Label it *FOR THE HANDSOME ONE*—capital letters."

I roll my eyes and jot an invisible note on my thigh. "Tomorrow night. Green cooler. Got it. And the intel?"

"I'll have it." He tips an imaginary hat. "Pleasure doin' business, counselor. And, Lane—move fast. Pixie tempers curdle quick."

Before I can retort, he blurs at the edges, shrinking into a haze of sparks that wink out with a faint *pop* of brimstone and burned caramel.

I push off the wall and head for the louder arteries of the Underground. Somewhere overhead, Chicago's nightlife is ordering charcuterie boards and IPA flights. I'm negotiating pastry-for-breadcrumbs deals with creatures who rate curses by the syllable.

"Partner track never covered this," I mutter, pulling up my hood and forcing my knees to keep moving.

Now it's time to stake out a food truck.

CHAPTER 9

Someone is trying to break into my apartment—politely, using the door instead of a crowbar, but with the enthusiasm of a SWAT team on double espresso.

I surface from four hours of sleep that did nothing for me, still wearing my outfit from the night before, the hoodie now reeking of fryer oil and victory. My bank account is decidedly thinner, as the price of twelve Fudge-Me-Once bars, two pints of honey-goat gelato, and a few other bars just for me was obscene.

But worth it if Wilkin's breadcrumb isn't a joke. Less worth it if I'm dead before lunch.

Pound-pound-pound.

"Emily Lane, you'd better open up before I take the door off its hinges!"

Danielle. Great. Someone who can clearly out-shout an angry landlord.

I untangle from the sheets and stumble to the entryway. The peephole shows a blur of dark curls and flashing canine eyes—cop-werewolf panic mode. I unlatch, yank the door open, and get a fistful of Danielle's pea-coat in my face as she barrels inside.

"What is *wrong* with you?" she snaps, slamming the door behind her. "You ghosted me. You ghosted everyone!"

It's too early to remind her ghosts aren't real. "Define 'ghosted.'"

She brandishes my phone at me—when did she snatch that?—the screen lit like Times Square: 12 missed calls, 37 texts. Most are from *Danielle Greene*. The rest? Megan. Brian. Matty. *Sara*. My stomach does a slow, unhappy cartwheel. If Sara texted, Lucian definitely knows his (*hopefully*) favorite lawyer went spelunking solo.

"I thought you were dead," Danielle growls.

"Okay," I croak, steering her to the kitchen and the life-saving coffeemaker. "I'm not dead. Just financially maimed."

She sniffs. "You smell like fair-food and mildew."

"Underground eau de cologne. Limited edition."

While caffeine drips, I give her the bullet points: Sweet Cheeses stakeout, Wilkin's dessert ransom, breadcrumb delivery promised tonight.

"Unbelievable." She scrubs a hand over her face, claws half-out from stress.

I fish out two brownies, slide one across the counter. Peacemaker pastry. "Sorry. Adrenaline crash. Fell asleep."

Danielle eyes the confection, then me. Finally, she bites. Victory.

"Look," she says around chocolate, "I got what we needed."

"You found a map to the Archive?"

"Better." She dusts crumbs from her badge holster, straightens. "Someone with the political clout to walk you through the Archive's front door."

I blink. "Lucian told me the only people who get in are House insiders or their pet representatives. And last I checked, I'm not on anyone's payroll."

Danielle's smirk doesn't budge. "Some people just like you, Em."

Which makes zero sense. Nobody in the Archive knows me well enough to like me—unless we're using "like" in the same way the House probably uses "favor," where the bill always comes due. But, considering I just learned about the House and the Archive in the last seventy-two hours, the connection seems weak. People don't hand out golden keys unless they expect something back. And if this mystery benefactor is willing to cross the House to let me in... either they're suicidal, or they think I'm worth the trouble.

And I've been alive long enough to know that kind of trouble usually comes with teeth.

I squint. "Who is it?"

Danielle shakes her head, eyes gleaming with the satisfaction of a magician about to pull a rabbit from a hat full of subpoenas. "You'll find out tomorrow. Six a.m."

Coffee nearly sprays from my mouth. "Six a.m.? Is that even legal?"

"It is when you're rescuing a teenager from extradimensional loan sharks." She folds her arms. "The difference between a 6 a.m. meeting and an 8 a.m. one could be the difference between a rescue and a recovery."

And that's the thing—Val doesn't have the luxury of banker's hours. Somewhere, she's living second to second, counting them down without even knowing the number left. Every minute we're not moving feels like we're already too late.

"You're right, you're right," I say, rightfully cowed.

"Be at the south end of the Riverwalk," Danielle says. "Under the Franklin Street bridge."

I run a hand through my pastry-scented hair. "Can't you at least tell me if this mysterious benefactor drinks blood or black coffee? I need wardrobe parameters."

"Wear something that doesn't scream 'I bribed a hobgoblin with baked goods.' And please, for the love of silver bullets, keep your phone on."

I salute with the mug. "Yes, mom."

She snorts, mood finally easing. "Take a nap. And maybe shower—you smell like fried sugar and sewer."

"Best new fragrance of the year," I mutter, but I'm already moving—brownie in mouth, plans rearranging faster than a House hallway. Or so I'm told.

When she's gone, the place goes silent, just me and the coffeemaker's death rattle. I send the bare-minimum assurances—alive, not arrested, will explain—and step into the shower. The water runs brown for a second from Underground grime. Appropriate.

By late morning the adrenaline shakes finally settle and I decide to eat something that's not chocolate. I stare at oatmeal, decide it's an act of war, and gnaw a cold slice of pizza instead.

More texts stacked up while I was trying to feel human. The law school group chat seems like the least accusatory—relatively speaking. Megan (five-ish feet of espresso and opinions) has the latest.

"IT'S BEEN 2 HOURS SINCE U LAST MESSAGED!! ARE U DEAD?" Megan writes.

Maybe a bad choice to start with.

"Alive. Generally well and no longer smelling of sewer sugar," I reply.

"GROSS," she fires back.

"Good morning, Emily. Check the earlier messages," Matty adds. *"Megan's panic play-by-play is a novella."*

"Like u werent freaked too," she snips.

"Technically we wouldn't have freaked if Danielle hadn't texted Megan in the first place," Brian says.

Reasonable premise. I'm not the best at communicating. And Megan and Danielle are friends now—my fault. Megan used to side-eye supernaturals; now a werewolf is her favorite brunch buddy.

"Tbf, Emmy vanishing = trouble = panicking," Megan writes. *"U need to start checking in!!!! Maybe a shift board for who watches u & keeps ur phone ON LOUD."*

"All in favor of Matty making the schedule," Brian adds, and drops a fireworks emoji for some reason.

"I'm a grownup," I type back, fingers pressing hard on the keys. *"I don't have to be married to my phone every second when I'm out living life."*

"'Living life' = going to allegedly haunted houses ALONE w/ a wicked werewolf," Megan replies.

I groan and flop back on the couch. They will never let that one die. At least they're forgetting when I went to a second—locked and private—location with a murderer, aka Mayor Peterson.

"+1 to Megan's point," Brian sends. *"See also: Peterson."*

Drat.

"Although," Brian continues, inadvertently saving me from another lecture, *"I wasn't actually worried."*

"...EXCUSE ME?" sent from (who else?) Megan.

"The hobgoblin in my walls said you were fine," Brian writes. *"He tapped the vent and said—quote—'Your lawyer smells like brownies and poor impulse control, but she'll bounce.' Then he ordered lemon bars."*

"Tell him to invoice me," I type.

"And u will explain EVERYTHING at bar night TO-MORROW," Megan writes, adding four martini glass emojis.

"I have a 6 a.m. thing, and there's a kid on a clock," I text. *"Getting distracted with alcohol feels wrong."* Especially since I already did that for Stardust's shindig last night.

"Not distracted. HELPING!!!!" Megan types. The exclamation marks are starting to give me a headache.

"This is a contract case," Matty adds. Ever the ADA, he can't help being accurate in describing my crisis—points for brand consistency.

"PERFECT," Megan adds, *"We drink and interpret contracts! Just like Ks class!!! Will bring my "Do Not Let Emily Die" notebook!!"*

"I'll bring index cards," Brian adds. *"And possibly my wall-goblin if he insists."*

I huff a laugh. *"Only if he buys the first round."*

I mute the thread before they can schedule my funeral, set two alarms—7:30 p.m. for Wilkin's drop and 5:00 a.m. for the mystery dawn meet. I try to prep for tomorrow's meeting—wardrobe triage (competent, not desperate), rapid mental review of everything I know about the House (not enough), and a page of questions I'll probably be too intimidated to ask.

The mail comes again, and I throw the pile on the coffee table. Ads, coupons, glossy mailers for preschools and music lessons. The last one sticks—thick cardstock, pastel balloons, somebody's first-birthday invite addressed to the old tenant. The photo on the front is all frosting cheeks and tiny paper crown. I turn it over before I can think about it too long.

At one, Victor calls. I let it go to voicemail, then immediately feel like a monster and call back. He answers on the first ring. "Any update? Officer Greene said you were meeting with someone who can find the house?"

"Tonight," I say. "And maybe. I'll call if I have a thread to pull."

A pause. "Thank you."

"We're not celebrating yet." I don't say *we might have to make a deal with something worse than Wilkin,* because why make it worse?

By three I'm exhausted but incapable of sleep. I lie on the couch anyway, staring at the hairline crack in my ceiling, listening to the building's pipes argue with one another. The brief nap I fall into is the kind where you dream you're answering emails you can't read. I wake up less rested and somehow hungrier.

Danielle texts right when my alarm goes off: *"I'm putting your mystery escort in my calendar as "pre-dawn surprise." Don't fall asleep again."*

I send back, *"her? them? could be a sentient filing cabinet."*

She replies with a wolf emoji and a coffee cup.

The sky tints toward evening. I double-check the cooler: twelve brownie-cheesecake bars still lined up like soldiers, condensation beading on the lid. I wrap them in another layer of foil because it feels like doing something.

At 7:30, I slide the cooler into the backseat, tuck a spare hoodie over it like pastry camouflage, and drive through a city that is far too normal for what's happening under its skin. Couples on patios with hot chocolate. A jogger with a Weimaraner. A billboard with Brian Fulton's smile reminding me that some faces don't age and no one seems to care.

The townhouse still looks exactly as it did the night Frank Mitchell bled out on the hardwood floor. It anchors the block like a lemon-colored palace—marble columns flexing for attention, gold trim flashing in the sun, and balconies puffed up with self-importance. Those oversized windows, each corseted in gilt, hide behind velvet drapes thick enough to muffle gossip and daylight in one swoop. But the hydrangeas are brittle husks now, rattling when the icy chill threads through.

I circle to the shadowed north side. The second-story siding bulges as if breathing; Wilkin's subtle signature. I set the cooler down with exaggerated ceremony.

"Delivery for one obnoxious hobgoblin," I whisper.

Silence until the light snaps on behind me.

"Emily?"

I freeze—half-kneel, half-criminal—and pivot to find my former assistant Liz on the back steps, arms folded, eyebrow cocked to maximum skepticism. Liz always reminded me of a postcard from Galway that learned how to type: a riot of red curls, green eyes that clock a room in three seconds, and pale freckled skin the color of "SPF 70 or die." She's in linen slacks and a silk cami, looking effortlessly like she fits into the elite. At her shoulder lingers her husband Camden, a sweet and smart bookkeeper at Johnson & Marcus, but the sort of man who collects vintage weather instruments for fun.

"Liz!" I rise too fast, knocking my knee on the cooler.

She rushes forward, hugging me and somehow managing to pull my hair from its signature pony. She never did like it. "O.M.G. It's been too long. Did you know we lived here?"

"I... didn't."

"We moved in after the probate finally cleared. I needed to get out of the suburbs, too dull. The firm tossed our bid to the top—apparently my references were immaculate." She winks but I catch the faint flush of pride. Good for Liz.

"The entire neighborhood whispered murder house, but a discount is a discount," her husband says, grinning obliviously.

"That poor Mr. Mitchell," Liz tsks. "And his wife! All because of creature problems."

"Creature-adjacent problems," I correct before I can stop myself. "Lucian was exonerated."

"He was *your* client," she reminds me—same touch of disdain she used when partners questioned why I risked the firm's reputation on a vampire. "Why you left Johnson & Marcus," she adds.

"It was—no, I—no." I shrug. Liz never understood. "Water under several bridges. How's life there, anyway?"

She lists new staff members, updated billing codes, and the fresh young hire who took over my original office. No one's replaced me as a partner yet. With every word, more distance yawns between me and my past life.

After she finishes, her gaze softens. "So... why are you here?

My brain sprints through alibis and selects the least incriminating.

"Paying respects." I clear my throat. "Frank Mitchell's... birthday would've been this week. Figured I'd, uh, leave something sweet. Gesture of closure."

Camden peers at the hydrangeas. "Rather solemn place for a picnic." Liz waves him inside with a well-manicured hand. He shrugs and disappears.

"You look... tired, sweets," she says, pursing her lips. "Are you still chasing the weird cases?"

"I'm *defending* the weird cases." I gesture at the house's trim. "Somebody has to."

She laughs lightly. "Well, if you ever want to rejoin the living, Utilities just poached two associates. Davenport might—"

"Thanks," I interrupt, gentle. "But my docket's full."

A small silence stretches. Night insects buzz in the hydrangeas.

Liz clears her throat. "Lunch sometime?" she offers, a little too brightly.

"Absolutely," I say with a smile we both understand, and she retreats inside, porch light snapping off.

I exhale and slide into the narrow shadow between house and hedge.

Wilkin unfolds from the siding like a shadow unpeeling from wallpaper, grin already smeared with chocolate he definitely hasn't earned yet.

"Mortals performing social calamity on porches?" he chirrs. "Fuckin' delectable. Nearly as sweet as your tribute."

"You set me up."

He pops his brows, all innocent rot. "Did a humble hobgoblin know precisely who bought the place? Perhaps. Should a humble hobgoblin be denied enrichin' entertainment? Never." He cackles, a sound like nails shaken in a mason jar.

I fold my arms. "Information. Now."

Wilkin drums claw tips on the cooler lid, listening to the thud like it's a heartbeat. "A collector down in the Loop tunnels is late with the juicy bits. But I did pry loose a crumb. Collateral for expirin' contracts—bagged by February first. Ledger liquefied on the second."

I skip past *liquefied collateral* because I want to sleep again someday. "So... Groundhog Day?"

"Adorable." His eyes gleam. "Mortals and their rodents. Imbolc."

"Im—what?"

He beams like a substitute teacher who loves pop quizzes. "The cross-quarter. Halfway from winter solstice to spring equinox. It's an old calendar hinge when the light remembers how to climb. The House loves liminal bookkeepin'—solstices, equinoxes, quarter days. February fuckin' first."

"And every expiring contract's 'collateral'—people, memories—gets collected before then?"

"Tick-tock." He snaps up another brownie, talks through crumbs. "Contracts run at midnight New Year's Eve. January's for scoopin' loose debts into tidy jars. By Imbolc, books shut, souls shelved. Eternity stamped and filed. Crunch--time."

Cold slides under my ribs. "Where are they staging the collections?"

He gives me a shrug so theatrical it should have footlights. "Don't know. Yet."

"Fantastic."

Wilkin's already sinking back into the siding, smile thinning to a crack. "Sweet dreams. Try not to listen to the clock chewing."

The siding goes still. Night insects take their cue.

I head for the car, cooler empty, deadline loud in my ears. Tomorrow at dawn I meet an ally whose name I still don't know. Tonight, I add Imbolc to my vocabulary and promise myself that a kid won't end up itemized on a cosmic spread-sheet.

Chapter 10

The river tastes like rust and bad decisions at six a.m. I'm under the Franklin Street bridge, pacing and breathing steam like a busted radiator. Danielle and the escort are late, but the city's waking orchestra—garbage trucks, gull cry, the line clattering overhead like it needs coffee more than I do—keeps me company.

A car door thunks nearby. An old brown Crown Vic—vintage enough to be charming if it weren't idling like I need to call a tow truck or a priest—is at the curb. The driver steps out: tall, trim charcoal coat, black driving gloves. Everything about him screams *airport shuttle,* except the eyes—the red of fresh blood, and too calm for pre-dawn Chicago.

"Ms. Lane." His voice is level, accentless. "Your conveyance."

"You're the escort?" I ask. I don't recognize him.

"I am only the driver."

He offers a small leather pouch. Inside rests a bronze token the size of a silver dollar, heavy as a doorstop. There's a House spade on one side, a feather on the other, etched so fine it looks ready to float off.

"Keep it visible," he says, and whips out a black silk blindfold.

"You have got to be kidding. You couldn't just slap a GPS tracker on me and call it a day?"

"House policy." Not threatening, just... inevitable.

I let him tie it on. It smells like lavender and peppermint, which is great if you're a pillow, less great if you're on your way to a myth library run by carnivores.

We pull away, tires hissing on wet pavement. Danielle's voice is still there in the dark—*Some people just like you, Lane.*

Which sounds almost flattering until you're in a stranger's car, blindfolded, heading toward a building you shouldn't be able to enter. If this is what "liking me" looks like, I'm not sure I want to find out how they treat their enemies.

The car turns, slow and deliberate, and I try to count the corners, but the sound goes weird, like the engine hum puts on a blanket and pretends to be silent. Gravity tilts. This is either magic or Lake Shore Drive at rush hour.

The ride ends with the click of a handbrake. The driver removes my blindfold. Dawn is gone; so is Chicago.

We're parked on a marble landing the size of a church vestibule. No way the Crown Vic fits here, but here it is. Ahead is a corridor that's less "hallway" and more Escher on steroids. Shelves climb floor to ceiling—stained oak with brass fittings, wrought iron with rust patina, tightly packed obsidian shelves that suck up every watt like they charge by the proton. Lanterns float untethered, flames the color of absinthe throwing shadows like bad intentions. Beyond our marble island, absolute blackness yawns—a void so complete it makes me wish I had night vision goggles and therapy.

The driver opens my door like we're going to prom. I take his arm because my legs have turned into interpretive dancers, and I really don't want to test the structural integrity of the space outside the marble. He walks me three steps to the threshold.

Flanking the entrance are two ghouls in white suits tailored to accommodate their hunched shoulders. Their skin has the texture of river clay left too long in the sun, with jaws too broad, yellowed teeth visible even with their mouths closed, and milk-pale eyes reflecting the lantern glow. One leans forward, nostrils flaring; the other taps a ledger with quill-sharp nails that click like typewriter keys. When I hold up the metal token, they relax—or as close to relaxed as apex scavengers get without a corpse.

Beyond them, brass-rung ladders slide around by themselves with the oiled precision of clockwork. Balconies climb into the dark with catwalks made of linked iron keys crisscross like a spider had OCD. Somewhere in the distance, a trolley rattles along unseen tracks and delivers scrolls with the distinctive sound of dice tumbling in a velvet-lined cup.

I'm calling it: this is the Archive. It crawled out of reality, chewed through a wall, and built itself a spine.

"Remain here," the driver says.

I turn—for questions, for reassurance—but he's already halfway back to the vestibule. The marble landing ripples, swallowing him and the Crown Vic is simply... not there. Either the area closed behind it or it never occupied ordinary space to begin with.

The ghouls are still in statue mode. I'm alone with indexed infinity and no escort.

"Hello?" I try, voice echoing like I'm yelling in a cathedral. "Emily Lane. Appointment at dawn?"

Nothing answers audibly but a ladder glides into place three stacks down, like it heard me and decided to be helpful. The token in my palm flashes lantern light off its feather.

No Danielle, no mystery ally—just a clock I can't see, ticking toward a holiday I had to Google yesterday, and a library that eats trespassers.

I square my shoulders, slip the token into my coat's breast pocket, and step over the compass seal. Dust and dead ink choke the air, that sweet-rot paper smell clinging to the back of my tongue. Under it runs a metallic tang—old coins, fresh nosebleed—that pricks the nerves and says, very politely, 'some of these books bite back.' Somewhere overhead, a book shuts with a thunder-clap finality—like the Archive acknowledging a new entry: Lane, Emily—Status: do not resuscitate.

I wonder if Val's somewhere like this—doors without exits, corners without windows—waiting for someone to find the right turn.

If the escort never arrives, I'll have to navigate this place solo. Good thing law school taught me one universal rule: *When in doubt, read everything.*

I grab the nearest ladder. It grabs me back—more glide than climb—and we're off.

Except the Archive won't let me read whatever I want. Of course it won't.

The ladder moves on its own until it clicks against a shelf that smells of cedar and thunderstorms and starts sliding. I can't tell if the Archive is guiding me or if the brass token in my coat has hijacked the steering. Either way, the coin is behaving like a supernatural dowsing rod: pleasantly cool against my collarbone while I cling to the rungs, then searing if I'm too nosy at a new set of stacks.

"Great. You're basically a paranormal GPS with attitude," I say, shifting left. The metal cools. I step back right and—ow—instant blister bloom.

"'Hot' is supposed to be the right way, you brat," I tell an inanimate object. It doesn't care.

I follow the temperature gradient—cool good, branding-iron bad—letting the token drag me deeper into the stacks. Lanterns drift higher here, their green flames thinning to candlewicks. The stacks grow older: oak gives way to worm-eaten walnut, hinges forged when Chicago was still swamp and ambition.

Halfway down a narrow aisle I pass an alcove where a single folio, chained open, rests on a marble stand. The page heading gleams in red ink:

ON THE MAINTENANCE OF ANCHORS

My blood spikes. Sara's séance peeled "anchor" out of Victor's contract like a splinter. Emily, meet rabbit hole.

The token stays pleasantly warm. Permission granted. I lean in.

> *The House maintains one living Anchor per century to stabilize its betting ledger. Anchor status confers jurisdiction over collateral equilibrium and insulates ledgers against temporal flux. Anchors must become signatory over all contracts subject to his or her ledger.*
>
> *Pursuant to Veil Covenant, the House must maintain human legitimacy. Thus, anchor identity rotated upon century close or upon catastrophic breach...*

The rest curls into sigils that swim like live eels across parchment. My brain feels two seconds from ejecting from my ears—until the token flares against my skin, heat radiating up my collar. Smoke wisps from the edge of my collar.

"Alright, alright!" I backpedal, fanning my neckline. The coin cools instantly, a passive-aggressive jerk that's angry I went off-trail.

So, an anchor is creepy bookkeeping with a pulse: one person so the bets don't wobble. Weird, but I can swallow it. It's the rest that throws me: Veil Covenant. If it's like the Fae Accords, I don't want to touch it. "Maintain human legitimacy" reads like *don't spook the mortals*. And "rotate at century close or catastrophic breach" gives me a trapdoor without telling me where it's bolted. What counts as catastrophic—getting caught without the mask on?

I don't know the mechanism yet, but I can almost smell leverage.

I press on. The ladder skims sideways across an invisible rail and stops at a row of midnight-blue ledgers whose spines bear constellation motifs instead of titles. The token falls ice cold. This is the stop.

One drawer glides out and stops with millimeter precision. Inside lies a single oversize contract wrapped in red silk, wax seal unbroken. I set it on the brass lectern that swoops down like a stage prop and break the wax.

Indenture of Fortune and Lifespan the title says.

"A cheat sheet," I tell nobody. I read:

> Beneficiary: *Victor Little*
> Consideration: *Winning stake, sanctioned game of Hazard—31 Dec*
> Term: *2 Standard Human Lifetimes*
> Termination: *31 Dec, 23:59 CST*
> Collection Window: *01 Jan—01 Feb*
> Collateral: *Retrieval of lineage due to Principal's failure to appear.*

Administrative Summary of Post-Term Events:

Notice of Termination. On 31 December 23:59 CST, the Term under the Indenture of Fortune and Lifespan matured. Formal Notice of Termination and Demand for Surrender of Principal was served upon Victor Little at his last declared locus.

Evasion / Non-Appearance. Between 00:00 CST 1 January and 23:59 CST 14 January, Principal failed to appear at any designated House ingress, declined countersigned interview, and undertook material acts of concealment and interference. Such conduct constitutes a technical breach of §11 ("Good-Faith Surrender").

Activation of Collateral Clause. Pursuant to §7 ("Collateral on Default or Evasion"), Custodian initiated collateral retrieval. First-degree familial extant at Termination was identified as Valentine "Val" Little (DOB redacted), biological relation to the Principal line. See Genealogic Schedule A, verified via House-grade sanguine assay.

Collection Action. On 15 January 16:13 CST, authorized agents (Ghoul Marshals Clyde et al.) executed Lawful Extraction Protocol at off-ledger location [REDACTED], securing remaining essence consistent with §3(b) ("Quantum of Consideration, Human Issue").

Escrow / Anchor Relation. Essence transferred to Soul Escrow Account AB-1999-FULTON to mature upon Imbolc or Anchor completion, as stamped on final folio. See *Anchor Bets Side-Note Ledger, Century 2000–2099.*

> *Status.* Ledger reflects Debt Outstanding: satisfied by collateral seizure, pending Anchor reconciliation and final Tribunal audit at Imbolc (1 February, sunset).

I stop because if I don't, I'll rip the page and feed it to the ghouls. Like shredding it would magically delete the universe's copy. The Administrative Summary reads like someone vacuum-sealed a kidnapping inside Latin and ledger codes.

Remaining essence is how they say "kid." It sounds like something you'd note about a candle before it goes out. *Technical breach* is "Victor ran because you threatened to take his life."

And then there's the part that makes my stomach drop: the Escrow Account, where the collaterals' *souls* get held until Imbolc or this Anchor completes. That's what's reconciled, but what's taken first? Do the ghouls get first dibs at her body?

My pulse thuds. The clock isn't just ticking, it's calendared, noticed, and blessed by whatever passes for a judge in this place.

I flip past the summary. No more euphemisms. Time to read the instrument they think is airtight and find the place where I can jam a crowbar.

But there are none. The only out was *before* the term expired. The thing is a legal bunker. Loophole-free.

The token starts heating, like it's done babysitting, but fury roots me. *There has to be something.* I scan margins, watermarks, anything—but the vellum drinks my hope like ink.

The only saving grace is the signature line:

Anchor Signatory: Brian Aloysius Fulton

The name hits like a surprise subpoena. I don't know how to free Val yet, but I know the man holding her anchor line. And if I can't pull her up, maybe I can sink his entire ship.

I reseal the bundle. The drawer swallows it and the ladder drifts backward. The token tugs me left—toward the exit, presumably—but I slide past a bookshelf written in English. My eyes catch on the most damning spine: *Anchor Bets Side-Note Ledger, Century 2000–2099*.

My hand shoots out faster than when I fight for the good elevator at the courthouse. The coin goes nuclear. I drop it—hah, loophole—and flip pages with scorched fingertips.

The first page opens on a full-width entry for someone I don't recognize—their photo all sharp cheekbones and eyes like a winter storm. Bets from the last two decades fill the columns: trade deals, elections, even supernatural disputes I don't have a glossary for.

Halfway down the spread, a black line rules them off. Below it: Ongoing Payouts; Former Anchor: Brian Fulton.

His bets end in 1999, neat as a page turn. But the payouts keep coming, each one initialed, each one feeding the same account number from Victor's summary: AB-1999-FUL-TON.

And then the photo: Brian Fulton. *The* Brian Fulton.

Cold does a horror movie crawl up my spine. It's the billboard face. The man in the 1927 photo. And now, the man still collecting on century-old wagers—one of them holding Val's life like a poker chip he hasn't bothered to cash in yet.

My collarbone flares like I lost a fight with an iron. The token is somehow back in my pocket because the House is a cheater. I slam the book shut, swear creatively, and lurch back onto the ladder. The temperature plummets. Three layers of fabric now feature a neat little burn hole. My skin matches.

"Message received," I pant. Too bad I got what I wanted.

The token leads me past the ghoul statues and out to the marble vestibule. No driver. No car. Just ozone and a folded blindfold like a party favor.

Fine. I pocket the token—cool and smug—and step off the marble. Black nothingness turns to asphalt, dawn haze, and the familiar clang of tracks overhead. I'm back under the Franklin Street bridge sans token. Time, it seems, hasn't noticed my detour into impossibility.

No loophole. No rescue clause. But I've got Fulton twice on the paperwork: the signer and the Anchor. If the House's precious stability lives or dies on him, that's something.

Chapter 11

By nine a.m. I'm wedged into a cracked vinyl booth at a River North diner that's been frying eggs since Prohibition. Victor sits across from me, hands locked around a mug he isn't drinking. Danielle commandeered the end of the table, badge clipped to her cardigan like a polite threat. The server drops a plate of pancakes the size of utility hole covers. None of us looks hungry.

I lay it out fast, before adrenaline curdles into fear. "Brian Fulton signed Victor's contract."

Victor blinks, slow. Danielle's pen is already out.

"The *candidate*?" she asks.

I shrug. "Or his doppelgänger or clone or nearly identical descendant. The Archive has Brian Aloysius Fulton tagged as the House's *Anchor* last century, but they didn't include a birth certificate."

Danielle underlines *Anchor* like it offended her. "Anchor like... ship? Weight? Metaphor me."

"Anchor like living escrow," I say. "They keep one per century to stabilize the math. Fulton's name is on everything: Victor's contract, the escrow account where they parked Val's... 'remaining essence.'" The phrase tastes like pennies. I shove my scribbled summary across the table. I wrote down everything I could remember the second I reappeared under the bridge. The print quality looks like a toddler wrote it, but the words land. "They time stamped her abduction at 4:13 p.m. on the fifteenth. Called it 'retrieval of remaining essence.' They dumped her into an escrow account under Fulton's name until his 'Anchor completion.'"

Danielle frowns at that. "Anchor completion... which means what?"

"No idea," I admit. "It changes at century rollover or catastrophic breach. His century's over, someone else is in the chair now." My brain wants to start a whole separate murder board just for that, but Val's the one drowning. Fulton's the rope in my hand, I can worry about who's on the other end later.

Victor stares at the page until the ink might as well be blood. "Is it the same man I took that photo with? The one you found in my storage unit?"

"Maybe. You said the name rang a bell but didn't remember him." I keep my voice even. "Get the photo out of storage. High-res scan, front and back, any captions. If we can prove he's the guy from 1927—and I mean identical, not 'looks like grandpa,' we've got something."

He nods once, already somewhere else in his head, inventorying boxes.

Danielle taps her pen. "Let's say it *is* the same guy—"

"It might be," I cut in, "but I'm not staking a case on 'Emily swears the cheekbones match.'"

"—*or* a descendant with the same name," she continues, unfazed. "Either way, you just said Anchor. If the House balances on a Fulton, rattling him rattles them."

"Exactly. If he falls, the House's books shake. Looks like they do all their business on fancy dates—solstices, equinoxes, and," I nod at Danielle, "Imbolc. February second. The collection window closes then. But the point is: everything they skim lands under Fulton. He's leverage."

"Leverage," Victor says hoarsely. "To trade for Val."

"It's our only shot right now," I say. "If we can rattle Fulton hard enough, we might trade the tremor for Val before they close the books."

Victor scrubs a hand over his face. "I'll go back to the storage unit. Get the photo."

"Good. Maybe get Sara to witch-OCR it, whatever she does," I say. "I'll see Fulton tomorrow night at his candidate dinner. I'm... on the list." (*Thank you, Montgomery.*) "I'll smile, shake hands, and see if a man with an unchanging face flinches. If he's only a descendant, maybe I can still learn how grandpa's connected to the House."

Danielle opens her mouth, closes it. Her pen clicks twice; her eyes do a quick side-cut like she's swallowing a thought. "Be careful what you say in those rooms."

Victor drags a palm across his jaw. "If it's him... if it truly is the same man... does that make him supernatural?"

"I don't know," I admit. "Fulton could be a victim the way you were, or he could be a collaborator. Or a well-groomed heir signing on the dotted line each century."

Victor flinches at *victim*. "I'll get the photo. Today."

Danielle's eyes flick to me, then away. "How did you—" She stops, rearranges her fork like it personally offended her. "How did you get in there, anyway? The Archive."

"A driver, a blindfold, and two ghouls with similar dental plans," I say. "Why?"

She schools her face back to neutral. "Just... checking. You were supposed to have an escort."

"I wasn't. Whoever you thought liked me didn't like me all that much." And if they did, then not enough to show up when it counted. Which means either they've washed their hands of me... or they're waiting for me to owe them. In House terms, that's just another way of saying *debt on layaway.*

Although the escort might have stopped me from going off-path to read about anchors, saving my skin but keeping us further in the dark.

I run them through the rest—the token that burned when I wandered, the Anchor folio that nearly cooked my collarbone, the way the Archive felt like it was grading me. Danielle's jaw clenches when I mention the burn. Victor just looks more tired.

The pancakes congeal. No one touches them. I slide cash under the syrup caddy and tuck my scribbles back into my tote. "Okay. Victor, storage unit. Danielle, see if your missing persons bulletin pulled any weird tips—anonymous calls, impossible sightings. Basically, try to find a ghoul. I'll prep for the dinner and ping Wilkin about a tail."

"Wilkin?" Danielle asks, a sliver of cop disapproval in it.

"Hobgoblin PI. Half the price, twice the stealth," I say. "We've got to use what we have. He's already looking for the House."

Danielle tosses an extra twenty on the check and hovers like she has more to say, then thinks better and leaves with a clatter of the bell. Victor thanks me in a voice too tired for hope and heads out to find that 1927 photo.

Back at my apartment, I'm fantasizing about a ninety-minute nap and maybe a doughnut when I spot it: a thick scarlet envelope squatting on my welcome mat like it owns the lease.

No stamp. No return address. My name, letter-pressed in black like an epitaph.

I crack the seal—and out slides a single red casino chip, warm as fresh toast. That warmth? Pure House menace. A small card follows:

Cease interference. Debt available.

For a beat I just stand there, heartbeat keeping time with the little chip's slot machine glow. The message is crystal: *We see you, Counselor. Nice apartment—it'd be a shame if something collected your essence.*

Nap cancelled.

Adrenaline suggests I leave. Ego suggests I dare them to knock. I compromise by double-locking the door, sliding the deadbolt with a flourish, and barricading with my rolling briefcase. Nobody barges in on a lawyer's paperwork mountain.

I snap a photo and text Danielle: *"House just doxxed me."*

Three minutes later the pounding starts—wolf-tempo again.

"Emily Lane, open this door before I huff and puff and—"

"Yeah, yeah." I drag the suitcase aside and crack the door. Danielle stands there in full police blues.

"Don't you work?" I ask, letting her in.

She clocks the poker chip between my fingers. "And we're swamped. That tells you how serious I am. They delivered a heat-seeking threat. You're leaving."

"I'm fine," I say. "I went after their contract, they mailed me a threat. Classic stalemate."

She arches one were-brow. "And the stalemate ends when they use keys instead of envelopes. Grab a bag."

I lean on bravado. "Please. They mail-slapped me. The building's still standing."

She flicks a finger, taps the chip. It hisses like a skillet. "Standing *for now.* You really want to test the deductible on supernatural arson?"

"I want to test my bed for a nap," I reply, trying not to whine.

"You can nap with a bodyguard." She shoulders past me towards my bedroom and starts yanking open drawers. "Where's your go-bag?"

"You hate my apartment decor that much?"

"I hate kidnapping paperwork delivered to my friends." She holds up the envelope, shakes it like evidence. "We have less than two weeks, Emily. They're escalating."

I fold my arms. "You don't have a guest room. Hotels cost money I'm uninterested in spending. Where, exactly, am I sleeping?"

Danielle pauses, she clearly hadn't solved that step. "You can't sleep on a couch?"

I sniff imperiously to cover the fact that my back will seize up on a couch. "I'm a princess."

Danielle rolls her eyes so hard I hear it. "Fine, Your Royal Highness of Snark—then pick a bed with real wards."

I groan. "I'll find something. I'll go to my second office and figure something out."

"Moonlit Haven?" She weighs it, then nods once. "Acceptable *for now.* Their wards are pretty basic, too many human and stranger patrons. I'll do drive-bys while on shift, but I'd better get an update before closing that you found somewhere with a bed and no open-door policy."

"Deal." I stuff my laptop, toothbrush, Victor's file, and the last few brownies into a tote while the poker chip goes into the trash. At the door I flip every light, set the coffee maker to brew at midnight out of spite, and lock up.

"Stay safe, Herle," I call from the steps outside. "Give 'em hell."

Mid-afternoon means the place is quiet: most of the chairs still flipped on tables, bar lights low, and only a few stragglers like me haunting the booths. I stake my claim with a legal pad, the Archive notes, and a promise to myself that I'll nap for twenty minutes and then be a responsible adult.

Eight minutes later I jerk awake to the sensation of being watched. The bar is empty. My table isn't.

A scarlet chip sits on my legal pad, centered like a period at the end of my notes. There's condensation around it in the perfect outline of a spade.

I didn't put it there. Obviously.

My stomach does an unpleasant flip. I text Danielle, "*Office compromised. Chip found me again. Inside the Haven.*"

Her reply lands in one beat: "Out. Now. Find real wards."

And yet... ego suggests I dare the House to try it again. Self-preservation suggests I stop auditioning for "*Final Girl: Attorney at Flaw.*" I open my contacts.

The problem is two-fold: no one but the supernatural have wards. At least, as far as anyone's telling me. And my supernatural allies are slim.

Although, my non-supernatural allies are *also* slim. Matty's a government lawyer whose "guest room" is a futon wedged between file boxes and I'm unwilling to open that can of worms just yet. Megan lives in a studio still paying off her loans; she'd rather buy something fabulous than spend it on what the rest of us would call essentials. And Brian... I honestly don't know.

But I wasn't kidding about the whole 'need an actual bed' thing.

Sara's first. Not that she has an open bed; you'd be surprised how little mortician's pay and how much of her salary goes towards black eyeliner and candles.

She answers on the second ring with her morgue voice—calm, efficient, possibly holding a scalpel. "Tell me you don't need more redactions. The last one ate through my counter. Not the cost I was expecting."

I wince. "Not yet... I was actually looking for another favor."

"Yeah, Danielle dropped by with a guy. Something about reverse-engineering a photo?"

Right. Fulton's 1927 glamour shot. My priority for the last few hours was finding four walls to keep the ghouls out, not on the reason the ghouls were tailing me. "What's the verdict?"

"I can't pull ink out of century-old sepia. What I *can* do is carbon date the stock, see if it's truly 1920s."

"That would still prove Fulton's face hasn't aged. Good enough for court-of-public-opinion. The book said something about human legitimacy under the Veil Covenant. Ever heard of it?"

Paper rustles, like she's reading something. "No, not in anything I've got."

"I'll keep looking." I shake my head. "But that's not why I called. Can you check with Lucian and see if I can crash at the coven in one of the guestrooms? One night only."

"Hang on." She sets the phone down. There's a distant murmur, with words I can't catch.

"Is he there?" I inadvertently ask aloud. I wasn't expecting an immediate answer but still.

"No," she says, her voice now having that echoey quality that comes with the speakerphone setting. "But I've got ways to contact him fast. Better for coven security."

I nod like I understand. (And as though she can see me.) "Is there a coven bat-phone?"

She replies, voice careful, clearly underappreciating my joke. "No. But I have an answer. He says it isn't wise."

"Oh." I make it light, like I absolutely expected that. "Because my pillow clashes with the drapes?"

"It's just... risky."

"Sure. Makes sense." It does, in the way that getting left off the VIP list always *makes sense*. Half the city's vampires and their buddies crash there, it's got a dozen empty beds, *and* he wanted to renegotiate our friendship after that nice note, but sure, I'm 'risky.'

"Anyway, thanks for asking," I say. What I don't say: I hate that I had to ask you to ask him because he doesn't text, and I don't rate a landline. "I'll find something."

"Do you want me to ask around?"

"I can ask," I say, a little too fast. Because what stings isn't just the *no*—it's that I had to ask someone *else* to ask for it. "Dinner soon?"

"And my three dozen donuts," she says. There's another pause. "Emily, he didn't say 'no' because of you."

"Sure," I say. "Tell him thanks anyway. And that I'll invoice him for emotional damages."

She snorts softly. "I'll pass it along."

We hang up. I stare at the chip until my reflection warps in the red.

The front door opens. Footsteps, a quick whistle, and Ray slips in carrying a paper bakery sack and a hoodie slung over one shoulder.

"Hey," he says, easy and warm. "Left my jacket here last night. Sev pretends he doesn't do coat check." His smile fades when he spots the red chip on my pad. "That supposed to be here?"

"Not unless Severin switched to mob-chic décor." I nudge it with my pen. "Long story short: someone powerful is annoyed I read a contract I wasn't supposed to. They left me these little valentines. Danielle says relocate. I tried Lucian via Sara." I aim for breezy but hit brittle. "Apparently I'm a warding headache."

Ray looks at me, then at the chip, then back at me. No theatrics. Just a nod. "Okay. You're not staying *here*."

"I can grab a warded motel, maybe," I say, even though my bank account just sobbed.

"Or," he says, simple as breathing, "you come to ours. Guest room's made. Good locks. Stardust did... whatever he does to the doors." He lifts the bakery sack. "Also, there are muffins."

I hesitate. "You don't even know what this is."

"I don't have to," he says. "But if you want me to, tell me on the way."

"It's called the House," I admit, keeping it quick. "Capital H. Think casino plus ledger plus very old grudges. They collect debts that look like lives. I poked the bear."

Ray winces. "I know the House. I know you don't want an account there. Or the guilt of working for them. So, let's not let them find you in a booth." He jerks his head toward the door. "You drive. You can brief me like I'm dumb and friendly."

"You're not dumb."

"Great. Then I'll just be friendly." He grins, and the knot between my shoulders loosens a fraction. "Safest entrance is the side alley with bronze fox knocker. It puts you under the wards. Say 'room service' at the peephole and the door unlocks. Don't ask me how. Stardust said it and now it's true."

I almost smile. "Will Stardust care that I'm bringing heat to your love nest?"

Ray bites his lip. "I won't tell him about the House part, but keeping you from becoming creature kibble? Come on." He slips into his Stardust impression—mock-British and faintly appalled: "Emily girl, I would be *put out* if you died and I wasted all that time cultivating you into my circle. And did you hear about Michael? He's back to wearing white velvet which, as you *know*, only looks good on me."

I huff a laugh that doesn't wobble too much. "I'll pay in pastries."

"Already accepted," he says, lifting the bag.

Ten minutes later, we arrive in Old Town, the area designated as the vampire quarter. The alley behind their brownstone smells like rain and bakery dumpsters. I find the bronze fox knocker, rap three times, and murmur, "Room service."

Air pressure tilts—cool and clean—and the door unlatches. Warm lamplight spills down the hall.

"You know where the guest room is," Ray says, hanging the hoodie on a peg. "Tea on the tray. If you can't sleep, there's movies."

I text Danielle, bypassing my plans for bar night, and set alarms for 6:30 and 6:45 (because I know myself). The wards hum against my skin like a cat.

And I finally get my nap.

CHAPTER 12

Last night's bar night tried to be a strategy session: Megan slapped down her not-a-joke "Do Not Let Emily Die" notebook, Matty stacked index cards like a tiny courthouse, and Brian drew a flowchart on a coaster. We walked anchor → escrow → breach until the bartender begged us to order something edible and still ended up with no loophole and a lot of swearing. The only actionable takeaway was "text when you go out or Megan calls 911." So tonight, I text—then put on a blazer to go rattle a candidate

The event is at the kind of townhouse that cosplays as Versailles, but a Versailles with better parking and radiant-heat concrete. Limestone façade slick as fondant, wrought iron balcony rails curling like judgmental question marks, and enough uplighting to give a vampire a tan. Valets form a phalanx of tuxedos, ready to whisk away German imports. Two marble lions guard the steps; each has better orthodontia than I do.

The moment I cross onto the estate, my skin prickles. Not danger, just that *watched* feeling. Because of the poker chip that's following me around or a hint of Fulton's connection, I'm not sure. All I know is that if I die in heels, Montgomery's going to write it off on his taxes.

Montgomery meets me just inside, immaculate as ever. "Smile, ask pointed questions with rounded edges," he murmurs, steering me beneath a UFO-sized chandelier into a room that's ninety percent gilt and ten percent family crest. There are floor to ceiling mirrors framed in gold leaf, damask drapes so heavy they could double as panic-room doors, and oil portraits of people who look like they charged Napoleon rent and tacked on late fees.

"I left my subpoenas in my other clutch," I say, trying not to trip over a rug that probably has an NDA.

He tilts his head. "Look."

Brian Fulton stands beneath a gilt mirror shaking hands like he's hydrating voters one palm at a time. And for a beat, my brain does that Windows-98 error noise.

Same jawline as the 1927 photo. Same cheekbone geometry. Same cautious dimple. If you told me the photographer shot him at the Aragon Ballroom yesterday and slapped a sepia filter on top, I'd believe you. My gut says *it's him*. My law brain files that under *inadmissible until proven beyond reasonable cheekbones*.

But it isn't the face that keeps me looking. It's the *nothing*. He radiates... dial tone. Not absence, exactly. *Null.* Like when your fridge dies and you only notice because the silence feels wrong.

Up close, he's glossy—navy suit, modest flag pin, tie that screams competent but not sexy—yet when no one's looking, he power-downs. Eyes unfocus, and posture stills. Face empties to factory settings. Then someone steps into his orbit and *click*—he's back, smile rebooted, handshake calibrated to "I see you, middle-class hope."

"Perfect candidate," Montgomery murmurs. "Unflappable. Everyone sees what they want."

"Because he's set to screensaver," I say. "If he starts showing the DVD logo bouncing, I'm leaving."

Montgomery's mouth curves, indulgent. "Play nice. He's *sensitive* to the needs of the city." His emphasis is deliberate, a little gleam in his eye. "*All* its citizens."

That's the tell. Montgomery doesn't just see a candidate; he sees a bridge. Someone polished enough to survive human politics and open-minded enough to stitch the supernatural into the civic fabric. To him, Fulton isn't null—he's potential.

Me? I'm not so sure. Ancient masquerader? House puppet? Or just another familiar face who could do good in the right hands?

But this is my opportunity to figure it out. The host does herding, Montgomery does the hand-off.

"Brian, this is Emily Lane," he purrs. "One of Chicago's more... useful minds."

Fulton's smile boots up on command. "Ms. Lane," he says in the voice of a thousand tasteful yard signs. "I've heard you're an asset to this city."

I meet his hand. Warm. Normal. The null hum under my skin spikes just slightly, as if my bones noticed something my fingers didn't. "I try," I say. "You've been in Chicago for ages, I bet. Ever run across any Aragon gala photos in the family scrapbooks?"

A hiccup—a blink half a beat slow—then the smile reboots. "We've *always* supported the city." He lands the word like it has a trademark. "Chicago's history is a treasured inheritance."

Not an answer. But a practiced one.

"Education, safety, stability," he continues for the small circle now orbiting us. "We build a city worthy of our grandchildren."

He could be selling vacuum cleaners. The room laps it up.

A council member leans in with a joke, Fulton laughs on the correct beat. When the conversation migrates toward the bar, he remains a half-step behind—facing a framed landscape. He stares like someone forgot to hit play.

I sidle up again. I'm not giving up yet. "Best jazz act you've seen live in the last century?"

"I try to be home for evenings with my family," he replies. The line is practiced, dustless.

"Cards or dice?" I ask, conspiratorial. "My uncle swore loved *hazard*."

"I prefer transparent odds," he says, voice half a degree cooler. "When the house always wins, we know who loses."

The words slip through me like a paper cut. Does he mean *the* House? Because it reads like he's not a willing collaborator. But something about the phrasing hums wrong, too clean, too rehearsed. Like a man who's repeated it often enough to forget where he first heard it.

I make myself smile like it's nothing. "You sound like a man who's played a few bad hands."

His reboot-smile clicks on again, flawless as a screensaver. "I only play when the rules are clear."

I shift the frame. "Every campaign needs an *anchor*—" I watch him closely "—the person everything routes through when the *ledger* gets messy. Who's yours?"

His gaze snaps to mine for a beat too long. "We have a disciplined team," he says. "No single point of failure."

"Healthy," I say. "You know, you've built impressive coalitions. Curious where your early support came from?"

His smile holds steady. "We're grateful to partners like the Solstice Educational Foundation," he says smoothly. "And I am deeply appreciative of all the work you put in with them."

I blink. *Educational?* I set up the Solstice Foundation—no middle name, a Super PAC, not any kind of nonprofit. PACs buy ads and headaches. "Educational" is a different creature. Either he slipped or there are two Solstices.

"A worthy cause," I say lightly, filing the slip behind my eyes in bold red ink.

Montgomery reappears at my elbow, dragging me toward edible status symbols. "He likes you," he murmurs.

"He likes not being asked about anything real," I mutter. "And he turns off when no one's watching."

"Discipline," Montgomery corrects. "He doesn't waste energy."

"Or personality," I say. "Unflappable or unplugged?"

He gives me a patient, sharklike smile. "Electable."

I do my job—listen more than I talk, watch where the candidate's eyes go, where his staffers' bodies lean. Everyone around him looks exhausted in the particular way of people who sleep in fifteen-minute increments and pretend it's a hobby.

But Fulton never wavers. When he speaks from the staircase, the room warms by five degrees on cue. When he stops, the air goes back to nothing. Like someone dimmed the lights and forgot to turn them back on.

I drift to the perimeter, inhale more canapes than is healthy, and do a staff lap.

A young comms aide with a thousand-yard stare and glitter on her wristband is my first stop. "When'd *you* first meet

Brian?" I ask, keeping it wide-eyed and interested in a benign way.

"He found me," she says, not looking me in the eye.

A veteran donor leans in when I mention Solstice Educational Fund. "It's smart packaging," she says, then sips. "Good for unlocking suburban wallets."

"Who set up the invite list?" I ask, faux-innocent. "I owe a thank you."

"Talk to Allison," she says, nodding toward a woman in a black sheath and a headset. "She knows every donor family tree."

I catch Allison between triage moments. "Solstice *Educational*—is that the 501(c)(3) or the PAC?" I ask, breezy. "I want to label my spreadsheet right."

Her smile flickers, internal contact list riffling. "We're grateful to many partners," she recites. "If you need compliance contacts, I can email the director."

"Please," I say, handing a card. "I'm old-fashioned. I like names that match filings."

She laughs, but it's the brittle kind.

Coats appear, checks change hands, and the quartet plays us out with a string version of a song that definitely started life in a nightclub. I thank our host, dodge a donor who wants to "pick my legal brain," and help myself to a centerpiece that costs more than my car insurance. Hell, more than *Montgomery's* car insurance. But it's doubling as a party favor and hall pass for the next part of my night.

Montgomery offers a ride, but I wave him off and skip the valet line. I parked my clunker two blocks away on purpose—valets judge, and my sedan coughs like a two-pack-a-day gremlin.

The walk back is quiet. Too quiet. Even the fountains along the street seem to hush when I pass. Of course I don't *see* anything. That would at least be real, and not me getting into 'afraid of her own shadow' territory.

The engine turns over on the third prayer, and the dash throws check-engine light confetti. Still, I make sure the doors are locked before I shift into drive. I point the hood toward my next stop, letting the heater wheeze me back to the murder house, hoping any ghouls tailing me prefer pithier prey.

Liz opens the door on the second knock, glossy hair, in silk pajamas that say 'I have opinions about thread count.' Camden hovers behind her, clearly thrilled to see anyone after nine p.m.

"Em!" Her gaze locks on the arrangement and goes wide. "Is that—"

"Centerpiece," I say, breezy as a flight attendant explaining turbulence. "Host said take them. I thought it would be a great housewarming gift."

She makes a noise normally reserved for proposal videos. "From that Fulton dinner?" She tries to be casual, fails adorably. "Come in—Camden, look!"

It's elegant, sure—also the floral equivalent of a quiet brag. White ranunculus stacked like tiny ballerina tutus, sprigs of winter berries popping out like Christmas punctuation, and enough glossy magnolia leaves to re-side a Mc-Mansion. The whole thing sits in a low stone bowl that whispers "four figures, pre-tip," dusted with fake frost and threaded with a skinny gold wire of fairy lights for the tasteful rich-people glow.

We do the dance—she asks who I saw, I give her the harmless celebrity list. She drops more firm gossip, I nod like it isn't completely irrelevant to me now.

But Liz glows with proximity. She's always wanted the in-crowd, she deserves a little sparkle. She name-drops me twice in her stories and I take it as the compliment it is.

"Lunch?" she says, angling a berry like she's docking a spacecraft.

"Absolutely," I lie kindly. "You can tell me why Camden now owns four barometers."

"Five," Camden corrects, delighted.

"Ambitious," I say, backing toward the door. "I love a man with a weather plan."

They wave me into the night, the flower arrangement glowing in their front bay window like proof I'm still in the room.

I slide into the hedge's shadow. The clapboard bulges, then peels, and Wilkin oozes out, grinning like he's raided someone else's dessert tray.

"Status bouquets to the ladder-climbers," he chirrs, his grin like he's just discovered the secret to happiness, or at least to getting under my skin. "Delectable. Almost as sweet as your tribute."

"Had to tidy the cover," I say. "Any leads?"

"Dick Fritz," he says, leering at me.

"The flyer guy?"

He shrugs, barely containing his self-satisfied grin. "Heard he's got a way in."

That's something at least. "And you found him?"

He taps the side of his nose, looking like he's cracked the Da Vinci Code. "His name."

I stare at him, blinking slowly. "That's the lead? A name I already know? Not where he is or how to find him?"

Wilkin shrugs again, the picture of smug indifference, like he's just handed me a treasure map, and I'm too dense to read it.

It figures. If I ran secret casino, I'd make myself harder to subpoena too.

I *should* ask Wilkin what he knows about the ghouls. I should ask if he's seen them tailing me, or if my shadow has started twitching wrong. But Wilkin loves irritating me like raccoons love trash. So, I plaster on a smile that's a little too wide and a little too fake and push past it.

"I have a new job," I say, adopting a tone of official business, even though the only thing that's official right now is my ability to barely tolerate Wilkin.

"Bigger than pixie bounties?" He licks a claw. "Convince me."

"Tail Brian Fulton," I say. "If he's the same man from 1927—or just the heir with the same face—I want patterns. Where he goes when the lights are out. Side doors, shadow meetings, who he eats with when he eats alone."

Wilkin wrinkles his nose. "He did a puff-piece photo shoot here. Somethin' about 'honoring the dead.'" He snorts. "If Fulton's supernatural, Mitchell would've wanted him laid out in the ground beside him."

Now it's my turn to wrinkle my nose. "I remember the discourse." Something I only paid attention to after I roped myself into the case. Mitchell was a hypocritical creature condemner and proud of it.

"I'm in," he trills. "But it'll cost you."

"Two dozen Fudge-Me-Once," I say. "Honey-goat gelato if your notes are specific. And Wilkin—he name-dropped something called the Solstice Educational Foundation. Not the PAC I created called the Solstice Foundation. If you find anything in his office, let me know."

Gold flecks jump in his eyes. "Two Solstices. How festive." He taps the siding. "Breadcrumbs go on your tin can's hood. If I get bored, I'm makin' art with your wipers."

"I'll risk modern art," I say. "You gave us the countdown clock, so move fast."

He grins too many teeth. "Vacuum like that? Sucks hard." Then he snaps back into clapboard with the sound of a deck shuffling.

The dark folds around me as I tug my coat tighter and head for the car.

CHAPTER 13

Stardust's house wakes up like a disco with a hangover—quiet, expensive in an outdated way, and still sparkling in all the wrong places. The Wi-Fi, of course, is NASA-grade. After waving Ray goodbye before the sun rose, I stake out the pristine and never-used kitchen island. For the next few hours, the only sounds are the clack of my keys and the occasionally exasperated huff when another database coughs up nothing useful.

Shock of shocks, Allison from the night before came through, sending me the contact information for the Educational Foundation's compliance section. (Gold star for punctuality.) I fire off a polite lawyerly request—*Dear Mr. Wallace, pursuant to public-inspection duties...*

The bounce-back arrives before my inbox finishes reloading: *Brad Wallace is unavailable to provide that information at this time.*

Either the director has weaponized their out-of-office reply, or they've got a hair-trigger set to *deny, deny, deny*. I try a second email, tweak the wording, add a smiley face like a professional. Instant denial, same wording, different timestamp. He's clearly got a macro keyed to "Nope."

I get three tabs of "Solstice Educational Foundation" open and, of course, none of them are the thing I actually set up.

Mine was *The Solstice Foundation*, big-kid PAC with teeth. This one wears a halo. Charitable. Educational. Vaguely smug. Their site is a single page of stock-photo children reading in sunbeams and a Donate button that looks like it refuses anything under five figures.

I pace the kitchen, past a crystal decanter of something I'm not brave enough to label and a framed poster of some Fritz Lang/Henry Fonda noir film, *You Only Live Once*—which is very on brand for a vampire and low-key mean-girl to mortal houseguests—and try to dredge up everything I remember from my white-collar days.

I'm not hunting for killer memos or villainous mission statements. Shell outfits never write those down. Shells are a husk of real, solid, organizations. (Really? "A shell is a shell." Why yes, I do have a professional degree.)

What I need are the fingerprints every hollow nonprofit leaves behind: a mailing address that's really a mail-drop warehouse, board "members" who share one Gmail and no resumes, articles of incorporation that list a purpose so broad it could fund either after-school tutoring or death-ray R&D, Form-990s showing ninety cents of every donated dollar boomeranging back out as "consulting fees," and, if I'm lucky, a wire trail from those fees to somebody's campaign chest. Stack enough of those slippery puzzle pieces together and you don't get a smoking gun—you get the outline of the gun, the smoke, and the guy whistling while he hides the bullet.

I plug in every search term that won't land me on a watchlist: Solstice Educational Foundation + "articles," "charter," "ledger," "board." I pull the easy fruit: public records all businesses, even shams, have to keep. But the public 990 stub? *Unshockingly* skeleton. Numbers, no guts. Anything juicy—donor lists, private ledgers, internal minutes—lives on paper in someone's locked cabinet. Every road ends at *visit in person* or *records unavailable online*. The internet shrugs: cute story, come touch paper.

Stardust appears in the doorway like a cat materializing out of velvet. Robe, slippers, hair that defies gravity and shame. He clocks my screen, the coffee, my frown.

"Some of us are trying to age backward, darling," he rasps. "Could you glower more quietly?"

"Research whisper-glare engaged," I say. "Go back to bed, your highness. I'm just trying to figure out whether the 'Educational' charity is legit or a front with better fonts."

He yawns delicately. "If it asks for recurring donations, it's evil. If it sends free calendars, it's worse." He floats towards me like a dandelion with opinions. "And if you're going to sacrifice your mortal looks to exhaustion, at least do something with your hair."

Then he disappears in a slow ripple of silk, leaving the faint scent of lavender and judgment hanging in the air. I sip my coffee and nudge my notes into a neater pile, willing the murder board in my head to shut up for five minutes. It's clear I won't uncover anything else in this garish—and unused—kitchen. Touching paper, here I come.

Matty pings just as I'm shrugging on my coat. It's either fate, or someone put a trace on my aura. Could go either way with this crowd.

"Lunch?"

"Trawling microfiche," I reply. *"Too boring even for you."*

"I prosecute fraud for fun. Which office?"

"State AG's Charitable Trusts," I tell him. *"Maybe Secretary of State filings if I get lucky."*

"Meet you in 20," he sends.

We rendezvous at a government building that smells like toner and long marriages. After flashing our bar cards, he gets the reels; I get the gloves. The place hums: fluorescent lights, a dehumidifier that wheezes like a lifelong smoker, and a row of microfilm readers the size of microwaves. Drawers labeled FOUNDATIONS—FICHE and CHARITY REGISTRY—INDEX screech open to reveal reels that smell faintly of vinegar and history. Within minutes we're back in our native habitats: his white-collar ADA brain wiring timelines and vendors, mine sniffing out alter egos and shells thanks to a past life of fraudulent-transfer scavenger hunts.

"This is the charter and amendments," I say, scrolling until my finger cramps. "Reinstatement paperwork. Look at this—it was called the *Equinox* Educational Foundation once. Inactive tradename."

"Does that mean something?"

I shrug, already thumbing out a text to Victor. "Maybe. My client hit a fundraiser for that outfit back in the day—might shake something loose in his memory."

Matty tugs another drawer. "Trade names and agents." He threads a fresh reel; I crank to the right year. A card flits by—Equinox Educational Foundation d/b/a Solstice Educational Fund (assumed name)—with a rubber-stamp date that screams hasty rebrand. The listed address is a mailbox store, and the purpose clause is so broad it could underwrite after-school tutoring or a doomsday bake sale. Board list? "Vacant pending," typed twice, as if that makes it less suspicious.

I jot the highlights and flip through the rest. "Every page that could tell us who bankrolled this thing might as well say 'kiss off.'"

"This is why white-collar cases take months," Matty says with a sigh. "Paper trails only talk if you have subpoenas."

"I have sarcasm and a deadline," I say. "Does sarcasm come with subpoena power?"

"Alas." He gives me the look that means *you're about to do something ill-advised, and I cannot endorse it.* "I'll file a couple public records requests on related city grants—it won't be fast, but it might offer other names. You... don't break into anything."

"I would never," I say.

He snorts. "That would be more believable if I didn't know you."

"I'll have you know that anywhere I've... entered, I did with permission. From someone."

"From someone that counts?"

I shrug. "Adjacent."

His smile is warm and slightly resigned. "That word gets a lot of mileage," he says. "Text me if you find something spicy. Or even mildly jalapeño."

"Careful," I say, rolling back to replace the frames. "I might start thinking you like research dates."

He taps the table. "I like you." A beat. "And research."

We split on the sidewalk—Matty back to court, me back to my borrowed safe house—his hand warm on my elbow for an extra second.

It's just after two when the front door opens and Ray stumbles in, hoodie half-zipped, a burrito the size of a newborn tucked under his arm.

"Shift took forever," he announces to the house in general, then to me, surprised: "You're still up."

"Dead ends breed insomnia," I say, shutting my laptop. "Foundation donors are locked up tighter than a vampire's diary."

"Vampires don't do diaries," comes a muffled voice from the hallway. Stardust drifts in, hair still gloriously wrecked from sleep, pajama pants that deserve their own stage. He looks at Ray like the sun just rose in his kitchen, which is weird since it would kill him. He kisses Ray, turns to me, and pretends he didn't just thaw a glacier with his eyes. "We journal."

"Semantics," I say. Turning to Ray, I ask, "Why so late today?"

Ray rolls his shoulders. "Three extra appraisal tickets, two broken scales, and one lady who tried to trade me her grandfather's Purple Heart because 'he'd want the cash flow.'" He rubs his eyes. "We're swimming in storage unit specials. Dust-choked jewelry boxes, wedding china that never met a dinner, trunks with monograms no one remembers. Everybody's suddenly 'liquidating an estate'—only the estates sound suspiciously alive last time rent was due."

The reminder clicks behind my ribs: the January fallout Danielle mentioned. People melt off the grid; their leftovers surface in pawnshops.

Ray props a hip against the island. "It's like half the city found out their relatives evaporated over Christmas break and decided sentimentality's overrated."

Stardust's smile flickers—there, then dimmed by a shadow only he can see. "I've been dying for a new set of vintage cufflinks. Do keep your eye out."

Ray's gaze softens and I know there's a subtext I'm missing. "Done."

Stardust flashes a fang-bright grin, a real one this time, then flicks a glance at the phone on the counter. "Also, Emily, Armand rang in his own insomniatic tizzy. He wants yet another contingency in his will. If the airboat venture in Biloxi stalls, his snuff boxes are to go to the Musée des Arts Décoratifs. But only the ones with griffins. The cherubs are 'for commoners.'" He rolls the phrase in a perfect Parisian accent, then slants me a look. "*You* asked for the introduction."

I shrug, tapping the space bar hard enough to rattle the keyboard. "Hey, billable hours are billable hours. If Armand wants a griffin-only exit strategy, I draft it—then cash the check before he changes his coat of arms again."

Stardust's laugh is all midnight velvet. "He will. The man changes his mind the way I change playlists."

Ray props an elbow on the island, entertained. "You two go back how far—flappers and bathtub gin?"

"1923," Stardust says. "He mistook my backstage for a speakeasy. I mistook his boredom for charm."

I lift a brow. "Why isn't he in your coven if you've been connected that long?"

"Because I was gloriously unattached in those days," he says, flipping a hand. "Armand pledged to House Verani; I didn't swear fealty to Lucian until '68. Commitment *grew* on me." He tilts his glass toward Ray, all adoration and a wicked grin. "Now I'm positively domesticated."

I hum and turn back to my laptop while they melt into each other like fondue—sweet, sticky, and hazardous to bystanders. Watching them makes something in my chest pinch: envy wrapped in relief, salted with the reminder that I've never been anyone's century-long constant. I literally couldn't be.

But deadlines don't care about feelings. Instead, I stare at the black-screened laptop, replaying the Compliance Director's rapid-fire brush-offs and the blank donor columns mocked up on microfiche. When the polite routes—emails, FOIAs, Matty's subpoenas-in-waiting—take too long, it's time to use the crowbar in my contacts list.

Only days ago Montgomery told me he was my 'in' for introductions sans paper trail. Ominous, but necessary now. I thumb out a text before I can overthink it:

"Hit the wall with Brad Wallace at Solstice Educational Foundation. Got any connection there? I need in their office for board ledgers, historical donors. Today if possible."

If I'm calling in my own personal mob boss, I may as well go big. Because a kid is still missing and Imbolc looms.

And if the ghouls are still lurking, they're clearly taking their time. Two full days and nada. It's like a weather report. Ghouls: 40% chance of eerie vibes, zero actual bite.

So, it's time for a field trip.

But the phone stays stubbornly silent. I keep checking, willing a three-dot bubble to appear. Nothing.

The afternoon stretches. Ray showers, Stardust disappears with him and reappears with inexplicable glitter on his collarbone. I reread my notes until the words flatten into soup. I do not nap. At some point when they've disappeared yet again—where and why I'm not asking, that's the rule as a houseguest—I head outside to sweet-talk a nearby hobgoblin into acting as my messenger.

Lucian's got a deal where they can't infiltrate *his* HQ without permission. But that arrangement doesn't extend to the rest of his coven.

By 5:30, when the sun is just saying goodnight, I'm on the side entrance steps. I wave one of Ray's leftover muffins in the air and whisper-yell.

"Anybody of the hobgoblin variety there? I've got a job for you."

Quicker than I expect, he fades into view from the ductwork next door—three feet of soot, brass-button eyes, and opinions. He eyes the muffin like it owes him rent.

"Courier run," I whisper. "Find Wilkin. I can't get to his place until later. Tell him: update?"

"Price is two things that work and one thing that leaks," he rasps.

Could be worse; at least this barter doesn't require anything difficult or illegal. I hand over my worst pen, a fresh AA battery, and a spare sewing kit from Stardust's junk drawer, adding the muffin as a tip. He inhales it, vanishes the other items and sluices back into the vent like espresso through a straw.

Five eternal minutes later, he reappears and slaps a lipstick-smeared cocktail napkin into my palm and disappears before I can blink. One side of the paper is typed—actual ribbon ink, smudged at the serif:

> "It's there all the time,
> driving me out to wan-
> der the streets, following
> me, silently, but I can
> feel it there."

The flip side is handwritten scratch in block printing: *Have a lead on the location. Will leave another breadcrumb on your car.*

"Another?" We've had exactly one breadcrumb—the Imbolc clock—and maybe, if we're grading generously, the Archive non-hint. Dick Fritz—a name I already know—isn't it.

And the typed bit? Either he's quoting something noir to feel tall, or he's needling me about the ghouls shadowing my reflection. Only he'd turn my paranoia into performance art. I shove the note behind the unmentionable decanter.

At 7:58 p.m., the house changes temperature—the way places do when night people start their engines. Stardust is buttoning a waistcoat that defies basic tailoring when my phone *finally* buzzes.

"*Records room,*" Montgomery writes. "*Thirty minutes. Ask for the east elevator; tell them you're there for Foundation review. And keep your calendar open, looking at a fundraiser for Blake next week.*"

My lips purse. Blake must be Montgomery's backup candidate.

Montgomery continues, "*I want unvarnished thoughts on which horse to back.*"

Anyone but the House's lapdog, I think, though that's still circumstantial.

"*Will do and I owe you,*" I reply.

"*I'm keeping track*" is his swift response.

But I'm on my feet before the threat lands. "I've got a date with a filing cabinet."

Ray's brows knit. "Is that legal?"

"Adjacent," I say, already shoving files into my bag.

Maybe I do need to retire that word for a while.

Stardust leans on the doorframe, amused and concerned in equal measure. "Emily girl, if a locked cabinet looks at you with bedroom eyes, avert yours."

"I'm more into digital nowadays," I quip.

"I mean it. You're fragile."

"Like a grape," Ray adds.

Stardust steps closer, fusses with my collar like a nitpicky aunt who can also bench-press a Buick. "Darling, you've got—what—forty mortal years left on the meter? Try not to fritter them away in advance, hm?"

"It's a charity's file room," I say. "The worst I'm expecting is a paper cut and maybe a ghoul popping out of a closed door."

"*Ghouls*?" Stardust echoes, sharp now.

"You sure you're okay going alone?" Ray asks, watching me zip my bag like I'm loading for a heist. "Isn't that why you're staying here?"

I wave a hand. Bravado is free, after all. "It's fine. No one's tried to eat me in *days*."

Ray doesn't look convinced. Stardust doesn't look amused anymore.

I sling the bag over my shoulder like that settles it. "Seriously. I got invited to a very dull room."

Ray squeezes my shoulder. "Text if it stops being dull."

Stardust kisses the air near my cheek, still frowning. "If someone offers you a free calendar—run."

I'm halfway out the door when I call back, "If Armand calls, tell him griffins are also for commoners."

Stardust huffs a laugh. "Heretic. Go."

Chapter 14

The "records room" Montgomery wrangled me into isn't a room so much as a climate-controlled bunker dressed as a nonprofit. Reception is all tasteful oatmeal—neutral carpet, ficus with trust issues, a framed mission statement about "civic literacy"—but past a keypad door the air drops ten degrees and smells like lemon cleaner, toner, and old money in a hoodie.

Security waves me through on the strength of a text from Montgomery and a badge that smells like fresh lamination and money. The elevator dings B-2, and opens to RESEARCH—AUTHORIZED where the door hums like a beehive. Inside, there's a rolling ladder, a date stamp still tacky with ink, a handheld embosser that makes everything look official, and a copier the size of a coffin humming like it's heard things. The only splash of personality is a box of logo swag—mugs and tasteful lapel pins—half-opened on a credenza beneath a tiny security dome camera. It's quiet in that way only paper can be quiet, like thirty years of conversations got and filed under Do Not Disclose.

An envelope waits on the counter. Inside is a brass key, and note in Montgomery's tidy hand:

B-2. Records. C-4 then E-12. Ledgers by decade.
No photos, notes only. –FM

Door C obliges. I unlock, step into the fluorescent glow—and stop.

Lucian stands at the center table covered in files wearing rolled shirtsleeves, reading glasses he does *not* need halfway down his nose, looking like a museum decided to manifest a dreamy docent with cheekbones. He glances up, perfectly composed.

"Hello, Emily."

My brain blue-screens. "How are you... here?" And then it hits me. "Tattletales."

"Indeed." His mouth tilts. "Ray knocked on my study door and said, 'If you like Emily alive, go stand between her and poor decisions.' Stardust added embroidery." His gaze skims my face for scorch marks. "You're surprised."

"That you got in? Yes." I fold my arms. "I had to practically sign a deal with the devil,"—not sorry, Montgomery—"to get access."

"You aren't the only one with connections," he says. "Although in this case, I may have sweet-talked security."

"You?" I arch a brow.

He pushes the glasses higher, all innocence. "I have a wide and varied history, Emily." He gestures to the stacks. "Shall we?"

I remember the letter he left me, careful and restrained. I remember the silence after Sara's secret spilled. I remember almost believing he was pursuing me until I realized how much distance he could create without moving an inch. Like refusing me a safe house.

"Not yet," I say, "declining to let a friend crash at your very warded mansion and then popping up in my file room as a chaperone is... a choice."

His expression doesn't shift, but the temperature of his voice does. "January yields fledglings. Too many covens are careless at the year's turn. I could not guarantee your safety among the newly turned as an unbonded mortal. I did not say no to you, Emily. I said no to circumstances." A beat. "So I came here to control the ones I can. "

It's a tidy apology and I don't have time to chew on it. So, I ignore the subtext and tip my head at his glasses. "Fine but lose the specs."

"They make mortals cooperative." He pushes them higher, shameless. "Don't you agree?"

Unfortunately, yes. "Weaponized hot librarian. Rude."

His eyes light up, pleased. Calculating. "It is useful for those who no longer swoon at the sight of fang."

Which would have been me. Months ago, he'd just need to smile, and I'd bare my neck. But I arch a brow and lie through my teeth. "You may have sweet-talked security, but you're not sweet-talking me."

"That would be inefficient," he says mildly. "You prefer provocation."

"Only when it's well-dressed." I tap the bridge of his glasses. "These are entrapment."

"They inspire compliance." He doesn't remove them.

I pluck them off anyway and slide them on my head. "File that under unfair advantage."

He leans in just enough to fog my composure. "If I used my other advantages, we wouldn't read a word."

"Promises, promises." I step back before I do something regrettably educational. "Fetch me C-4 and maybe I'll forgive you for the no-crashing edict."

"Conditional absolution," he murmurs, sliding the ladder like he owns gravity. "My preferred kind."

"Of course it is." He hands down the first ledger; our fingers skim, and a little static misbehaves. I don't drop it. "Stay where I can see you, Lucian. The books can bite and I'm not on the menu."

His mouth tilts at the opening I handed him. I pretend I didn't and slide into a chair, spine straight, eyes on the page before he can make it worse. "Read," I tell the ledger. "Behave," I do not tell him.

The Solstice Educational Foundation entries are all choir-robe wholesome: scholarships, "learning fellows," endowments. Then a thinner book: Founding Instruments.

"Here," I murmur.

1925: Initial capitalization: confidential underwriting—see private ledger.

Same year Victor won his wager. My pulse does a drumline.

Lucian's eyes flick, all business. "Invisible capital buys very visible policy."

The "private ledger" turns out to be a manila folder with exactly one sheet inside. No words, but a single, stylized spade—inked so black it swallows the fluorescence.

I look at Lucian. "That's not accounting."

"No," he says softly. "That's ownership."

Maybe it's not proof the House *owns* Fulton, but it's proof they're involved somehow. My conscience reminds me of Montgomery's instructions, but my fingers snap a clandestine photo with my phone anyway.

"This is just... silly," I say when the incriminating evidence is hidden away. "A supernatural bureaucracy preparing all these documents, recording minutes, with a capitalization record that's a logo." I thumb the thin minutes, then glance at the spade page. "I guess this is the 'human legitimacy' part, or whatever the fine print calls it. Banks, ballots, permits—doors in human society that only open if you've got receipts."

Lucian's mouth tilts. "And donors. Foundations. Audits. Daylight likes paperwork."

"Props to keep mortals nodding."

"Sunshine camouflage," he agrees.

"Camouflage I can subpoena," I say, sliding the flimsy minutes back and running a finger along the shelf tabs until I find Montgomery's next breadcrumb.

E-12 is where the modern plumbing lives: cross-refs, flow charts, and all the polite euphemisms for money. Solstice Civic Advancement (c)(4). Solstice Action (§527). I flip and scribble until a donor-summary binder lands with a thud big enough to register on seismographs.

"Randall Prescott. Anthony Erskine. Dior Porter, Mark Goldman," Lucian reads, voice gone archival. "And onward through the decades."

"Ring any bells?"

He looks at me flatly. "Your willful ignorance of public events is going to be a detriment at some point in your career."

I barely hold in the eye roll. "Educate me, Count Encyclopedia."

The expression turns withering. "Former mayors. All of them."

"Sorry I missed Chicago: The Prequel," I mutter. I moved here post-law school; for me it's been Peterson all the way down.

I run a finger down the newest column. "Friends of Michael Peterson. Peterson for Chicago. Re-Elect Michael Peterson—"

"—continuing through his tenure," Lucian says, cool sharpening to ice. His fingertip stops on the bottom line. "And ending the week Frank Mitchell died."

And a few months later, Brian Fulton appears. You'd think they'd choose someone else to bribe—Tom Turner likely would have accepted in a heartbeat. If they needed someone slick with shifting supernatural opinions, he'd likely have changed his entire personality for the payday. But this time, they aren't greasing politicians; they're trying to install their own.

My stomach does a low, ugly turn. The House has been propping up mayors for a hundred years. Whatever the House is anchoring this century isn't just a ledger.

It's the city.

Which means, I need to talk to Peterson.

"No," Lucian says. He isn't guessing; he's stomping on the thought. "You will not walk into a prison and speak the House's name."

"I wasn't going to—"

"You were. I know your mind well enough by now." He closes the ledger, covers my hand with cool fingertips—brief, grounding. "Peterson is not merely a felon; he is *a message.* Now we know his connection, we know the House will be watching. They will have ears on him and the men who guard him. If you trigger those ears, they will write your name again."

The contract's love note flashes in my head: *Watch what you bargain for, Emily Lane.* I swallow, stare down at the grid. "You know about that one, huh?"

"I have known Sara longer than you have known your coffee order," he says, dry as paper.

"Fine." I tuck ink-spattered index cards into my tote and re-square the stack like a model patron. "I won't visit tonight."

"At all," he says.

I hum noncommittally; I'm not making extra promises. On my way past him, I hook the reading glasses off my head and tuck them into his breast pocket with two fingers and a tap. "Your prop. And for the record? I'm still annoyed about the houseguest policy."

"Noted." The corner of his mouth tips.

We kill the fluorescents, lock up, and ride the elevator in mirrored silence—me with a pocket full of leverage, him with a pocket full of... glasses.

In the lobby, winter air knifes through the revolving door. He falls into step until we reach my clunker.

"You will go home," he says, calm as a court order. "You will not go to the prison. And you will call upon me before you decide to antagonize the House."

"I heard you the first time," I say, climbing in. "No prison dates tonight."

"Good." He taps the roof—old-fashioned, absurdly protective—and vanishes into the darkness.

I ease into traffic, index cards fanned on the passenger seat like a losing hand that just learned how to bluff. Tomorrow I start cashing them in. I only promised *tonight.*

I thumb my phone to my ear. "Yeah," I say when the line clicks live, "I need one more thing..."

CHAPTER 15

Apparently when you open the door to "favors" from Montgomery, the smart move is to wedge your foot in and yank it wider. Although, if I've already put a yoke around my neck, what's one more shackle?

By nine he's texted, *"You're on Peterson's list for tomorrow."* Like it's a brunch RSVP and not sliding me a backstage pass to a maximum security prison.

But with favors come demands. Like his latest casual lunch invitation that I know isn't casual.

I'm already seated by the time he sweeps into the restaurant, silk pocket square immaculate, that faint citrus-and-clove cologne that says money but not cologne-counter money. He sits like the chair was built for him. Honestly, maybe it was.

"Emily," he says warmly. "You've been busy."

"Bills do need paying," I say, folding the napkin into my lap.

"You enjoyed your stroll through the archives, then?"

My neck nearly cracks from how fast I look at him. "What?"

His smile tilts, not quite amused. "The records I gave you access to last evening. The Foundation."

I relax, a hair. "*Stroll* isn't the word. Try breaking and entering with a permission slip." And a vampire chaperone.

He doesn't flinch. "And yet, you got what you wanted."

"Yes," I say slowly. "But with the grand tour of the Solstice Foundation's sketchiest corners, plus a front-row ticket at the prison tomorrow, I'm wondering what the fine print says about what I owe you."

Montgomery folds his hands like he's at confession, not lunch. "Emily, you still think of these as favors. They're not favors. They're opportunities. You wanted access, I gave it. You wanted sunlight on the shadows, I opened a curtain. This is how it works. People like you and me—we move faster when we stop pretending we're on the guest list and admit we're already on the committee."

I eye him. "Committees usually come with dues."

He smiles without warmth. "And dividends."

The server arrives, pours water, and flees. I flip the menu shut without looking. "Let's cut to it. What's the dividend today?"

"Fulton." Montgomery says it like he's announcing a toast. "He is looking stronger than ever. Donors are steady. Polls are tightening. He could be the one who finally bridges the gap, making the human-supernatural coalition more than a theory."

I lean back. "Bridges built on casino money tend to collapse."

A flicker of irritation crosses his face. "Yes. That was news to me as well."

My brows rise at the admission, and he catches it. He leans in, voice pitched lower. "You didn't think you were able to access anything I hadn't already rifled through, did you?"

I cross my arms, aiming for poised and probably hitting petulant. "Next time, maybe just give me the notes instead of doing the digging myself."

He exhales slowly, patience sharpened into warning. "We can't choose who supports us. That's politics. What matters is the candidate. Fulton has presence. He has vision. He could stand at a podium tomorrow and talk about dual citizenship, shared legitimacy, and the city would listen."

"Or he could stand there and rot from the inside," I say flatly. "You don't know what he is, Montgomery."

"And you do?" His eyes sharpen, suddenly steel. "You think you see more than I do?"

I don't answer. Because right now, I don't. Not yet.

The silence between us is a gavel strike. Finally, he leans back, signals for espresso. "You wanted to play in the bigger rooms, Emily. The records room, the prison visit—that wasn't charity. That was me staking you in the game. You can walk away, if you like. But don't confuse access with accident. Doors open because I open them."

There it is. Not a threat. Not even a demand. Just the reminder that I'm not as free as I pretend.

"Good to know," I say. "Next time you hand me a key, I'll check what it's cuffed to."

He actually laughs at that, soft and surprised. "Always the sharp tongue." Then, leaning forward, quieter: "Don't waste the access I've given you. It costs more than you realize."

I swallow that one, because the truth is, I can already feel the costs racking up.

"Now," he says briskly, checking his watch, already moving past the warning. "Let's talk about Blake. I've penciled us in for a private meeting next week to test their campaign's supernatural perspective."

I huff out something that isn't quite a laugh. "Always hedging your bets."

"Always planning for contingencies," he corrects smoothly. "That's how you win."

My evening wraps up at Moonlit Haven. No ghoul sightings all day, so I'm feeling pretty smug about the House's threat being more hot air than horror.

Severin clocks me the second I slip in. He's in ink-black, cuffs knife-sharp, face arranged at that angle that reads "civil, not forgiving." The only concession to humanity is the bar rag over his shoulder, the only concession to whimsy is a single gold pin at his lapel shaped like a very small, very judgmental crescent moon.

"Ms. Lane," he greets, with that smooth formality that always sounds like he's about to scold me for existing. But tonight there's something else in his tone—something rare. Weight.

He slides a glass of water across the bar, then a coffee, as if I ordered both. "Prairie Trust confirmed the account. Routing number. Checks. All of it." He meets my eyes, steady as ever. "I haven't had a legitimate bank in... longer than I care to measure."

I grin, I can't help it. "Congratulations."

His mouth twitches. "It's... significant, Ms. Lane." A pause, deliberate. "And I recognize that." Then he smooths his cuffs, breaking the moment like it never happened.

"Now if you'll excuse me, someone just snapped their fingers at my staff." His gaze cools, sharp enough to slice deli meat, before he moves away soundlessly.

I shake my head and cut toward the booths, claiming mine and waiting for Armand.

It feels a little... off... spending brain cells on non-Val work, but until I get Peterson or a location from Wilkin, I'm parked at a red light.

Armand arrives before I can think too much about it. Today, he looks like he's been poured into his suit and left to harden, skin nearly translucent like he hasn't had a healthy day in about two centuries. His snowy hair is combed straight back, as though gravity signed a nondisclosure agreement.

"Ms. Lane," he says, sliding into the booth across from me with the grace of a man who never once stubbed a toe in his undead life. "You've finished it?"

I push the slim folder across the table, resisting the urge to say *abracadabra*. "All the paperwork your afterlife could want. Wills, trusts, and one very boring binder tab."

He places a gloved hand over it, then looks up at me with aristocratic curiosity. "You insist these... trusts... will safeguard my chairs and curios?"

"Absolutely. You name a trustee, you spell out what happens to the assets, and voilà—no family feud, no estate sale at Sotheby's."

He glances at the papers again, then at me. "You make even tedium sound... vital."

"High praise from someone who doesn't breathe."

The faintest curve tugs his mouth. Then his gaze lingers on my throat a second too long. "You would forgive me if I... asked?"

I slide the coffee carafe across the table like a shield. "Caffeine is all that's on the menu in this booth."

He chuckles—low, polished, not even embarrassed. "Your willpower is stronger than most who parlay with our community, Ms. Lane. Very well. Show me where I sign."

I turn the page, hand him a pen. "Here. And here. And if you have the cousin's information, that would streamline things."

"You require... his account information?" The word "account" comes out like I've suggested necromancy at brunch.

"No," I say slowly, "like his Social. For transferring assets and tax stuff."

Armand blinks. "Social?"

"Security number." I lean in, remembering a moment at another table when talk turned to accounts. "What kind of account did you think I meant?"

A pause, then he tilts his head, amused. "The kind everyone meant, once. Though no one with any sense has them now. We've moved on from the barter system in polite society and no longer need accounting from ne'er-do-wells and tricksters."

I frown. One: supernaturals still barter. Two: that didn't answer my question. "You mean like a supernatural bank? Or?"

But Armand's having his own conversation now. "They were interesting times. You wished to bargain, you brought it to the table. Coins if you had them, heirlooms if you were bold. And if what you offered was yourself, then you were the stake. Sit, sign, and surrender. Nothing invisible about it." He pauses, distaste shadowing his mouth. "No long drawn out deals and contracts. No intermediaries. Merely your honor and your pen."

I slide the paperwork back and don't mention he described... a *contract*. "And yet, without trusts now, who knows what might happen to your griffin collection."

He shudders delicately. "Indeed. Now, if you will excuse me," he stands, sweeping the folder into a deep inner pocket of his suit, "I require refreshment. Thank you, Ms. Lane."

I give him a jaunty salute, and he meanders away, white hair trailing behind him.

Danielle slides into the booth two minutes later, smelling like cold air and squad car upholstery, curls half-tamed by a pencil she probably stole from the evidence room. She's in jeans and a gray sweater that makes her badge look accidental. She steals my water, swallows, then points the glass at me like a threat.

"You left the wards again."

"I missed you too."

Her glare could dent steel. "You want me to start writing obituaries? Because that's where this is heading."

"Relax. I had company outside the Haven," I say, lifting my coffee like it's evidence.

Her eyes narrow. "Lucian Belmont doesn't count as a bodyguard."

Heat prickles my cheeks. If he doesn't count, then Matty won't either. "I didn't say—"

"You didn't have to."

"Anyway," I say primly, trying to sound like I didn't just get caught sneaking in after curfew. "It's gotten me somewhere. I'm close to something, I think."

She sighs, pulling out a folder from who knows where. "Better than I've gotten. We've had three 'she's staying with friends' tips and one guy who tried to sell me a haunted doll.

Nothing that smells like real." Then she flips open the folder and pushes it across the table.

"Victor asked me to run background," she explains, gesturing to the pages. "Not much to find, but there's a pattern that keeps repeating. Property deeds, tax slips, even a life insurance payout that never closed. They're all still in the name of Valentine Little. The elder—Victor's mother."

I glance at the page. "The one that died a century ago?"

"1905," Danielle says. "But no probate, no estate transfer. Everything just sort of... stopped. Paperwork still cycles through her name sometimes, like the system thinks she's overdue for a census form."

I flip the folder closed. "So, Chicago clerks are bad at their jobs. Stop the presses."

She smirks. "Tell me something I don't know. I'm not saying it's important, but it's odd." She taps the folder. "Anyway—Victor wanted it flagged. I'm keeping an eye."

"Thanks," I say quietly. "I know this isn't your lane."

Her mouth quirks. "Missing kids are always my lane. Doesn't matter whose paperwork they're caught in."

Severin materializes long enough to set a small plate of salted almonds on the table like a treaty. He inclines his head at Danielle. "Officer Greene."

"Severin," she says with a smile. "Got anything non-alcoholic that tastes like alcohol?"

"Water," he says, deadpan. "With ice."

She rolls her eyes. "When did you learn banter?"

He ghost-smiles and disappears.

When I look past Danielle, Victor is at the door.

Danielle follows my gaze, murmurs under her breath, "He's running out of rope."

"Or already out," I say.

He looks like he slept in his clothes—good cloth wrinkled wrong, tie a suggestion. He beelines towards us, and I wish I had more to tell him. His eyes flick to me, then to Danielle.

"Any progress?" His voice is low, but urgent.

Danielle rises, gathering the folder. "I'll walk you through it."

He hesitates a second, looking at me directly this time. "Thank you, Emily. For staying in it for Val. I know this isn't... simple work."

"Nothing worth doing ever is," I say, though my throat feels tight.

My parents never said it out loud, but they lived the idea that I was an accident, a burden they hadn't budgeted for. And here's this half-broken immortal telling the world she's worth the fight. That kind of belonging? It's rare. Precious.

He inclines his head, gratitude and grief in equal measure, before leaving with Danielle. The space he leaves behind feels thinner.

I sit with my cooling coffee, trying not to picture how much more hollow he'll look by the time I can actually help.

I don't notice Lucian until he's already sliding into the opposite side of the booth, shadows parting like they're giving him space.

"You look," he says, studying me the way some people study case law, "more tired than yesterday warrants."

I laugh under my breath. "Tired's the new chic."

"Not on you." His tone is quiet, and suddenly the din of the bar feels very far away. "You carry it like it belongs to you. It doesn't."

I swallow. The letter he sent me—the one I've read too many times—burns like a phantom weight in my pocket. "Careful, Belmont. That almost sounded like concern."

"It is concern," he says simply, like there's no use denying it. "And it's more than almost."

My cheeks feel like they're on fire, so I hide in my coffee. "So, you came to warn me off my next steps, or just to brood in better company?"

"Neither." His gaze stays steady, unreadable. "I came to provide you a reprieve."

I smirk. "From what, despair? Or that terrible ABBA rendition?"

His mouth twitches, almost a smile. "From thinking too loudly." He gestures, and suddenly there's a deck of cards between his hands, the backs patterned with silver stars. I don't ask if he brought them or if they simply appeared.

He shuffles with long, precise fingers. "What shall we play?"

"Spite and Malice?" I suggest.

He arches a brow. "Too mercenary."

"Go Fish?"

That earns me a look—dry, imperious, the kind that could curdle milk. But then, softly: "Rummy."

He deals. The cards whisper across the table, catching the lamplight. The noise of the bar hums around us—laughter, glasses clinking, someone now butchering Sinatra at the mic—but my booth feels sealed off, private.

I pick up my hand. "Fair warning: I cheat."

"I would expect nothing less," he says smoothly, laying his first meld with unnerving efficiency.

And just like that, the bar disappears for a while. It's only the two of us, hands brushing when we reach for the discard, the low current of banter sharper than the cards. Each glance feels weighted, each silence more telling than the words we manage.

When I finally win a round—barely—he looks at me like the game was never the point.

Chapter 16

The prison squats in the prairie like a brick-red warship run aground—four stories of 1920s ambition, limestone trim trying to pass as frosting, every window gridded tight as ledger paper. A thirty-foot wall curls behind it, dull concrete the color of old snow, as if the prison decided a moat was too subtle and built a dam instead. The main block has the proportions of a Victorian boarding school, but the watch-towers—capped in gun-metal gray—kill any storybook day-dreams on sight.

Inside, the air is thin and over-heated, the color palette government-issue ecru. Metal detectors beep, lockers slam shut, all of it designed to make you feel like contraband. A sign warns me not to smuggle in romance, gum, or hope. I hand over my phone, my pen, and whatever illusion I had about this being routine, then follow the yellow footprints to Visitation—one long strip of bolted tables under fluores-cents that buzz like a bad verdict.

Families fold themselves into plastic chairs that were de-signed by someone who hates knees. A CO calls names like a bingo caller who'd rather be anywhere else. Through the glass of a side room, I clock the attorney booths—no, thanks.

Peterson arrives with the remains of a mayoral glide and the full weight of a plea deal that called itself "generous." But twenty years on a tidy plea looks different up close—less "second chance," more "slow calendar." He's thinner, grayer at the temples, and wearing the uniform that does nothing for his style. But the blue eyes still count votes when they land on me.

"Ms. Lane," he says, like we're at City Hall and I'm here to discuss potholes. He slides into the chair across from me, shackles whispering a reminder. "To what do I owe the pleasure?"

"Curiosity," I say, because *justice* would be a lie and *gloating* would be gauche. "And a mutual acquaintance who can oil open doors."

His smile twitches—there and gone. "Montgomery does love a hinge."

We let that hang there until the CO drifts away. The room fills and empties on tides of supervised affection: a toddler squeals; someone laughs too loud and stops. Behind Peterson's eyes, you can still see the campaign posters peeling off the walls: Leadership, Integrity, a skyline at sunset. He was good at being a city, before he murdered a man on a hardwood floor.

"Ask, Ms. Lane. You must want something more specific than closure," he says, not bothering to soften anything. "You didn't brave our hospitality for nostalgia."

"I need to understand how the House operates and why they've got their hands in City Hall." I keep my voice even. "And whether Brian Fulton is their man or just their paperwork."

He studies me, weighing which answer buys him the most oxygen. Then: "The House doesn't haunt the city, Ms. Lane.

It governs it—very politely, for thirty-one days a year. Outside that timetable, it legally doesn't exist."

"Is that the Veil Covenant then?" I fold my arms. "Hide the House's deals, rake in the cash?"

He blinks. "Veil what? That sounds like one of their inside jokes." A beat. "We never had names, only rules. Keep it polite, keep it human-facing, don't make anyone say the quiet part on camera. If there's a covenant, it's above my clearance and outside the municipal code."

I drag my thumbnail along a crack in the laminate, redlining the phrase in my head. "So why do it then?"

He splays hands that once held beautiful but deadly ink pens. "January isn't a mystery, Ms. Lane. It's a settlement window. The House keeps its trades off our streets for eleven months. Then, they balance the books—debts called, memories skimmed, the unlucky relocated. We label it hypothermia, voluntary psych holds, runaways. Transit finds sleepers who can't recall their stop, hospitals log 'acute confusion.' The victims don't count on paper—runaways, the undocumented, the newly turned our statutes won't even regulate. It files neatly."

He flicks his eyes toward the ceiling cameras. "Why tolerate it? Think of it as a controlled burn. The House is the biggest bully on the playground, and bullies like rules—they want to know when lunch money's due. Hold January still and the rest of the year stays quiet. Push too hard and you don't just get the House, you get a supernatural coalition. If they ever unified, we'd be negotiating in daylight with people who don't need it."

My brows hitch. "Meaning to avoid a supernatural united front, you hand over a month of collateral damage?"

"Correct." His smile is thin. "You and I call this Chicago. They'll call it a buffet if we ever look too weak. Our three-hundred-year-old republic can't out-legislate creatures who've had constitutions older than Latin. Most humans still think supernatural jurisdiction is a campfire story. That illusion is fragile, and useful. Break it, and every vampire who once owned a century-old deed, every witch with a grudge, every House accountant with a calculator full of souls remembers they out-vote us in time, if not in bodies."

"Silence for stability," I translate.

"Exactly. We're both ants and grasshoppers, Ms. Lane—just none of us want the other side to realize which."

Cute Aesop, but I didn't bring my moral-of-the-story decor. Instead, I tilt my head. "That doesn't track. When you ran for re-election, you had the supernatural-friendly vote in your pocket. After Mitchell's murder, you courted the creature-hating bloc like it was a prize. Why burn supernatural goodwill if you were already in bed with the House?"

Peterson's smile twitches. "You think the curfews and ordinances were about keeping creatures in check? That was for the voters. The House doesn't care what speeches I give in September, as long as January runs smoothly. Mitchell would've started a war in October just to win an argument. I gave the mob their bogeymen and kept the real ones off the ballot."

"The pendulum will swing," I tell him. It always does.

"It's worked for at least a hundred years," he says quietly. "The best landlords are the ones who leave you in peace if the check clears on time."

The fluorescent bulbs hum overhead, too loud for a room this tense. I picture Val's face, Victor's hollow eyes, Fulton's perfect smile.

"And what happens," I ask, "when the landlord decides rent isn't enough?"

Peterson's gaze slides to the clock, then back to me. "Then you pray the tenant union you've been ignoring finally lets you in the meeting, Counselor."

"The so-called greater good," I say, shaking my head.

"It's the game," he replies, repeating his excuse for the night he murdered Mitchell and called it policy.

"Well, the landlord's looking to expand. They're changing the rules," I say. "One of theirs—Fulton—is running for the slot you left open. Seems like less of a controlled burn, more intentional arson."

Peterson's gaze goes cold. "They're putting a *face* in City Hall?" For the first time, he looks genuinely thrown. "That wasn't the deal. The House stayed off the ballot. Influence, yes. Fronts, yes. *Electeds,* no."

"He's the Anchor."

At that, a flicker—confusion or calculation, I can't tell. "Anchor?" he repeats, like tasting a word he hasn't ordered.

"You don't know what it is?"

He blinks, not faking it. "I know what a donor is. I know what a guarantor is." He leans in. "I know the House prefers one face per era when it's time to shake hands with daylight. If he's this era's handshake, he's either a pawn who thinks he's a bishop... or a bishop who remembers he started as a pawn."

"So, he's a baddie."

"He's a tool," Peterson says. "The House is the hand. You'll try to break the tool. Fine. Just know the hand owns the workshop." He tilts his head, eyes tired and sharp. "Which vampire are you fighting for this time?"

"For a human girl," I say. "Valentine Little. The House took her as collateral. I need a loophole to pry her out before their month is up."

"That is the trouble with loopholes," he muses. "They're doors for people who already have keys. You think this Fulton is your in?"

"You tell me."

He sits back. "People will bargain everything for power, Ms. Lane. Titles, blood, daughters. They'll call it legacy while they hand over the receipt."

I exhale, temper fraying. "If I can expose Fulton somehow—does the House blink?"

"The House blinks when ledgers do." He studies me, then adds, almost kindly: "Weren't you balancing your career against Lucian's life not so long ago? We all make trades. Some are more comfortable than others."

The barb lands; I pretend it doesn't. "You got twenty on a tidy package. You're telling me you're relieved."

"I'm telling you I wake up and the phone does not ring," he says. "I'm telling you I shake fewer hands." A beat. "I'm telling you that if you go loud, make sure you've already built the quiet that gets your people out."

"Meaning?"

"Meaning you'll need a promise before you strike a match. A counterweight. Someone who can open a door the House didn't plan to open." He tilts his head. "You don't have that yet."

"Working on it," I say, which is lawyer for *no*.

He glances at the clock the way men glance at tides. "Then work faster. Your month is nearly up."

The CO calls time. Chains murmur. He stands, and the mayor transforms into the inmate.

"Advocacy aside, remember which roster you're on, Ms. Lane. When the strike whistle blows, you're just as breakable—and expendable—as the rest of us."

I make it back to the parking lot with the sour taste of recycled air still coating my tongue. I replay every word like hot evidence, when I thumb a call to Danielle.

"Got something," I say, skipping the origin story. "Remember your January rush? Someone finally spelled out how it works. It's not random—it's the House's authorized settlement window. They call debts, skim memories, shuffle people like they're receipts. And the city lets it happen."

On the other end, there's a beat of dead air before she says, low, "Lets it happen?"

"Keeps it contained. Says it's better than the House going year-round."

"That's not containment, that's surrender," she snaps. "You're telling me we write off a month's worth of disappearances so we can feel in control the rest of the year?"

"That's the math."

Her voice sharpens. "Do you know how many of those 'disappearances' I've taken reports for? How many families I told we'd keep looking?"

I close my eyes. "More than I want to think about."

She's silent long enough that I think she's hung up. Then, quietly: "It makes me complicit."

"But we can still break it. It's a long game," I say. "Right now, we focus on Val."

"A win record of one is still a win," she says, almost to herself. To me she adds, "I'm not letting Val be another loss."

The line goes dead. I slide the phone into my pocket. That's when I feel it—the quiet bending. Not breaking. Bending, the way sugar glass warps before it shatters.

Two figures detach from a DOC maintenance van. Same beige jumpsuits as the laundry detail I'd seen inside, but too pristine, too loose in the shoulders, as if they'd borrowed skin as a costume. The faces underneath bubble slightly, like latex left too close to a space heater.

The sensible part of my brain—the one I gag during adrenaline spikes—whispers, *you should already be in the car.* I fish out my keys and keep walking. Head up, shoulders square. Predators—dead or otherwise—love a flinch.

They close in.

"Ms. Lane," the taller one calls, voice dribbling gravel. He's broad through the chest, charcoal bruise under each eye where the makeup didn't stick. "House wants a word."

"The House can leave a voicemail." I thumb the fob. Only five steps separate me and the car. The driver's window is smeared with something dark and tacky: a spade symbol drawn in (what I hope is) molasses. It's too much to hope that it's a puerile 'breadcrumb' from Wilkin.

Shorter Ghoul angles right, blocking the line between me and the driver door. Perfect, the car's out as an escape hatch. "You've been collecting paperwork that isn't yours," he growls.

Where's a hobgoblin bodyguard when you need one? I clock the prison transport two lanes over: closer to the guard shack, bigger windows, and every emergency bus kit in Illinois. More eyes, more toys. Good enough.

"Well," I say, "clerks never answer after five." I pivot, pretending to fumble my purse, and snag the chunky metal pen that wasn't allowed inside. Heavy, steel barrel—Peterson would certainly approve.

"But House wants a word," Tall Ghoul repeats. His fingertips dangle, jointed wrong—like someone rewired a mannequin with copper. Close up, I catch the wet-cellar smell—grave dirt dampened with battery acid.

"Back off." I plant my feet on the frozen tarmac. Left shoulder forward, pen hidden along my wrist. My heart is doing a drum solo against my ribs, but my voice stays in the lawyer register: audible contempt, half an octave from boredom.

Tall Ghoul inhales—an ugly, sucking sound. "House says deadlines are *dead-lines*. Come with us and we leave the marrow where it is."

"Counter-offer." I drive the pen into the hollow beneath his collarbone, making Peterson proud.

The impact is dull—like stabbing a beanbag—but he *feels* it. Bellowing, he reels. Short Ghoul lunges; I dodge left, slam the key fob into his ear like a brass knuckle. Cartilage crunches. He howls, clawing at air.

Momentum is mercy. I sprint, boots skittering on black ice. Cold air razors my lungs. Behind me are curses, the wet slap of feet gaining. They're slower than a vampire, faster than me—a bad median.

I beeline for the bus parked two lanes over. The side emergency hatch is padlocked, while the back door is chain-looped but glass panels intact. I swing my bag by the strap and smash the nearest pane. Safety glass beads scatter like rock salt. I climb through, snagging my coat on the jagged rim, and tumble onto linoleum floor sticky with slush and other unmentionables.

In the narrow aisle, bench seats become barricades. I crawl fast toward the driver's partition. A box of road flares nestles behind the seat. *Hello, lovely.*

Glass explodes in front of me; Tall Ghoul slithers in, tearing metal with bare hands. Short Ghoul slips through the shattered panel opposite, fencing me in a coffin-shaped corridor.

I pop the flare cap. Magenta fire jets to life, spraying smoke that smells like burned crayons and hellfire. I brandish the mini-torch like a lightsaber.

Short Ghoul recoils with a hiss. Tall Ghoul hesitates, one palm shielding lidless eyes.

"Come. Now," he growls.

"Pass." I wing the flare underhand. My aim's terrible, but he's close enough for it not to matter, pitching right into his ribcage. Nylon meets magenta, and the jumpsuit whooshes like a bad soufflé. Tall Ghoul howls, his arms windmilling, violet fire spider-climbing his torso.

Short Ghoul vaults a seat to reach me. I grab the nearest weapon—a stainless fire-extinguisher the size of a toddler that nearly drags me to the floor—and yank the pin. CO_2 blasts his face. Frost blooms on bubbling skin; he shrieks, half-blinded, and slams backward into a window. The cracked safety glass finally gives, coughing him onto the asphalt outside.

I scuttle past the last row, ducking Tall Ghoul fumbling towards the back, over the driver's seat and shimmy through the half-open side window. The landing's signature me, knees kissing pavement, shoulder taking the rest. The pain demands payment, but adrenaline cashes the check and keeps me mobile.

I crab-scramble beneath the bus chassis just as Tall Ghoul—now a walking bonfire—lurches out the rear hatch, swatting at flames.

Above me, his molten footfalls sizzle on snow-wet concrete. Acrid smoke crawls under the bus, eye-stinging and hot. I belly-crawl to the far side, pop out by the front bumper, and sprint—limp-shuffle—back toward the car.

The parking lot is suddenly siren-lit: guards yelling from the watchtower, radios barking "fire on transport." Good. More witnesses.

Short Ghouls staggers in from the right, face rimed white where the extinguisher tagged him. I slam my shoulder into his sternum. He's heavier than he looks and the momentum nearly flattens me. But the frosted flesh fractures, skin cracking like over-frozen mud. For good measure, I rake the key across the gnarled flesh of his neck. He screeches and jerks back, giving me the window I need to escape.

The key hits the lock and I dive in, slamming the door. The engine coughs—once, twice—because it always chooses melodrama. The third time it growls awake. Tall Ghoul, still flaming, has spotted me. He lumbers towards the hood, arms ablaze, leaving blackened shoe-prints. Short Ghoul follows, limping, shards of frozen flesh tinkling off him like sleet. I punch the gas. The car fishtails, tires shrieking on ice. Tall Ghoul leaps aside and I barrel past the kiosk as the guard hut alarm shrieks.

The exit gate drags halfway up before I smash through, shearing metal and sparking like a Fourth of July firecracker. The rearview mirror shows no pursuit—just fire crews fanning toward the bus and two half-charred ghouls limping for the skeletal tree line into a prairie no one's paid to patrol.

The shoulder I rammed earlier throbs; adrenaline starts the slow fade that heralds real agony. Still, I laugh—high, shaky. Because I'm alive, because Peterson's trivia is alive inside my head, and because I just pitched a road flare into a corpse that tried to threaten billable hours.

"House wants a word," I mutter, still giggling. "Buy a dictionary."

The laugh dies when the pain crests. I brace the wheel one-handed—the other arm nearly useless. Chicago's skyline flickers in the distance like a jury just starting deliberations. I just need to make it home.

Chapter 17

The room smells like rosemary, rubbing alcohol, and whatever anger smells like when it's been simmering for three hours. I'm lying on Sara's couch, a butterfly bandage on my cheek, ice against my knee, and waiting for her to fix my shoulder. My coat is now a crime scene prop, the fabric scorched, covered in road flare *and* propellant soot, with one sleeve almost torn completely off. At least it gives Sara the opening she needs to do her witchy wonders. Her fingertips pulse gentle heat over the bone. Then she tugs and I hate her for four seconds, then love her when the stabbing stops.

She pulls out a scarf in—what other color—black linen and wraps it around my forearm and chest in a makeshift sling. "I've popped it back in and used some localized healing, but it needs to be immobilized for a while. After that, your HMO's on its own."

"I don't have an HMO," I mumble. Health insurance is a luxury for solos.

"The morning paper will spin it as 'unidentified intruders posing as contractors attempted to access restricted vehicles,'" Matty announces over speakerphone, his cadence pure newscaster. "Quote 'Civilian visitor assisted in repelling assailants, resulting in limited, but necessary, structural loss to Department of Corrections property.'"

"Necessary," Danielle echoes from a wing-back chair, arms folded, badge glinting. "Care to define necessary, Em?"

"Road flare versus corpse seemed necessary at the time," I say. "Plus, I left the bus mostly intact. Call it historic preservation."

"Do you *ever* hear your own nonsense?" Danielle snaps, eyes drilling holes through me like she's sizing up a suspect who just swallowed the murder weapon. "You were actively threatened by the House and left your bolt-hole alone *multiple* times. And look what happened!"

I bite back the defense—that I tried escalation-avoidance until escalation found me. It wouldn't play well with the audience.

"For the record," Matty cuts in, smoothing the edges. "Your statement did land at DOC Legal, but since it's the weekend and I know the GC, I managed to get it and massage the draft myself. I've dressed it up as heroic civilian intervention. The county won't press charges." His tone sharpens. "But the prison wants compensation for the gate."

"Send them the House's billing address," I tell him.

"Funny," Matty says flatly. "Don't set anything else on fire until I check in. Sleep, Em." The line clicks dead.

Lucian leans in the doorway like a reprimand sculpted in marble. Cuffed sleeves, no tie, and a glower that could sour good wine. "You promised," he reminds me, voice velvet over gravel. "No prison dates. No heists without accompaniment."

"I promised no prison Thursday night, and I went this morning." My grin is paper thin. "Lawyers live in loopholes."

"Loopholes," Lucian repeats, as if tasting something bitter. His gaze drops to the bruises spreading under the torn sleeve. Something flashes there, swift and lethal. I'm waiting for our pattern to emerge: Emily does something Lucian doesn't like; Lucian yells and shuts down.

Victor derails it, hovering behind the sofa, clutching the key to his storage unit like a blankie. He looks like he's been whittled to scraps. "It's the twenty-fifth," he says, voice raw. "Val's ledger closes in less than a week, Emily."

Technically still a week. "I know." I sit straighter, and pain snaps along my ribs. "But we finally understand why City Hall keeps January quiet. The House buys thirty-one days of latitude, keeps the other factions at each other's throats, and everybody looks away."

"How does that bring my daughter home?" Victor's voice shakes.

"It doesn't—yet." I inhale. "Our research also confirmed that Solstice fronts bankrolled every mayor since the '20s. That trail ends the week Mitchell died until they decided to install their own. That's the key. If we show Fulton's face hasn't aged a day since 1927—"

Sara lifts both palms. "I can carbon date the photo—and I did. It's the real deal, old photo. But that's all I've got. Temporal forensics on hundred-year-old photographs is outside my lane."

"So we find someone whose lane it is."

Danielle leans forward, elbows on her knees. "Even if we do, you're still one abducted minor short of probable cause. Val's nowhere in that trail."

The weight of the truth slams home: the bus fire bought me nothing for Victor. "But she's in the books," I say, trying to convince myself. "Which means rattling the books rattles the cage they parked her in."

Danielle frowns, unconvinced. "And your plan is?"

"Wilkin's looking for the House and tailing Fulton." I shrug and immediately regret it. "I get his map, prove Fulton's ageless, leverage a trading position."

"And wind up in another parking lot knife fight?" Danielle's eyebrow climbs. "Absolutely not."

I drag my uninjured hand through my hair, hitting every knot the adrenaline sweated in. "Okay—alternate plan. We *kidnap* Fulton tonight, hold him till Imbolc, negotiate an exchange."

"No, Em," Danielle says, voice flat as gravel. "Let's review tonight's highlight reel. One former mayor who basically confessed to enabling supernatural racketeering. Two ghouls roasted medium rare in a DOC bus. Property damage already estimated at forty-seven grand and change." She ticks the list on her fingers. "Also, my phone has melted from the number of captains demanding to know why Crime Scene found a spade symbol smeared on your car in—" she checks the note "—'unknown bio-material.'"

"It might be molasses," I offer.

"You're benched," she snaps.

The word benched hits harder than the bus floor. "I'm not an intern you can order around."

"You're human," Lucian says. "A talented, exhausting, beautifully stubborn human who bleeds too easily. This part shifts back to us."

The pronouncement momentarily stuns me. I really need to watch that Fischer TV show because the pattern seems officially broken.

Danielle plants palms on the table and leans in even more. "This is supernatural now. My badge can't cover you. I'm sorry, but you need to sit and let the immortals drive the next leg."

"I've been in *every* leg," I protest. "It's my damned race. If you sideline me now—"

Victor's knuckles whiten on the chair back. "If she quits moving, Val dies."

Silence.

Danielle's jaw is tight. "I don't want to sideline her either, Victor. I *know* she's gotten us this far. But Val doesn't get saved if Emily ends up in the ledger next to her."

"You all realize I'm still in the room, right?" I glance between them. "Fully capable of voting on my own funeral arrangements?"

Sara inhales like she's bracing for a punch. "Then we make her harder to stop." She kneels, rolling back the rug to expose inlaid runes in the floor that glimmer when candlelight hits them. "I'm going to try a personal ward."

Lucian's brows knife together. "Sara—"

Her looks brooks no argument. "What else can we do?" she asks. "There's a kid on the line. It will be worth it."

A shiver slides down my spine. Worth it for who? She hasn't said what the price is, just that she's decided to pay it.

Danielle asks what we're all thinking. "What'll it cost?"

"Something I'm willing to give," she answers. Lucian disappears from the room.

Pattern back on schedule.

Sara starts drawing chalk circles in precise concentric rings. The runes already carved into the floor begin to thrum, faint as a power line. She pricks her thumb, presses the blood against my sternum and pushes. Cold blooms under my skin, oozing through bone, making my breath fog in the candlelight. The room tilts.

A filament of mercury races through Sara's platinum hair, shimmering like liquid magic. My stomach drops. Whatever she's pouring into me, it's taking from her.

Guilt slices colder than the ward. "Sara, pull back," I say. "Cost-benefit on this is lousy."

"Benefit is you breathing," she rasps, trembling. "Don't cheapen it."

Victor darts forward to steady her; she waves him off, but the tremor in her hands stays.

The pressure builds until my body thinks it's standing in the eye of a hurricane—dead calm, relentless force pressing in from all sides. Then it breaks. The blood vanishes, replaced by something heavy and sure under my ribs. Not comfortable, but solid. Safe.

A final spark leeches from Sara's irises, and she sags. Lucian reappears, offering her a crystal vial of something dark and thick. She drains it without comment, color seeping back into her cheeks.

"How strong is it?" he asks, hand gentle on her back.

Her answer is directed at me "You get hit with anything tougher than a bus next time, it won't help. But this will keep you from being on the menu. And useful side effect," she adds, gesturing to my arm, "you'll be out of that sling by tomorrow instead of twelve weeks."

I open my mouth—to thank her, to apologize, but she keeps talking.

"It needs twenty-four hours to settle. Thirty-six would be best." The quicksilver strand in her hair glitters like diamonds. "Think you can sit still until then?"

Thirty-six hours. A lifetime in crisis math. I swallow the pride poisoning my tongue. "Can I go back to Stardust's?"

She cocks her head, thinking about it, before nodding. "I need to take you, keep the locus steady. Right now, it's keyed to me. Give me a few hours to nap and we'll go."

Danielle plants herself in front of me. "Here's the shape of it: Until that ward sets you *do nothing* that bleeds. Lucian keeps Sara vertical. Victor—"

"—will go insane waiting," he mutters.

Danielle's tone gentles. "You're with me, looking for any hint of Val. We're not wasting any time, I promise."

"And Emily?" Lucian asks.

"Research," I lie. Mostly I'll sit here tasting copper and plotting how to slip the leash.

He hears the lie—or smells it. "Emily."

"Lucian."

We lock stares. The ward pulse between my ribs echoes his heartbeat, slow and inhuman. Something softens at the edges of his eyes. I swallow all the things I shouldn't say in front of an audience.

Danielle's fingers ghost over her service piece, tension still wired through her shoulders. "Text me before you hatch the next stunt," she warns. "Or after, because why even pretend? Just leave enough body intact for identification. But I'd better not hear from you until Monday."

They disappear into the corridor and the front door thuds shut. Sara vanishes down the hall into her bedroom, leaving me alone with Lucian.

He produces his absurd spectacles from an inside pocket and sets them on the coffee table.

"Still making mortals cooperative?" I ask.

"If they truly worked, I'd use it on you." The intensity in his eyes makes the ward throb. "You breathe danger as if it's oxygen, Emily. One of these nights it will stop being generous."

"I'm still breathing, aren't I?" It comes out softer than I mean it to. "And I had a plan."

"A plan that ended with road flare flambe." His mouth quirks—half exasperation, half something else. "Remarkably 'on brand,' as the fledglings say, if utterly unacceptable."

"What can I say?" I murmur. "If people keep trying to board-up the windows, I'll just pick the lock on the cellar."

A low laugh slips out of him, genuine and surprised. "Of course you will."

His hand hovers—just for a second—then settles lightly over mine. The ward flares cool and sharp, but neither of us moves.

"Reckless," he murmurs, thumb smudging the pulse at my wrist.

"Worrywart," I shoot back, though it comes out more breath than words.

He inclines his head, conceding the point. "Please take the thirty-six hours, Emily. If not for yourself, then for what Sara poured into the ward."

I squeeze his fingers—brief, electric—then pull away before the moment turns into something I can't pocket.

"Thirty-six hours," I promise, leaning back against the couch.

"Thirty-six hours," he echoes, standing. The candlelight etches every line of him into something I'm not ready to read.

He leaves, following the path Sara took into the house. The ward flares along my collarbone—silver light, quick as a wink. And for the first time since the prison parking lot, the cold in my chest feels a degree warmer.

Chapter 18

The ward's 'locus' being keyed to Sara is a nice way of describing my three yards of glowing house arrest. It lets me reach the fridge, the sofa, and the bathroom—nothing else. A magical studio apartment. Outside the circle: the front door, freedom, and a shoe I kicked in protest. If I toe the boundary, the ward hums like an electrified "nope."

Lucian left an hour ago for the tunnels after verifying—twice—that the tether held. Danielle texted a parade of siren emojis for emphasis. Even Vivvy appeared from wherever she was hiding to stare me down on the couch. Everyone's version of "waiting" apparently involves surveillance.

Fine. If I can't cross the rune line, I'll treat the space inside it like a war room.

I sweep the coffee table clear with my good arm, flip the legal pad to a fresh page, and start laying out the case—one sticky note at a time—until the surface looks less like furniture and more like an evidence board.

I spread my notes across the table like forensic photos:

Photo Proof: 1927 Fulton (witchy carbon dating, may not qualify in civil courts but enough to rock the boat)

Anchor: catastrophic breach swaps it out; *human legitimacy* is the lever (Veil Covenant?)

PAC Misdirection: Solstice Educational Foundation→ probable fraud, false filings, 527 violations.

January: Compile missing persons spikes; correlate with House rumors.

Personal Liability: Locus leash, ward expiration T-minus 33 hrs. 17 min.

Lawyers can't throw punches any more than we can toss a flare, but we can choke a monster in paperwork. If the House is going to play with mundane laws and interfere with human elections, they can damn well drown in discovery. The statutes were written for flesh-and-blood grifters, not soul-collecting casinos, but paper is species-agnostic: campaign-finance rules still flag laundered money, FOIA still pries open "charitable" ledgers, and perjury is perjury whether you breathe or just pretend. I'll swamp them in subpoenas, audits, and injunctions until supernatural meets super-bureaucratic—and watch them drown in the fine print.

We're make paperwork their natural predator.

Sara shuffles out just as I'm sketching out a lawsuit which may or may not work and may or may not end with me as ghoul grub. Her platinum hair now sports two silver streaks, bright as tinsel.

I jump up, sling protesting. "Lie back down. You've been vertical for ninety seconds and that's eighty too many."

"Pot, kettle," she mutters. "Or cauldron, if we're being technical."

"If you're stealing my jokes, you're clearly still in recovery. Now, bed."

Vivvy hops off the coffee table, plants herself between Sara and the rest of the room, emitting a decisive meow. Feline quorum achieved.

Sara sighs—equal parts fond and defeated—and pivots back toward her room. "Bossy," she grumbles, but she's already halfway down the hall.

"I'll bring you dinner," I call after her. "Vivvy's here to make sure I don't burn the place down."

Vivvy blinks at me, unimpressed, but follows as I limp to the kitchen.

My quota of open flames was met for the day, so I stick to (mostly) cold assemblies: sliced baguette and jarred tomato bisque nuked to lukewarm. I plate everything, add a chocolate-chip cookie for moral damages, and balance the tray one-handed.

Her bedroom smells faintly of sage and ozone, like someone tried to air out a lightning strike. Every surface is busy—stacked books, candle stubs in jars, neat bundles of herbs hanging upside down from the curtain rod. A map of the city is pinned above her desk, dotted with pushpins and string in a pattern only she can read. Her quilt is patchworked from old band T-shirts and velvet scraps, and the floorboards creak like they've got secrets. It's not cozy so much as *armored*—a witch's war room disguised as a bedroom.

"Gourmet," she croaks, collapsing against a mound of pillows. Up close, her skin is parchment thin, pupils slow to track.

"Don't mock the chef, she bites." I set the tray on an avalanche of books.

She huffs and nibbles on the bread. It doesn't come back up, so that's a win in my book. "I'll be back to normal by nightfall."

"What *was* the cost?" I ask, parking at the edge of the bed.

"A month of life," she answers. "My entire January, iron-ically. But I'll earn it back, eventually."

Guilt settles like wet cement between my shoulder blades. Friends shouldn't come with depreciation schedules. Rule of consideration: all contracts need exchanges. I've over-drafted, and she's footing the bill.

She doesn't give me the luxury of wallowing. "What plan did you concoct during my down time?"

I could demur but I am who I am. "A lawsuit currently. Probably won't work, which laws apply are squiggly. And it doesn't help Val, but it's all I could do on that couch."

She waves a shaky hand at the surrounding sea of books—tomes on city-scale warding, consecrated geometry, something handwritten in ink that looks suspiciously like gall. "We'll figure it out."

"Anything in those about mayoral magic anchors?" I ask.

She snorts. "These are my mother's. The index stops at *altar salt*. I've written to other covens but no dice so far."

As though saying it made it happen, the mail slot clacks from the front foyer. Vivvy trots in like a tiny courier, a wax-sealed envelope clenched in her teeth. She hops onto the quilt, drops it with a proud *mrp*, and sits on it for good measure. Sara nudges her off it and breaks the seal with a fingernail. The paper smells like sea air and old ink.

Sister Sara,

Your letter found us, though it had far to travel.

You asked what we know of the House and its "anchors."
We did not learn the word from books, but from grief.

Two centuries ago—Lammas of 1824—one of our mortal children went to the city to work in a counting-house. The House chose her for our region's anchor: a mortal face to stabilize collections. They do not always choose the strong or the trained; they prefer the steady. She was kind, punctual, and beloved. That is enough.

We tried to pull her out. We learned the hard rule: to remove an anchor by force is to snap the web. Every bargain tied to that person—debts, reprieves, safe-passage clauses—breaks at once. Our magic could not undo it.

Since then we have understood: once the House names an anchor, there is no clean undoing. Anchors are not chosen to be rescued. They are chosen to be irreplaceable.

There is no gentler undoing. If you are too late, the only mercy is to limit the damage. Keep the secret contained. Prevent the city from seeing how the House roots itself. They prefer order to spectacle. Remember that—they like rules, even cruel ones.

I am sorry for the sharpness of these words. We buried our hope with her, and our grief still teaches us caution. If you are too late but determined to bargain, bring a steward the House respects, offer clean security in hand, *and write the smallest promise you can live with.*

—In solidarity, Aoife Ní Runaidh, Coven of the Wind-Hewn Stones

Sara's eyes are wide when she finishes reading. "I'd never even heard the term until last week." She pushes the grimoires aside. "I've written to every coven that'll answer a stray. Only Aoife bit. The rest sent blessings or blank parchment."

"Here's what's stumping me," I confess. "We know Fulton's tied to the House even if he's not the anchor anymore. But why the mayor's face? The House already gets their month. They've still got the ledgers, the contracts, the machinery. Why drag a retired anchor into politics?"

"Is that the legitimacy you mentioned?" she asks. "They need to be in the system to work it?"

I lean back. "Some nameless all-powerful supernatural conglomerate needing human legitimacy seems weird. And if that's the case, what changed? Why now?"

She shrugs and we sit in silence, each chewing on the possibilities.

"If winning is 'completion,'" she runs shaking fingers over her new highlights, "would they accelerate every contract?"

The words hit the air like a knife tossed by someone with bad aim and worse intentions. What if "completion" isn't just an ending, but a trigger?

I picture a thousand IOUs maturing at midnight, souls vacuumed up like loose change. "Or consolidate them? Stitch every outstanding debt into one civic-sized lien. Or take the bargains *outside* the casino?"

A galaxy of consequences could spiral out: landlords who demand years, not dollars; police precincts writing off disappearances as tax; supernatural tribunals arguing jurisdiction over human lives because City Hall granted it.

Although human courts have been trying that lately in reverse, so maybe it's a good-for-the-gander scenario.

Sara's left eye starts drooping and fresh guilt comes with it.

"Go back to sleep," I order, softer than I intended. "I'll try to make some very messy problems for a very tidy House."

I straighten the tray, ruffle Vivvy's ears—she's posted sentry at the door—and tiptoe back to the living room, where sticky notes and legal pads wait for their next round in the ring.

Sara wakes after sunset, declares me fit for one field trip, and marches me out the door—only for us both to freeze. Something's stuck to my driver's-side window. Again.

Not the House's spade in unknown 'bio' matter (the substance of which I never want clarified). But what looks like... chocolate. And ice cream. Melted together and smeared into a crude stick figure with—what better be—a tripod between his legs holding... is that a magnifying glass?

Sara stares at it. "What am I looking at?"

"Someone's idea of subtle." I wipe a fingertip through the smear—yep, Rocky Road—and come away with a folded scrap of paper pressed into the mess. Two words, scrawled in a blocky print I recognize: COME NOW.

"Do *not* tell me you know who did that," Sara says.

"I know who did that."

Her sigh is pure homicide. "We were *going* to Stardust's."

"We still are," I say, tucking the sticky note into the ruins of my jacket. I open the passenger door and slide in, planning to ride shotgun like a dented airbag. "We're just making a...

pit stop on the way. He might have something on Fulton or the House."

Sara glares at me over the steering wheel like I've just suggested we swing by an active volcano. "You realize your wards aren't sealed yet. If he pulls something—"

"Then you'll drag me out by the scruff, got it."

Her jaw works, but she throws the car into gear. "Fine. One stop. No lingering."

We roll up to the Mitchell house and Sara shades her eyes from the yellow glare.

"You'd think Peterson would've been blinded by the décor and missed," Sara mutters, cutting the engine at the curb.

I scan the windows, looking for Liz or Camden to stroll past. I'm running out of plausible excuses for my presence. But the lights are off. Good. The less they know about my recurring visits to the house they still probably overpaid for, the better.

"I'm only extending your leash once," Sara says. "Come on, let's get this over with."

I clamber out one-armed and hobble to the side of the house, Sara close behind.

A seam in the siding pops open and Wilkin oozes out of it like he's been poured, all sharp elbows and the smell of mildew.

"You're late," he says, as if we had a set appointment. His eyes flick to Sara, then back to me. "And you've got a shadow that smells like embalming fluid. Fuckin' hate that stuff."

Sara's nostrils flare. "I work with embalming fluid. And you're standing inside a half-baked ward I threw up this morning, so maybe don't breathe too deep."

Wilkin snorts, unimpressed. "At least it's coverin' the burn."

I snap my fingers. "Focus. You defaced my windshield for a reason."

"Right." He chitters, gaze flicking between us like he's enjoying a private joke. Then, without warning: *"It's me, pursuing myself! I want to escape—to escape from myself! But it's impossible. I can't escape. I have to obey it. I have to run, run."*

Sara frowns. "What is that?"

"Is that a hint about Fulton?" I exchange a confused glance with Sara. "That he's stuck as the candidate? That he's a pawn?"

"It's a quote," he says, smug as a client who thinks search engines beat law degrees.

"If you're going ransom intel with monologues, start citing your sources," I say. "And I asked you to tail Fulton."

"And I did," he says. "Lost him between the Hancock lobby and a taxi that didn't exist. No driver, no plates, no heat signature. Keep following a guy like that, you end up as ledger ink. I'm givin' you tips on good ole' Dick."

I cross one arm—it's hard to pull off menace when the other's out of commission. "You could have just *told* me that instead of handing me half a noir monologue."

"Where's the fun in that?" he says, already melting back toward the siding. "If I give you the plot, you'll never find the twist yourself."

"Wilkin…"

Sara mutters something under her breath that smells faintly of ozone. "We're done here."

"Agreed," I say, heading back to the car. But the name—Dick freakin' Fritz—sticks in my mind like gum on a shoe: messy, persistent, impossible to ignore.

The wards she's spun around me hum faintly under my skin, still unsettled from earlier. The Rocky Road smear on my jacket sleeve is already stiff.

Sara starts the car. "Next stop, Stardust's. No more detours. If anyone else leaves dessert on your car, we're burning it on sight."

"Even if it's pie?"

Her glare could bend silver. "Especially if it's pie."

I lean back in the seat, rolling the name *Dick Fritz* over in my head again. If Wilkin's right and Fulton's a dead end, it's a thread into the House's archives that doesn't require a ghoul chauffeur or a blindfold. A thread I can pull without warning anyone I'm cutting the rope.

The wards hum louder as we turn onto the district's narrow streets. I tell myself it's just the magic settling—and not the sound of the House taking notice.

Stardust's townhouse glitters against the night like a champagne bottle about to pop—fairy lights in the window, soft jazz leaking onto the porch. But the usual Saturday sparkle feels paused, like someone pressed mute on the party playlist.

"Want the car?" I ask as we exit at the curb.

"I'll walk—slowly," she says, already setting off toward coven HQ.

Ray yanks the door open before I can knock—hoodie, some kind of powder on his sleeve, and smelling faintly of burned sugar and solder. "Knew that bus story was you," he mutters, hauling me inside. "Stardust wouldn't let us go dancing until you checked in alive."

"Sweetling," Stardust croons, sweeping me into a hug that smells of iron and very expensive worry, "are we required to post bail?"

"Merely a disagreement with faulty transportation policy," I say.

He cocks his head. "The news mentioned a prison bus barbecue involving a 'local attorney.'"

Behind him, Ray gives a tiny shake of his head: *not the whole story.* Message received.

I shrug one-shouldered. "Had a question for Peterson, that's all. Paperwork needed eyes."

That lands like a brick. Stardust's smile sharpens. "Peterson? The same mayor who teeter-tottered between enlightened tolerance and supernatural curfews?"

"Even a broken clock keeps transcripts," I say. "He owed me context."

Stardust flicks imaginary dust off his sleeve. "Next time you seek context, kindly avoid triggering prison lockdowns. Last citywide curfew was a bore—no decent after-hours, and the fledglings pouted for weeks."

"Look, it was a fact-finding mission, not a campaign rally. I promise not to trigger another lockdown." I glance at the kitchen—which looks like it lost a bet with a flour bomb—and the unmistakable evidence that someone tried cooking for the first time in history. "You paused Saturday night for me?"

"We couldn't let a headliner miss her set," Ray says, producing a mug of something that smells like actual cocoa. "Drink."

"I'm on a timer," I say, sipping sugar. "I can't go anywhere until Monday morning. So, raincheck on Moonlit Haven or anything outside these very glittery walls."

Stardust snaps on a brighter playlist. "Very well. Then we pretend nobody scorched a prison transport and decide whether tonight's plan involves house karaoke or cards."

"Karaoke," Ray votes, already dimming the lights.

"Cards," I counter. "One-handed advantage."

They groan in unison—perfect harmony—and for the first quiet moment in days I let myself believe the world can stay postponed—and intact—until Monday.

CHAPTER 19

By Monday morning, the ward's finished cooking. I spent the remainder of the weekend scouring the internet for any reference to Dick Fritz and polishing my lawsuit until the footnotes shine and the exhibits don't argue with each other. Two complaints prepped for good measure—election law and charitable fraud—because if you're going to poke the bear, use both hands. By mid-morning, everything is stapled—digitally, because *Illinois requires e-filing or it didn't happen*—and even my caffeine has a table of contents.

I crack my knuckles, open eFileIL, and type in the login I've had since the Jurassic.

"User not found."

I blink. I definitely exist, there are receipts. I try again, slower this time.

"User not found."

I reset the password, using the security image of a lighthouse I picked in a kinder decade. Answering a question no one else knows: *What was the first concert you attended?* Answer: 'Hanson. Don't judge.'

"No account associated with this email."

I blink at the screen like it just meowed. I have filed murder-sized motions with this login. I have fee-waiver receipts. *Tyler Technologies* did not dream me into existence.

Maybe it's my internet. Maybe the universe hates Mondays. Maybe I'll light Stardust's router on fire and see if it helps. I stare at the tiny spinning wheel until it starts to look smug, then drag the filings into a folder called FILE ME and decide to go shake information out of a hobgoblin instead.

It's daytime, which means people will wave and ask about recycling pick up. The sun is a bad idea, but waiting until sunset is a worse one. At least Liz and Camden are at work, which makes slinking along their hedges only slightly less weird.

The siding peels like a magic trick and Wilkin drags himself out of the wall—three feet of soot, teeth, and opinions. He looks out of place in sunshine, like a smudge on a wedding dress.

"You're early," he trills, delighted. "And formally warded. Naughty."

"News?" My voice comes out tighter than I mean. "I'm fresh out of time."

He smirks, stretching the moment like taffy. "I found the House."

The words hit like a brick through stained glass. "You *what*?"

"I sniffed it out doing my little now-you-see-me routine." He waggles long fingers. "Invisibility is a blessin'."

"And the door?"

He bares a grin with too many teeth. "Invitation only for forty-eight hours. But your name is not a favorite."

My stomach drops. "So how do I knock?"

"Find Dick Fritz," he sings, ecstatic to be annoying. "He's a key on legs. House hates him, but their doors recognize his stink. Get his token and get inside. Otherwise, you can't fuckin' see it."

"Of course." Dead ends after dead ends. I press both hands over my face. "Anything else?"

He plucks a crumb from nowhere and pops it into his mouth. "Bring more pastries."

"Keep hoping," I snap, because my patience died sometime around my password reset failure. "Text if you see Fulton."

"Screensaver smile?" he trills. "Hard to miss when he doesn't vanish."

I'm halfway down the sidewalk towards where I stashed my car when a voice booms from the sidewalk. "Ms. Lane?"

A woman in a parka jogs up, recorder already out.

Every instinct says keep walking—surprise hellos are how I met Rhett Baxter, Victor Little, and those damned ghouls. But... "Can I help you?"

"Tash Ruiz, WBEZ."

"No comment," I say, on reflex. How a beat reporter found me, and how I can explain my proximity to Mitchell's murder house is not something I'm interested in attempting.

"You should hear the question first," she says, too kind to smirk. "Who filed the twenty-page ethics grievance against you yesterday? And the fraud claim? And who walked a Sunday injunction through Chancery freezing your operating account and your IOLTA?"

I stop so fast she barrels into my back. "I'm sorry—what?"

"Temporary suspension pending hearing," she says, checking her phone. "The complaint cites 'pattern of deceptive billing practices' and attaches screenshots of your client trust ledger. There's a temporary restraining order enjoining you from transacting with 'any accounts in the respondent's name or under her control.' "Filed yesterday.

Sunday filing—which means someone sweet-talked eFileIL into a timestamp and a judge into weekend duty. *Citizens for Civic Integrity* signed the grievance. No names. Their counsel is—" she squints at her phone "—Brad Wallace."

The name hits like a thrown brick. Compliance Director. Solstice *Educational* Foundation. Denial auto-macro guy whose files I had my fingers in days ago.

"Care to comment?" she asks.

"Only into a pillow," I say, and bolt.

I haven't been home for almost a week. I need to see the papers. I need proof. Because this. This is...

No.

The mailbox is stuffed like a python. On the doormat: a green card from a certified delivery I missed, the kind that smells like consequences. Inside, someone has shoved an envelope under the door so hard it skidded across the floor.

I don't even make it to the couch, too many steps, sliding to the floor beside the coffee table.

I rip open the first: Attorney Registration & Disciplinary Commission (ARDC)—Notice of Complaint & Interim Relief Requested. It reads like a bad dream in Times New Roman. *Emergency petition for temporary suspension pending investigation.* The affidavit cites "pattern of inappropriate behavior" that sounds like they fed my Solstice research through a smear machine. Like Tasha said, there's even a screenshot of my client trust account line—how, I don't know—circled in red like I stole from myself.

Second envelope: Cook County Chancery—Temporary Restraining Order. It's got the Sunday seal, the judge's cramped initials, and a list of banks that makes my blood turn to slush. *Respondent is enjoined from transacting with any accounts pending hearing.* Service by email, text, Sunday certified mail I somehow didn't get.

Third: Bank—Urgent Compliance Notice. *We have received a court order. Your accounts are temporarily restricted.* My operating account, my IOLTA (which legally holds all client funds), my emergency Visa. Rent due next Monday. Malpractice insurance autopays on Wednesday. My personal account I've never let drop below a five-figure buffer—now "temporarily unavailable."

I sit on the floor like my legs forgot the plot. My phone buzzes with a call from an unknown number; I let it die. It buzzes again—different number. Then three emails ping in a row: Password reset request, Suspicious activity detected, Welcome to eFileIL.

Welcome.

Someone just re-registered me.

I try my old login again, the screen smiles blankly. But again, "no account associated with this email."

I call the bank. I get a chipper human who turns to stone when she pulls up my file. "Ms. Lane, an injunction is in place. You'll need to contact the court for modification. Also... there's a fraud alert attached to your Social."

"My—what?"

"Identity theft," she says gently. "We've placed a protective hold."

Nothing says 'protective' like freezing a lawyer's trust accounts, but sure. Still, I thank her because she's not the one trying to unmake me, and hang up on a world where my hands are empty.

The ARDC letter flutters in my grip, official as a funeral. **You have fourteen days to respond.** Sure. But the reporter said "pending hearing" and the TRO says "immediate."

The House didn't come for my throat. It came for my keyboard.

It's still January. The city's "controlled burn." Today it feels like a trap door. The machinery that's supposed to protect the rest of us just helpfully paved their road. So *that's* their human legitimacy: turn the rules into a leash when they don't like the dog.

The building radiator clanks like a dying submarine. I sit in the middle of my floor surrounded by paper and hear my heartbeat counting deadlines. Rent. Insurance. Trust account. ARDC. Chancery. eFileIL. The letters multiply when I blink.

"What am I going to do, Herle?"

Instead of an answer, there's a knock at the door. It's a courier with a clipboard and that green certified-card I missed earlier. I sign without reading and get another thick envelope: Notice of Account Review and Enhanced Due Diligence from the trust bank. It's a stack of questions that would be insulting if I had spare pride left: *Have you recently solicited funds for any non-client purposes? Do you maintain political committee accounts? Provide all client names and amounts held in trust.* I lay my forehead on the doorframe and consider leaving my body.

I am built of law and paper. I breathe motion practice and footnotes. And now what am I?

My hands text the law school group chat before my brain catches up. I should call in another Montgomery favor. I should hire my own lawyer. I call Danielle.

She answers on the first ring. "Tell me you're not in handcuffs."

"Worse," I say. "I'm in paperwork."

A beat. "Explain."

"They filed a grievance and got a TRO freezing my accounts and a quasi-suspension. My efile login vanished. The bank says my Social is flagged. Someone took my *practice* and... erased it."

She swears in cop. "Text me the orders. Don't touch any money—"

"I *can't*," I say, voice breaking. "That's the point."

"Where are you?"

"At my place. The ward's settled."

She hisses. "I'm patrolling in the area. Stay put."

Where would I go?

My phone pings, a text from an unknown number. *"We can discuss a path forward. Foundation counsel would welcome a conversation. -B. Wallace."*

Of course. The House is a monster with accountants. It likes rules. It knows exactly which threads will strangle you when pulled together. They've shown me elegantly, efficiently, that "human systems" are clay if the right hands pinch.

I laugh—one ugly syllable that tastes like copper. Then I forward the text to Danielle with, *"If I disappear, start with him."*

But there might be options. I stare at my phone, thumb hovering over Montgomery's name. Three months ago, he was the anchor client that let me launch my own practice—my scaffolding when everything else was held together with tape and caffeine. Calling him should be the obvious move. But it doesn't feel like one. Because I know how this works. Montgomery doesn't bankroll charity cases. If I can't practice, if my legal reputation is meaningless, I can't deliver. And if I can't deliver, then I'm not useful.

Back on the floor, I drag my laptop out of my bag. For the first time since law school, my superpower feels like a liability.

I work anyway. I send a confirmation email to the ARDC like I've been doing this since birth. **Received. Will respond within the fourteen-day window. Requesting copy of all exhibits.** I keep my sentences clean and boring. Then I open a blank: **Emergency Motion to Modify or Dissolve Temporary Restraining Order** and start typing like oxygen depends on it.

Danielle arrives with snow in her curls and two coffees, reads the orders once, twice, then folds them like they're crime scene photos.

"This is bad," she breathes. No cop-voice, just Danielle. "The TRO especially. Freezing the IOLTA is… cruel."

"It's efficient," I say. "It makes me a ghost with bills."

She sets the cups down and crouches so we're eye-level on the rug. "I don't… fully get how deep this hits. I hear 'license,' and I think badge."

"It's my name on the door," I say, voice doing an uncontrolled wobble. "My hands. My work. They wiped my login like I was a typo."

Her face cracks. "I'm so sorry." A breath. "Okay. We will fix it. But we triage. You've got fourteen days. You can make it fourteen days."

I nod because she's right and because if I don't, something will break.

Her voice gentles. "I know your practice is your lungs, Em. But, it's a long game, remember? Val's clock is still ticking. We can't let this paperwork pile become the fire we stare at while she burns."

She's right. My identity may be my life, but Val's a kid. "I can compartmentalize."

"And don't text Wallace," she adds, catching my glance at the phone. "He wants you off-balance. We answer on our terms."

"Copy. No dancing with Compliance Dracula."

She huffs a laugh, then sobers. "Tell me what Wilkin said."

I give her the short version: We've got a location, invitation only, open for forty-eight hours, Fritz as the key. She doesn't like it; her mouth goes thin in the way that means *I will arrest a building if I have to.*

My phone buzzes. I expect another Wallace text but it's Megan. Calling. Megan never calls; she treats phone calls like radioactivity.

"I called the court," she says without a hello. "You've got 9:30 a.m. Thursday, Room 2408. Bring three copies of everything and a pulse. I'll meet you at security. I'm filing my appearance—your lawyer, basically."

"Megan—"

"No speeches," she cuts in. "Email me every exhibit you've touched. And you're buying drinks once your account re-opens." Click.

Danielle's eyebrows climb. "Megan?"

"She hates calling," I say, dazed. "She got us a hearing date."

"See?" she says. "Fixable."

"It'll stick," I say, fingers worrying the edge of the TRO. "Even if we unwind it, the smear smears."

It's not like I'm starting from zero. With Lucian and Peterson's case, half the humans decided I'm Nosferatu's pet, the other half decided I'm dangerous with a subpoena. And with the supernaturals, I outed Sara as a witch in the wrong room—spectacularly bad manners—bringing heat on her and stamping myself reckless. Clean it up in court and it still lives on in the record books; scrub it in the coven gossip and it echoes for a century. All press isn't good press when both rumor mills have eternity on the clock.

"Then we wash *louder*," she says. "You've got a choir now, remember?" She pauses, looking at me like she's making sure I'm still here. "You are more than a BAR number, Emily Lane."

"I know," I say, meaning *I'm trying.* The truth is uglier: my superpower is law and paper, and the House just turned both into a cage. It's hard not to feel like a rabbit who got out-warranted.

"I'll drive you to Stardust's," she says. "You're not using your accounts, you're not calling rideshares, and you're not going alone."

"Bossy," I say.

"Alive," she corrects, reaching up to tuck hair out of my face like a sister. "My shift ends at five. Then we go poke a man named Dick because apparently irony is our religion."

I pull on my coat. The sleeves feel wrong—like they were tailored for a person whose name matches her login. It'll do.

My phone pings: "*We are available this evening. -B. Wallace*"

Danielle reads it over my shoulder and snorts. "Block him. I'm serious."

At the door, Danielle hesitates. "I am sorry," she says again, and it lands. She gets that she doesn't get it, and she's still here.

"Me too," I say. "But Val first."

"Val first," she echoes.

The House can have the clay. I'm keeping the kiln.

CHAPTER 20

Stardust's place at 11 a.m. is a mausoleum for perfect taste. Curtains drawn, music off, silence doubled. I spread out my arsenal: yellow pad, two pens that aren't cursed (hopefully), and a draft script for responding to Dear Mr. Wallace. Underneath, a Dick Fritz refresher: *Secret casino. House-adjacent. Looks like a key with eyebrows. Annoying in bulk.* I underline annoying twice for morale.

Someone knocks at the side door. I freeze; nobody here orders DoorDash before sunset.

"Anybody home?" rasps a voice that sounds like sandpaper flirting with a hinge.

I peer through the sidelights. A hobgoblin—the little barter fiend from last week who passed along my message to Wilkin. He air-taps the glass and points down. Stardust's threshold glyphs are lit faintly like buried wire: no entry for the uninvited.

I crack the door three inches. "I'm out of muffins and batteries."

He bares teeth. "Courier service. Your clapboard friend says: *come to him.* He has more. Must be quick."

Of course Wilkin refuses to cross the city to help me. "Can he come here?"

Hob shakes his head hard enough to shed lint. "He says no. He says you owe him two Fudge-Me-Once and one honey-goat besides."

"Unshockingly on brand." I glance down the empty street—vampire district when the sun's out is tumbleweeds and tasteful townhouses. "Two minutes." I step over the line and lock the door behind me.

The air shivers. Two figures detach from the daylight like bruises—not the prison-lot ghoul duo, but close cousins. These wear city-maintenance vests over thrift-store coats, and the light makes them look *dry* instead of melted: skin gone pewter and papery, seams showing at the jaw like somebody reattached it with duct tape. Their eyes are fish-white, no pupils to negotiate with, and when they move there's a lag—like bad buffering in a corpse.

"Delivery," the taller one says, voice like sand through a vent.

"I didn't order anything I can't return," I say, shoulder tucked toward Stardust's door.

"Come along quiet," Short says. "House wants a chat."

"Put it on the calendar," I answer, edging my heel back toward the threshold. The glyphs hum under my shin; Sara's ward hums under my ribs.

"We don't need inside," Short says, taking two slow steps that smell like turned earth. "We only need you outside."

Tall's hand snaps out—too fast for that bulk—and clamps my forearm. The ward Sara stitched under my collarbones flares—cold bands cinching tight—blunting the pain like I'm wrapped in tempered glass. Sturdier, Sara promised, but not invulnerable.

I do the stupid thing that's saved me before: I aim for cartilage. I slam the heel of my shoe into Tall's knee. It's like kicking a packed freezer bag but the joint gives a grudging inch. He grunts, grip loosening.

Short lunges for my shoulder. I pivot into the door, ricochet off the jamb, and grab the brass lion doorstop from the stoop. I feed it to his wrist. Bone cracks like pond ice. He howls, a ruined-violin sound, but stays too close.

"Ms. Lane," Tall says, leaning close enough for the penny-smell to make my eyes water, "we are on a schedule."

"So am I," I wheeze, palming a fist of dirt and the rock salt Ray scatters outside for the mortals without vampire grace walking on ice. I fling the mix into Short's face. He recoils, hissing as salt etches those fish-white eyes, stumbles into the closed door, ruining my escape route.

Tall takes another swing. I slam the doorbell and scream, "Room service!"

Somewhere deep inside, a chime rings that wakes no vampires but definitely wakes the house. The threshold glyphs flare brighter. But I can't get the door open.

Short recovers, feints left, then drives a shoulder into my ribs. The ward catches it—makes my body ring like struck iron—but I stay upright. I grab the handrail and yank; it's secured like a bank vault.

But they're both too close, eight limbs against warded-but-still-clumsy-me. Tall manages to slap something black and glossy against my sternum, right over the ward locus. Cold bites through fabric, needle-sharp.

A spade.

The patch drinks light.

My ward coughs—once—then drops to a whisper. Tempered glass becomes thin ice.

"Contractor trick," Tall rasps, satisfied. "Private ledger meets public nuisance."

Short ducks in low, loops a strap around my ankles, and yanks. I go down hard; the threshold saves my skull from the stone, but pain flares bright along my elbow. I kick—connect with shin—and earn a grunt and a smear of papery skin on the step.

Zip-ties bite my wrists before I can swear properly. I scream but Tall slaps a palm over my mouth—heatless, powder-dry—and my cheek stings.

As they haul me upright, I twist my bound hands toward my coat pocket, pinch a business card free, and let it slip into the alley. Breadcrumb, meet gravel.

"We're late," Short says, blinking tears, and between the two of them they frog-march me down the lane. The spade patch keeps the ward smothered. My body feels like someone let the air out two PSI at a time.

My phone is still in my coat pocket; I slam the side button five times with my bound hands and pray the Emergency SOS is braver than I am.

No sirens, of course. No one regulates the vampire district. But maybe a ping flies to Danielle. Or Megan. Or someone. Maybe.

"Contract is clear," Tall adds, almost conversational. "You come. You talk. No marrow."

"Charming terms," I snap. "Add 'no ghouls' and I'll consider."

The hobgoblin hovers at the curb, greedy eyes bright. "Payment," he rasps. "Two things broken, one thing melting."

Short grunts and out comes a rusted key, a cheap cigarette lighter, and a lipstick already sweating. The hob weighs them, pockets the lot with a satisfied growl, and vanishes into a drain like scheming sludge.

My stomach turns. Bribed with my own barter rules. Great.

A sliding door thunks open. The van wears a magnetic CITY OF CHICAGO—WATER sign that would fool exactly no one with a pulse. Hands shove, gravity tilts, and I'm in—onto ribbed metal and the faint clink of tools. Cable ties cinch around the seat posts. Something cold taps the spade patch, and the ward goes from whisper to nothing.

No witnesses. No vampires. No cavalry.

"Hey," I say, because my mouth runs on adrenaline. "Just so you know? Last time someone offered me a quiet chat, I set a bus on fire."

"Not a bus," Tall says. "A schedule."

The van laughs in rattles. I tighten my grip on the seat post and count breaths. Sara's ward is buried under a spade. My superpower is paper. And the House has now proven they can steal both.

We head south, judging by the skyline bleeding away in the rearview. I count turns—left, right, right, left—until we descend into an underground garage.

The walk is down a corridor so narrow I could brush both walls if I stretched my arms. The panels are matte-black, no knobs, no hinges, but they flex almost imperceptibly as we pass—like lungs holding their breath until we're gone. And with Sara's ward cracked off me, I can feel it. The air skims my skin like static, cataloguing me, waiting for a gap to slip into. Every step is a reminder that I'm a guest here only in the hostage-negotiation sense.

Panel seven exhales open. The air has weight, like a court-room right before the jury files in. I don't walk in so much as get shepherded—my two ghoul buddies behind me, a new one in front, the choreography of "voluntary" attendance.

The office itself is textbook prestige-drama lawyer: walnut paneling with grain so perfect it might have been painted on, leather-bound law books arranged by height rather than subject, and a brass lamp with a green shade that casts a pool of light just bright enough to make contracts legible but dim enough to hide the fine print. Set dressing that's meant to say *trust me, I bill $700 an hour,* even though the walls probably eat intruders between depositions. Worse is the paperwork: bland manila file folders stacked in neat little piles, each tab labeled in the same meticulous block lettering that hasn't seen a smudge in decades. You'd hope legal supernatural powerhouses had moved past physical filing, but no dice.

And behind the desk sits Brad Wallace.

He looks like he was sketched by a corporate illustrator who specializes in boardroom villains: tailored charcoal suit with a thread count higher than my monthly rent, blond hair in a perfect side-part that requires either imported gel or seventh-level sorcery, posture calibrated to suggest authority without effort. His olive skin is too smooth, like someone buffed out all the pores with fine-grit sandpaper, and the shadows under his razor-sharp cheekbones don't move with the lamp, staying fixed like they were applied with contour-ing makeup. His pupils ripple like oil-slick on water, never quite settling into a single shape. Not a vampire—the shaft of sunlight flicking over his crossed arms confirms that with-out a wisp of smoke or flinch. Not a ghoul—his manicured nails are too clean, his teeth too white when he smiles. But also not a human. Something else that passes well enough you could sit next to him in court and never realize until you notice he hasn't taken a breath in three minutes.

I've never seen him before, but I know the type—slick, composed, the same easy economy of movement Montgomery uses when he wants you to forget he's the most dangerous person in the room. Apparently the House is *selling* legitimacy too, as his BAR number is as real as mine.

Or it was.

I know his name from the bottom of the automated rejections for the Solstice Educational Fund. Brad Wallace, Compliance Director. The guy with the macro that kicked back every emailed request I made for House-adjacent records.

Like he promised, Montgomery was my "in" to those records, slipping me through a locked door with permission and a map. He made it sound like brunch reservations, access on half a day's notice, not a one-way pass into the wolf's den. Which means either he greased the hinges without mentioning the teeth on the other side, or he knew exactly whose office I'd land in.

Assuming I get out of this room, he'll be getting a hell of an accusatory text from me.

And looking at Wallace now, I can't decide if he's here to collect a grudge or congratulate me. Part of me suspects he let Montgomery pass me through—just to see what I'd do once I got my fingers in his files.

"Ms. Lane." His voice is warm, measured. "We need to talk."

I take the chair without being asked. "About my kidnapping, or are we skipping straight to the pitch?"

That smile—half amusement, half calculation—doesn't budge. "You've made yourself... inconvenient. The House doesn't appreciate your interpretation of the rules."

I lean back, as though this is a friendly chat and not me auditioning for the role of 'cautionary tale.' After all, humor's my shield and sarcasm my weapon, even if it's more butter knife than broadsword right now. "Guess I'll cross them off my holiday card list."

His brows tick up, lazy as a metronome. "Cute. But you've done more than bruise feelings, Ms. Lane. You've walked into offices where you don't belong. You've handled contracts you shouldn't be able to read. And yesterday you put yourself on more than one list that doesn't forgive easily." He steeples his fingers, eyes rippling. "Frozen accounts, a profession about to disown you, and colleagues who will swear they never learned your name. That isn't a bad day. That's the rest of your life."

My skin prickles, not just from the speech but because without the ward, I can feel the room tasting me, measuring exactly how human I am. Like I've already been seated for sentencing, and the walls are leaning in to hear me plead.

Then he leans in, warmth dialed back on. "Unless you'd like another option. I can make all that go away," he says smoothly. "Your frozen accounts, your grievance hearings. More than that—we could keep you in practice."

"In practice?"

"Permanently." He lets the word linger just a fraction too long. "No aging out, no illness, no one closing your file when you're... done. You could keep at this another fifty years. A hundred."

I blink. "You're offering me immortality."

And God help me, for half a second, it lands. Because I've been the only mortal in the 'courtroom' of my supernatural pals, outvoted by people who won't ever wrinkle. Immortality would level the field. No more sidelong glances when

I don't know the lore, no more running on borrowed time when I step into the Underground, no calling in favors.

But the catch flashes neon: no one offers forever unless they mean to own you for it.

His smile widens, like he's hooked me. "I'm offering you the right kind of permanence. Legitimacy. With the right adjustments, you'd be untouchable—part of something much older, much stronger, than the city's little courts."

"That's a lovely brochure," I say, "but you stole a girl, kidnapped me, and froze my accounts. You'll forgive me if I'm more interested in *her* release than your pension plan."

A pause. The shadows under his skin twitch like they want out. "You've already seen the ledgers. You know the rules. She is in escrow until her term expires."

"She's not collateral, she's a person," I snap. "So, either you're bluffing about your power or you're choosing not to use it."

His smile doesn't budge—half amusement, half warning—but his fingers flex once against the desk blotter, almost human. "Not everything is negotiable, Ms. Lane."

I lean forward, sharp enough to cut myself. "Says who? You build contracts for permanence, but permanence isn't static. Lifetimes are longer now. Centuries stretch further. By your own rules, Victor Little's contract should be renegotiated. What's the harm in giving him five more years? Ten? If your machinery is so flawless, why not flex with the market?"

That gets him. A flicker in the eyes, oil rippling sharper. "The machine works because it does not pause. If one thread slackens, the weave collapses. Time moves forward. The House must move with it."

I let a bitter laugh scrape out. "So kidnapping is just... what? Your standard operating procedure? January hits, you pull out the net, and drag in the next crop?"

"Every January," he says, with the eerie calm of someone reciting case law. And then, almost too soft to register: "It's tradition."

"Tradition," I repeat, flat as paper. "Kidnapping children is nasty business. You know that, don't you?"

Something shifts. His pupils ripple like spilled ink, but it isn't just the usual slick performance—there's a crack in it, a beat too long where he doesn't speak. His gaze flicks, unthinking, toward the corner of his desk. A folder sits there, its edge lined with neat black type: *Little, Valentine.* His hand moves almost unconsciously, sliding the folder half an inch under a blotter as though I hadn't noticed.

Then it's gone, smoothed out into that immaculate, corporate calm. "Not everything is negotiable," he repeats, but the edges are tighter now, defensive.

"Then why bother dangling forever?" I press. "If the House wants me, it's not for my litigation record. What do you *actually* want me to do?"

"That depends on which side of history you'd prefer to stand on."

"History has a lot of wrong sides," I say, but my eyes catch on a framed letter behind him.

It's not just old—the paper's the deep, uneven cream you only get from a century of oxygen and bad storage. The date at the top is clean enough to read from here: *March 4, 1918.* The handwriting is all confident loops and sharp downstrokes, ink gone to sepia.

From my angle, I can make out a fragment:

> *"...in accordance with the Covenant's terms, the bearer shall be afforded all rights and dignities of a citizen in perpetuity..."*

My brain pings on *perpetuity*—it's one of those words that lives in contracts and wills, not casual correspondence. I think of Victor's storage unit, the carbon dating, and Brian Fulton's smile in a 1927 newspaper photo. The gears grind and refuse to catch, but the shape of it is there: the House doesn't just write contracts. They write permanence. I just need to exploit it.

When I look back, Wallace is watching me—not moving, not smiling, just holding my gaze for a second too long. Then the warmth snaps back into place, like he's smoothed a wrinkle I wasn't supposed to see.

I drag my eyes away first. I've already had one kidnapping today; I don't need to start a second. "You'll forgive me if I don't sign up for the Forever Plan after a thirty-minute sales pitch," I finally say.

"You'll change your mind," he replies, as if it's already decided. "Once you realize your human leads are gone and your supernatural allies can't help you anymore."

It's meant to sound like prophecy. It feels like a warning.

The ghouls are already moving before I can decide which.

The world snaps back hard, like a rubber band catching skin.

One second, I'm in Brad Wallace's law-drama office, the air thick enough to chew; the next I'm standing in the alley beside Stardust's where they grabbed me, knees aching as though I've been dropped from a height. If they could just 'plop' me anywhere they wanted, you'd think they wouldn't need the van-kidnapping performance.

And my body swears it was an hour, tops. But I went in with daylight, and I'm coming out to a skyline gone black. Either I blacked out time—or the House took it. I fish my phone out of my coat with fingers that don't feel steady. One number.

"Sara," I say when she answers.

Her voice is tight. "Where are you?"

"Back at Stardust's. The ghouls just—dropped me. The ward's gone."

"I know. I felt it go. I'm with Lucian at his." A pause, then the scrape of a chair. "Stay where you are. We'll come to get you."

"It's only a few blocks—"

"Stay. Put."

But staying put has never been my strong suit, and Lucian's place is only four blocks away in the vampire district. I start walking, the high-gothic rooflines and narrow gaslit streets closing in around me.

I'm a block from his door when the tall, dark shadow of him steps out of an alley, coat snapping behind him.

"You walked," he says, voice flat. Not at me—for once—but at the situation.

"I walked," I admit. "I figured if they wanted me again, they'd take me."

His jaw tightens, but he doesn't lecture me. Instead, he falls into step, herding me toward the front door.

Inside, the foyer blooms into cathedral-sized grandeur: all dark wood and soft lamps that make shadows behave. A sweeping staircase curves up to a mezzanine where a massive, gilded family tree dominates the wall. Branches scroll out in elegant script, each name an echo of Belmont lineage.

Someone—not Lucian—has stuck a neon pink note on the end of one branch in blocky Sharpie: *murderous mayor Peterson.*

It shouldn't make me smile, but it does. Briefly.

The parlor's already a war room. Sara's crouched over a tangle of chalk lines, muttering under her breath. Danielle's pacing with her phone glued to her ear, every step tight enough to creak the boards. Victor stands near the window, coat collar up, hat brim low enough to hide his face from anyone glancing in. Even Severin, who takes his position as Lucian's second in command more seriously than a judge, is there, stone-faced and ready for whatever might be coming.

The air's sharp with tension and the faint tang of ward-smoke.

"Emily—" Sara's on her feet the second I step in, fingers hovering an inch from my chest.

I glance down like I'll see the switch for the ward. And maybe I do. The spade over my sternum curls in one corner and I can peel it off like a cheap sticker.

"They didn't break it," Sara says. "They turned it off."

"Brad Wallace," I tell them, and Danielle stills mid-step. "Compliance director. Or whatever the House calls it. He's the one whose macro bounced the record requests I sent last week."

Lucian's voice is a cool blade. "And now you've met him in person."

I nod. "They took me to him. Offered me immortality. I'd be *legitimate.*" I spit the word like it tastes wrong. "Problem is, damned if we can't find this Veil Covenant to know what 'legitimate' even buys. Oh—and he's got a little wall art: letter dated 1918, promising someone 'all rights and dignities in perpetuity.'" I rub my temple, the image burned in. "It means *something*. I just can't make the gears catch yet."

Sara's already chalking sigils on my skin without touching me. The ward clicks back into place with a muted thrum, and she exhales in relief—no mercury flashing in her hair this time.

Severin gives me a sharp nod and stalks back towards the foyer, doing whatever he does when he's not at the Haven or scheduling security drills for the fledglings.

"Brad might be our way in," I say when the room settles. "I can retrace the way they took me."

"No," Lucian says. "They can turn you off just as easily. You have no leverage."

Danielle slides her phone away. "Dick Fritz is our safest option. Victor's given us a description."

Victor's voice is low, precise. "Tall. Carries himself like the room belongs to him. Mid-forties maybe, dresses like he's auditioning for three different decades at once. Loud jackets, louder opinions."

"Supernatural?" I ask.

"Vampire, I think," Victor says.

My gaze slides to Lucian, who looks like he's rifling through a century's worth of memory. "Fritz," he says, tasting the name. "I don't know a Fritz. That name isn't in any Chicago coven, nor on any recent roster."

"He didn't have one," Victor says. "Loner. Showed up when he wanted, vanished just as fast."

Sara chews her lip, chalk still smudged on her fingers. "So, we've got a ghost with a loud wardrobe. That narrows it down to, what, half the Underground?"

Danielle's already typing on her phone, jaw tight. "Then we start the Underground. Paper trails, precinct whispers, the kind of people who remember the loud ones. Lucian, Victor, you're both with me."

Lucian inclines his head, though his eyes flick toward me. There's an undercurrent, like they had a conversation before I arrived and are only recapping it now.

Danielle nods, taking the cue. "Emily, you're not coming with us."

It slams harder than the first time they tried to sideline me. Then it was about buying me time. Now it's about cutting me out of the chase altogether.

"Absolutely not," I snap. "You want me to go sit at Stardust's like a house cat while you all run off chasing neon blazers?" I almost laugh. "Didn't we have this same conversation already? No. I've been in this from the start and the clock is ticking down."

"Emily," Victor says, quieter than I've ever heard him. "Last time, you were the only one actually moving the trail. If you stopped, Val was lost. But the last few days—" He looks away. "The House already got to you. They froze your accounts. You were gone for a weekend we couldn't afford to lose. You're not the only one who can move now."

The words hit like a gavel. It almost hits worse from Victor. Not because he hired me. He's a mess—half out of time, half out of hope—but he's trying. For Val. To make up for all the times he didn't try.

Which is why I can't walk away. Because if Victor can carve out space for Val in a world this merciless, can try after all, maybe—maybe there's hope for... for others.

And for one blinding second, I picture myself storming into the Underground anyway, consequences be damned. Going rogue worked before. It could work again.

Danielle cuts through the thought like a scalpel. "This isn't about proving yourself. It's about Val. One mistake—*one*—means she doesn't come home. The long game is how we win, remember? You're still part of it, Em. Just not right now."

The fight drains out of me, leaving only heat behind my eyes. They're not wrong, but it feels like being pushed off my own case. Again.

Sara folds her arms. "You go back to Stardust's. Wards hold there. Let us hunt the ghost."

No one argues. No one has to. The decision's already locked, and apparently I'm the liability in the room.

I bite down hard enough to taste copper, because if I open my mouth again, I'll burn every bridge left. It doesn't mean I won't think about slipping the leash the second they're gone.

Lucian's the one who peels away from the others. "I'll take her back."

I bristle. "Like I'm a package?"

"Like you're a target," he corrects, cool as frost. "And one I'd rather not see hit again."

So we walk. Stardust's house is only a few blocks away, but with Lucian shadowing me step for step, it feels like a perp walk. The silence between us is thick enough to bruise.

"You're upset with me," he says. It isn't a question.

"I'm *upset* about being sidelined," I mutter. "There's a difference."

He sighs. "You believe it's punishment. It's not. It's triage."

I laugh once, sharp and bitter. "Funny, because it feels like hospice." I peek over at him, pale as carved alabaster in the streetlight. "I was offered immortality today, you know." I don't say the rest: if I'd taken it, this wouldn't be happening. I'd have a later bedtime, no babysitter, *inter alia*.

His gaze is sidelong, unreadable. "Immortality is a leash, not a crown. Don't mistake one for the other."

"Easy for you to say." It comes out snide. But we're both too tired to file the edges down.

We reach the alley beside Stardust's place. The lion-head doorstopper sits cracked where I smashed it into a ghoul's arm; paper thin skin flakes are ground into the step. Lucky for me, none of my blood or unmentionables are decorating the scene too.

"Room service," I tell the fox knocker before shoving the door open and flashing a dry smile over my shoulder.

Lucian lingers just outside the threshold, shadows sharpening him into marble. "Stay inside this time," he says evenly. "You can't flip the table if you're the one nailed to it."

The door closes between us.

Chapter 21

Stardust is perched on the arm of the sofa in a smoking jacket that looks like it lost a knife fight with a fireworks display. Sequins glint like shrapnel whenever he moves. He looks me over like a critic summoned to review the uninvited. "Do you have a *systematic objection* to letting my evenings conclude like they were planned?"

Ray leans against the hallway doorframe, quiet, watchful. His eyes say *glad you're okay*; Stardust's say *entertain me*.

"Sorry to ruin the costume extravaganza," I mutter. Knowing Stardust, one is happening somewhere.

I head for the kitchen, because it's either pace or scream. Stardust trails behind, radiating the kind of theatrical annoyance only immortals and actors can sustain.

"You could at least *text*, Emily girl. Some of us immortals can manage this newfangled technology."

That's when I see it: my note, the one Wilkin left, delivered by a traitorous (or capitalist) hobgoblin, sitting on the counter. Only now there's fresh ink scrawled across the back.

"Who wrote on this?"

"I did," Stardust answers smoothly, padding closer. He flips it like a tarot card, clears his throat, and launches into full stage mode:

"It's there all the time, driving me out to wander the streets, following me, silently, but I can feel it there." His voice drops to a hush, then blooms again, echoing out his own additions, "It's me, pursuing myself! I want to escape, to escape from myself! But it's impossible. I can't escape, I have to obey it."

I blink. It's verbatim what Wilkin recited Saturday night. "That's... not the kind of annotation I was expecting."

His grin blooms, sharp and satisfied. "Fritz Lang. *M.* 1931. Sublime paranoia. We owe the entire language of noir to that film."

I squint. "You're telling me Wilkin quoted a ninety-year-old German movie at me?"

"Ninety-*plus,* darling. Vision ages better than governments." Stardust pirouettes away, robe dragging inexplicable smoke in his wake. "Lang saw everything—city as machine, man as commodity, morality as contract. He built the blueprint."

My gaze flicks to the framed poster—*You Only Live Once*—then back to the paper in his hand. A realization starts forming.

"You're a fan," I say carefully.

Stardust's brows arch. "I am civilized."

"Civilized," I echo. What did that one vamp say? "Or obsessed enough to quote Lang at your bonding proposal."

Ray coughs into his sleeve, failing to hide a smile as he sidesteps toward the bar. "She's not wrong."

And the pieces slam together.

Metropolis for a proposal. A Lang movie poster in the kitchen. Victor's voice in my head: *Loud jackets, louder opinions. Carries himself like the room belongs to him.*

"You're Dick Fritz."

Stardust doesn't even flinch. He just tilts his head, a cat presented with the obvious. "Once upon a badly dressed time, yes. Richard if we're being formal. Fritz if we're being tacky." His nose wrinkles. "Everyone experiments with aliases. Floyd was worse."

"You scrubbed it," I say, everything clicking into place with the subtlety of a dropped piano. "But you worked for the House."

The flicker in his eyes isn't brief—it's a storm shutter slamming down too late. "You've been doing homework."

Ray sets down his glass with a quiet clink. "She's a lawyer, Star. Homework's her kink."

Stardust musters up a smirk, trying for breezy. "You've come a long way, Emily Lane, from not even knowing my real name."

"So, what's the story?" I ask. "You used to bankroll them? Cheat cards? Run errands?"

"A finder," he admits, sharp smile turned inward now. "Every House needs a fool to feed the table. I was their showman, their door-opener bringing the good gamblers. One good bet after another until it bought me something rarer than chips: a walkout. Most don't get to leave."

I blink. "And that was that?"

"Not exactly." He slinks toward the kitchen drawer, the one where I'd stolen a battery last time, and rummages. When he returns, his palm opens to reveal a brass coin worn soft with handling, edges chewed down by time. Stamped on it, a spade and a single number: *one.*

"My marker. A final courtesy and good for one door." His voice drops. "That's all that remains of the incomparable Dick Fritz."

Ray leans back, studying him. "You always did love your dramatic exits."

"And my dramatic returns," Stardust says, but the usual lilt isn't there. His hand closes around the coin, almost protective. "If I ever have a need to get out from under the House again, I've got my path. One hundred years and I've never had to look back."

I stare at the coin, then at him. "So, you've had a century-long safety net."

The words come out sharper than I mean them to—probably because I'm thinking about Sara bleeding thirty-one days just to keep me standing. Stardust got to *walk away* from the House and carry a golden ticket in his pocket.

Me? The House already shredded my career, emptied my accounts, and gift-wrapped me for ghouls. My best exit strategy right now is prayer and caffeine. Seeing him hold a perfect out makes my chest ache like a bruise I can't stop pressing.

Meanwhile, Val's ledger is closing in a week. A girl barely old enough for a learner's permit doesn't get the luxury of an exit coin. She gets numbers on a page, her life boxed and signed away.

"But I don't need nostalgia—I need an entry," I tell him. "There's a kid in their ledger, and the clock's ticking."

His brows lift, skeptical, but I press harder: "Brian Fulton. Their man. He's not just lurking in shadows anymore—he's running for mayor. The House doesn't just want contracts this year, they want City Hall. You think they'll stop once they've got the chair?"

That cracks something. Stardust blinks, and for once the perpetual smirk doesn't arrive to cover the silence.

Ray watches him closely. "She's not wrong, Star. You told me you walked out because you didn't want to be their mascot anymore. If we get another mayor like Peterson—"

"Mayor," Stardust repeats softly, like the word itself tastes bitter. He turns the coin in his palm, brass flashing. "It was always cards and contracts before. A mayor's seat... that's daylight. That's the House moving upstairs."

"Which means," I say, leaning in, "your century-long safety net just got a lot more valuable. You want to spend it running, or help me kick in the door?"

The line lands harder than I meant. Maybe because part of me *wants* to give him an out—I don't owe Stardust my crusade, and a coin like that could buy him a century more of safety. But there's Val, and there's Fulton, and there's the ugly truth that safety for one vampire couple doesn't balance against hundreds of names in those ledgers.

For once, Stardust doesn't smirk. The robe, the sequins, the sarcasm—they all slip, and what's left is something stripped-down, rawer than I've ever seen him. He looks at Ray, and for a heartbeat, guilt hangs in the air like incense.

Ray's voice is quiet, not mocking this time. "You've been carrying guilt as long as I've known you. Maybe it's time you spend the coin."

Stardust exhales, long and slow, like velvet dragged over glass. "Emily Lane, you ruin everything. And fates help me, I'm going to let you ruin this too."

The guest room Stardust gave me looks like a jewel box idea got drunk and shacked up with an antique store. Blackout velvet drapes stitched with constellations. An absurdly low chaise. A mirrored vanity that turns one human into five slightly prettier ones. The air hums faintly—wards stitched into the molding, purring like a cat that prefers you don't touch it.

I close the door, lock it, and lean against it until my spine remembers upright. My shirt is a crime scene of ghoul dust and alley grit; there's a scuff at my collar where the spade patch tried to turn me into a paper doll. I stretch, wince, and breathe through the way my ribs complain. The vanity's glass shows a woman who looks like she lost an argument with a filing cabinet and then sprinted through a haunted craft store.

I scrub off the worst of the ghoul and the sidewalk, wrestle into a clean black tee I find in a guest drawer (Ray's: soft, stolen, blessedly mortal), and trade chewed-up flats for boots with tread. Hair up in my signature power pony. If I'm going to walk into a pocket dimension casino, I'm not doing it in eau de kidnapping.

It has to be me. Who else can carry it? Danielle has her family, Sara has Severin and the coven, they have each other. Stardust has Ray.

It can't be Victor. Val has someone who told her she wasn't a mistake. It matters that she gets to keep hearing it.

No matter how it sounds, this isn't a pity party, not like when I went to the Baxter house alone. This is because I can do this, for everyone else.

The brass coin sits on the vanity like it followed me. Small. Heavy. When I touch it, it's warmer than my pulse. I set it down again before I start reading it like tea leaves.

I'm not delaying, not really. But recent history tells me I might not be walking out of this one. My other... incidences... were never intentional. I finished those cases when I was locked in the room with danger. Now I'm forcing myself through the door.

The guest room is quiet, the kind that lets the last seventy-two hours stencil themselves in sharpie on the inside of your skull: Wallace offering me immortality like a loyalty program. Sara paying a month of her life to keep me breathing. Danielle's voice, low and furious, about January's "settlement window." Victor counting days on his daughter's ledger as if it's a rosary and he's out of prayers.

Okay. Breathe.

There's a little desk in the corner, lacquered within an inch of its life, with a fountain pen shaped like someone's favorite dagger. I drag the chair out, sit, and pull a sheet of Stardust's monogrammed paper. **R** embossed in silver at the top, smug as a crown.

Not a manifesto. Not a goodbye. A will.

I can still hear myself in Armand's parlor: *cheap insurance, vanilla law, not because you plan on getting staked next week...* Funny. Turns out I was pitching to the wrong room.

My hand shakes on the first line, steadies by the second.

Last Will and Testament of Emily Lane

I name an executor because that's what adults do (Megan, who will bully the probate court into submission). I nominate a successor (Matty, who knows where the bodies of FOIA are buried).

The rest is easy, because I don't own much of value. My laptop and the drive of case notes to Danielle—with a sticky: *file if I don't show, still file if I do.* My coffee maker and teapot to Sara, who'll at least put them to dangerous use. My client list to Megan, to scatter however she sees fit. My rolling briefcase to Matty because government lawyers really don't get paid enough.

Stardust gets nothing on paper, because he'd hate the sentiment. Lucian doesn't need anything. And Ray already lives in a dragon's (read: Stardust's) hoard of sequins and crystal. Giving immortals my thrift-store bookshelves would be like donating a toothpick to Versailles.

My hand hovers over the page. A new line takes shape before I realize I'm writing it:

To Montgomery: tell him I went down swinging.

I stare at it. Three seconds, maybe four. Because part of me still wants him to know I wasn't useless, not just some mortal pawn the House chewed up and spit out. That I was still worth the retainer, even without a license. That I had value as the infamous Emily Lane. That he backed the right horse.

But Montgomery doesn't keep souvenirs. He keeps pieces on the board. And once you can't move anymore, you're no doubt replaced.

I press the pen hard enough to nearly tear the page, then drag a line straight through the sentence until it's gone. The pad looks cleaner without him in it. Neater. Like maybe the end of my story doesn't belong in his files.

I do *not* write why I'm doing this, or Val's name, because that feels like tempting the House to practice penmanship. I write this instead: any residual cash to be split in equal shares among my friends as named above, for "emergency purposes only." If they squint, "emergency" can mean "rescue a teenager from those 'extradimensional loan sharks' however you can."

That's it. That's all. One mortal life boiled down to a couple hard drives, a caffeine ritual, and debts disguised as favors.

I add an email address and a line that will make some clerk blink: *If the decedent is missing in any realm for more than 180 days, presume death.* Grim? Yes. But competent. Competent is the religion that got me this far. Competence and sarcasm.

The words sit there. Black lines on expensive paper. Mortal as it gets.

Wallace told me I could be "in practice permanently." I'm sitting under someone else's monogram drafting proof that I won't be. The irony would be delicious if it didn't taste like pennies.

A soft knock. I freeze. "Yeah?"

Ray's voice through the door, warm and unhelpful. "Need water? A less haunted T-shirt? Permission to swear creatively?"

"I stole your shirt," I say. "And I'm already swearing."

"Proud of you." He doesn't try the handle—bless him. "Yell if you need a witness. Or a hug. Or a witness to a hug."

The corner of my mouth twitches. "Go be glamorous."

"On it," he says, and his footsteps fade.

I sign and date with the dagger-pen. The signature looks like me, even if the woman who wrote it is two days older than she should be. I fold the will, slide it into a plain envelope, and write **Megan: open if I'm obnoxiously late**. I tuck it on the vanity for exactly three seconds, then think better of it and wedge it under an abalone statue on the hall table, where a vampire's eye will fall first.

Back upstairs, the coin is still on the vanity. Still warm. Still a choice.

I am not brave by accident this time. Not running on adrenaline or because some asshole with a grudge boxed me into a corner. This is me picking the corner, chalking an X on the floor, and stepping onto it on purpose.

I take out my phone and thumb open a new text, a group thread of my mortal and immortal gang because I finally learned.

"Going in. If I make it out, I'll bring something back. If I don't, Richard Fritz says hello and knows where to find me."

If they hate me later for doing this solo, fine. They'll be alive to do the hating.

I add a separate ping to Megan: *"There's an envelope for you under the clam, just in case. Don't get sentimental, just be competent."*

And one to Sara: *"If I don't answer by sunrise, assume the House is cheating and flip the table."*

She might not know what I mean, but Lucian will.

I put the phone face down, palms on the desk, and make myself look at the woman in the mirror again. Bruised. Tired. Mortal. The outsider at the supernatural table who kept playing anyway.

"Cheap insurance," I tell the girl in the glass. "And one ridiculous bet."

I pocket the coin. It's heavier than it was a minute ago. Or maybe I finally feel it.

Downstairs, the house is quiet. Stardust and Ray are murmuring in some other room, a low duet of silk and judgment. The alley door breathes cold when I open it and the lion-head doorstop growls in sympathy, cracked and loyal.

I pull the door shut behind me, the wards purring against my skin like a 'don't-be-foolish' reminder. I pat the envelope-shaped absence in my pocket, the coin-shaped weight in the other, and choose foolish anyway.

I'm done waiting to be dragged under. Time to go where they live.

Time to knock.

Chapter 22

Midnight at the derelict El stop looks like purgatory with graffiti. The tracks are rusted through, the stairwell sagging, the clock frozen at 11:58 like it gave up trying. The only thing moving is me—and the clock in my chest, ticking louder every day Val spends in someone else's ledger.

Stardust's instructions echo in my head: *Put the coin in the turnstile. They'll come for you.*

I take out the brass coin, edges chewed soft by a century of nervous palms. It feels heavier than it did an hour ago. Heavier than I am.

"One way in, one way out," I mutter, sliding it into the rust-frozen slot.

The machinery groans like a grave shifting. A sound builds under my feet—low, grinding, mechanical—and then the floor of the station *peels open.* The cracked tile unzips into an elevator shaft, air rushing up as sharp as a lungful of snow.

Pocket dimension. Wilkin hadn't been exaggerating.

A funicular car waits, black lacquer and brass rails gleaming like someone polished it yesterday. There's no driver, no sound, only the creak of gears hungry for passengers. The door peels open with a hiss like a cigarette dragged too hard.

I climb inside, snatching my token from the slot before the opening seals. My ward hums faintly against my skin, like even *it* doesn't want to be here.

The car jerks, drops. It's not a smooth elevator descent—this is a plunge, like someone cut the cord but physics decided to indulge me. Brick walls blur past the windows until there are no walls at all, just a tunnel of black. I swear I hear roulette wheels in the dark, or maybe it's my pulse.

When it levels out, I step into velvet. Not the suggestion of velvet—*velvet everywhere.* Crimson draped from thirty-foot ceilings in heavy pleated folds, crushed into carpets so thick my shoes sink half an inch with each step, swallowing the sound whole like a confessional booth. The air tastes of cigar smoke and old pennies, every inhale coating my lungs with something heavier than oxygen. Before me, through gilt-edged archways as tall as brownstones, the windows to the House's casino stretch open.

Clockwork croupiers click across mahogany tables, hands assembled from polished brass gears and yellowed finger bones, faces cast in featureless porcelain that catches the light at all the wrong angles. Cards whisper across green felt, leaving phosphorescent trails. Dice roll themselves, obedient to gears no one winds. The wallpaper crawls with microscopic writing: thousands of contracts stitched so close together they become a damask pattern, clauses fading in and out like the walls themselves are breathing law into the room.

It takes effort not to gape like a tourist.

"First time?" a voice drawls.

He's waiting by the doors: the Pit Boss. I know without asking, because I've watched enough movies. Six and a half feet of suit cut from shadows, charcoal wool so black it absorbs the crimson light around it. His tie is the precise color of a scab three days old, knotted in a perfect Windsor. The hollows where his eyes should be don't blink—they absorb, like twin singularities carved into a skull of polished bone-china. He doesn't walk so much as *loom,* the kind of presence casinos cultivate so losers know when to fold. If that weren't enough, the rest of him confirms I'm not in Vegas: his shadow spills the wrong way, his tie drifts as though underwater, and when he smiles, his teeth aren't white—they're yellowed ivory rectangles, filed to perfect uniformity, like piano keys harvested from something ancient.

I hold up Stardust's coin. The brass glints like it's proud of itself.

"I'm here on a marker," I say, voice steadier than I feel.

The Pit Boss studies it, then me. His jaw works as if the machinery underneath needs oil. "That token hasn't hit the floor in a century."

"Guess you should have picked a better century," I shoot back, because sarcasm is the only thing between me and the urge to crawl back up that elevator shaft by hand.

For a moment, nothing moves—not him, not me, not the gear-driven world behind him. Then he smiles. It's not pleasant. It's the smile of a man who knows exactly how much you can lose and already has the chips counted.

"Very well, Ms. Lane," he says, voice like velvet cut on glass. "The House honors its bets. Enter and be welcome."

The doors to the casino peel open. Smoke, music, the soft chaos of fortune—all of it spills toward me, daring me to step inside.

I think of Val. Of Sara bleeding a month just so I could stand here. Of my career ground to ash by a single motion the House didn't even bother to sign.

I take a breath, set my shoulders, and cross the threshold.

We move across the mosaic floor, each hexagonal tile clicking under my shoes like the ticking of a hundred tiny clocks. At every table I pass, chips clatter and cards shuffle, voices hushed as if accusing me of trespass. Along the walls, every contract embroidered into the wallpaper emits a low, eager hum as I pass. The clauses ripple like living things, thirsty for my signature. They each have names—thousands of them—written in ink that never fades. I catch one: "Margaret Halvorsen." Then another: "Thomas Liu." Each signature pressed into perpetuity, each a promise as permanent as stone.

Perpetuity. The word burns.

I keep moving, ears tuned to what slips through the smoke. At roulette wheels, clusters of gaunt ghouls and writhing shadows mutter about "our man Fulton" and "the election guaranteed." Snatches of the campaign trail spliced with talk of ledgers, clauses, and what happens once Chicago belongs to them not just in shadow, but in City Hall. Every whisper clinks like a chained skull.

The Pit Boss stops us before a pair of double doors: black oak, brass inlays in the shape of spades, catching the chandelier glow like warning lights. His bone-pale hand presses the seam. The spades turn, listening.

"You are not here to drink," he says, voice low and rasping. "You are not here to play."

"Correct," I say. My voice doesn't shake. "I'm here to bargain."

"Incorrect," he replies. "The House does not bargain."

My pulse stammers. It was worth a shot. "Then I'll play."

The doors open.

The corridor beyond is a fever dream of geometry. The Archive, but worse: hallways that circle back into themselves, staircases that bend sideways then straighten, rooms opening into places that shouldn't exist. A labyrinth with rules I'm not supposed to understand.

A door breathes open and paper flies out like a hurricane. Sheets swirl around me—yellowed maps of precincts, steel-engraved blueprints of ballot boxes, campaign schedules stamped "Brian Fulton" in pristine ink. I catch contracts and clauses, the compliance paperwork Wallace signed to launder Fulton's candidacy. At the center, a spread of documents too fresh for parchment. *Compliance certificates. PAC disclosures. Solstice Educational Fund filings.*

Fulton's name repeated, decade after decade, century after century. His candidacy isn't just a vanity project. It's *airtight paperwork,* filed and blessed by the same man who suspended my license yesterday.

His *human* legitimacy in paper form.

The House doesn't just own shadows and contracts. They own *legitimacy.* They use human law to launder monsters into mayors, just like they used it to erase me.

Then the papers shift. For a dizzying heartbeat, the clauses ripple and re-form, letters bleeding into new shapes—my own name stitched into the pattern. *Emily Lane,* printed crisp in a font I've seen on subpoenas, already fading at the edges like someone half-erased it. Beneath it: disbarred, insolvent, deceased. The clauses hum, eager to make it permanent if I so much as blink.

This isn't a warning—it's a demonstration. Look too closely and you'll see how fragile your own name is. Step wrong and they'll file you out of existence the way they're filing Fulton into office.

But I've already drafted my will. Paper can't scare me. Instead, the puzzle pieces start to stray together.

Daylight camouflage, Lucian called it. Tied up with a bow in the form of the photo of their ownership still in my cell phone memory.

The Pit Boss watches me, impossibly smug even in his mask of indifference.

My gaze tears from the papers, from the contracts bled into the wall like festering wounds, and I let the silent gears in my mind whirr.

"Where is she?" I ask. "Valerie Little. You escrowed her under Victor. I want her back."

He reveals that ivory grin. "You want a great many things."

"And your wallpaper wants privacy," I shoot back. "Let's make this easier. Consideration for consideration. Let me sit at one of your tables. I'll stake something you want. You put her life and his contract in the pot."

He straightens, the air freezing solid. "You propose a gamble."

"I propose to make your machine do what it was built for. Adjudicate risk."

He chuckles, low and hollow. "We do not wager flesh."

"You do it every January," I snap. "You just prefer to call it tradition." It gives me no comfort to throw Wallace's words back at his underlings.

For a heartbeat, the world stills. Then he inclines his head with skeletal grace. "Very well. One game."

My mouth is dry. He thinks he can beat me at anything he picks. He's probably right. So, I don't let him pick.

"Not dice," I say, before he can gesture.

A thin lift of brows. "Poker, then. The elegant democracy of chance."

"No," I say. "Poker's too polite."

"Baccarat. It flatters the refined."

I shake my head. "I wasn't invited to be refined."

"What, then?" he asks, and for the first time there's the faintest curl of something like amusement in his carved-ivory smile.

"Spite and Malice."

His face doesn't move, but the chandeliers do. A shimmer runs through the lights like someone pulled a harp string over the ceiling. The Pit Boss blinks once.

"A children's game," he says. The House feeds on grandeur, on roulette wheels spinning like galaxies. To be forced into something small, mean and mortal—that's a wound to his pride.

"A patience game," I correct. "Stock piles. Building piles. Discards you can weaponize. You block me; I block you. First to empty their stock wins. Tell me this isn't your whole personality."

He leans back, folding his hands like origami gone sinister. "You choose a game named for rancor and ill will."

"I'm a lawyer in a haunted casino," I say. "Lean into the theme."

His hollow eyes fix on mine. "What do you stake?"

This is where he expects me to fold. To panic. To blurt something stupid: my memories, my license in perpetuity, my consent to be erased if I lose. He expects the desperate human with the trembling hands, begging to walk out intact.

I lean forward instead. Calm. Steady. Like I'm dictating terms in a deposition.

"I stake myself," I say.

The words land like glass shattering on marble. The wallpaper clauses ripple, listening hard. The crowd hushes the way juries do when the cross-examination cuts too close.

His teeth click once, a sharp ivory percussion. "You would indenture yourself?"

"No." My voice sharpens. The token in my grasp grounds me, my door, my backstop, my bluff. "I'd *write* myself. On my terms. No substitutions, no redrafting in the margins. I win, and Valerie Little walks free, and Victor's contract—renegotiated, fair time, no tricks. I lose..."

I let the silence hold. Let him imagine the paper version of me, penned and filed, a name he could cradle forever. My throat is dry, but my hand doesn't shake when I set it flat on the green felt.

"I lose, and you get me. In ink. In perpetuity. Clean. Legal. Yours. Your boss, Brad Wallace, seemed interested in the opportunity earlier."

The Pit Boss tilts his head, expressionless, but the flicker ripples through the room—like blood in the water. They like this. They like me making myself into a clause. *They* don't know it's a bluff. *They* don't know I'm already holding an exit in my pocket.

"You gamble your soul," he murmurs.

"No," I say, steady. "I gamble my *name*. And you of all people should know which is more valuable."

He weighs it or threatens to. I flick my gaze down to Stardust's marker. I still have my door and he knows it.

Then: a bone-pale hand gestures, and the corridor peels into a salon that shouldn't fit where it is. A small table waits in the middle—a parlor piece in clawed feet and too much shine—already set with a double deck. The backs are printed with spades and tiny mechanical hearts; the edges gleam like someone sharpened them. Two chairs face each other in an elegant threat. Around us, the walls swell with observing shadows. Word has moved faster than the chandeliers.

"Sit," the Pit Boss says.

"Where's your stake?" I ask, sliding into the far chair and not letting my eyes track the crowd. If I look at them, I'll see things I'll have to dream about later.

"Bring her out," I continue, because Armand and Aoife gave me the idea. "Put her and the contract on the table."

The Pit Boss looks at me for another second. They can't know my angle: get Valerie in my sights, hand her the coin, and let the chips fall where they may.

He signals again, and a croupier reassembles from geometry with a small glass case in his hands.

It isn't a case. It's a stasis box—a portable ledger page made solid. Sigils feather the edges, light pooling and folding over them like silk. Inside, curled small is Val.

It's horrifying. There's no other description.

Everything in me that can shake does. I stand without knowing I've stood, my chair flailing to the ground. No one flinches. Gravity feels optional in here.

The Pit Boss somehow manages to smirk. "Ready?"

My chair is back on its feet, and I slip into it. It isn't what I planned, but lawyers always have to be ready for surprises. If I can't get Val out with the coin, I'll get her out with cards. There's no other choice now.

"Let's play," I answer.

Poker's never been my game. But spite? That's practically my bar specialty.

CHAPTER 23

The croupier assigned to this room isn't brass and porcelain. He's a man, or something similar to one, in shirtsleeves whose cuffs never wrinkle and whose hair never moves. His skin is a smooth red-brown ochre color, and his pinkish white hair is slicked back with precision. He shuffles like a magician who knows you won't catch him even if you watch his hands. Cards whisper, the deck cutting itself under his palms.

"House plays first," the Pit Boss says.

"Of course it does," I murmur, because it always has.

The croupier deals: two thirty-card stock piles built face down, each topped with one face up to start; five cards into my hand, five into his. In the center, four blank spaces—foundation piles waiting to be born, the building piles we'll nurse from A up to Q. Kings wild. Four discard lanes for each of us, where strategy turns spiteful in a hurry.

He drags the top of his stock into view: a jack staring up, pretty and useless until ten shows. I glance at mine: a two, the little workhorse card every Spite and Malice player prays for. A mean, tiny miracle blooms behind my tongue.

The croupier's hands pause, hover, as if the room needs to take its pulse again. More onlookers push into the periphery, coalescing like fog against glass. A woman with a beaded dress that drinks light. A man whose pupils are wolf-slit and who never blinks. Two figures in civic-maintenance vests (my ghouls? no; cousins) who smell like turned soil even through the smoke. Every eye is a vector. Every vector is a rumor.

"Name your terms for victory," the Pit Boss says, even though we both know them.

"First to clear their stock," I say, keeping my gaze on his face and not on that useless jack.

"And the stake?" he prompts, as if we didn't just chisel it in the air.

I won't let me eyes fall to the box, but I can still see it through my periphery. "If I win," I repeat clearly, "you release Valerie Little, whole and unencumbered, into my custody and renegotiate Victor's contract. If you win, you get my name."

A ripple touches the crowd. The Pit Boss steeples his hands like origami folding into a blade. He gestures to the croupier.

"Begin."

I don't touch my hand. Not yet. I set my palm on my stock instead, feeling the press of the two against my skin as if it has a pulse.

Breathe. Open lanes. Make him choke. You're not leaving here without that girl.

He draws first blood, because House. A five, an ace, a wild king. "A," he says, and the croupier drops the first foundation pile, letter embossed in pale gold. He slides a two on top and discards a jack like a warning.

"Cute," I say, tapping my own stock. A two waits there like a tiny miracle. "Two." The pile hums when I touch it. Even the walls purrs, contracts liking order the way sharks like blood. I follow with a three, then park a queen deep in my lane as insurance. One more card down the middle, a dare.

"Blocking already," the Pit Boss drawls.

"Building is blocking," I say. "Ask any city council."

His smile is thin and old. He plays ugly and efficient—discards that answer my discards, a king slipped onto the foundation to leap numbers, burning a wild to steal tempo. He sits back when he has to, patience weaponized. It's not a poker face, but a courthouse facade. A man could fall asleep inside it and never wake up.

On the second round, I burn a discard pile with a king, forced patience calcifying into strategy. On the third, the Pit Boss blocks me with a ten that claps down like a book closing.

"Delaying," I say.

"Adjudicating," he answers, and it's a thin-lipped smile of a word.

The room leans closer. The whisper-stream shifts tones: "Fulton" again, "compliance," "Wallace," "ARDC," "injunction"—little flecks of my day thrown back at me from a mouth I haven't seen yet. They think I'll blink.

I don't.

"Three," I say, laying center. "Four." The croupier's hands move faster now, skeletons dancing. I peel the top of my stock and—bless it—a five shows. "And five."

The pile hums like a happy transformer. Somewhere behind me a slot machine I never saw stutters out a string of bells, the casino's version of polite golf clapping.

The Pit Boss puts down a wild king with too much grace, force-feeding his own pile past my block. He discards an ace I can't use yet, face up, daring me to overbuild.

"Tell me something," I say, mouth dry, eyes on the flow of his hands. "When you fold a child into a ledger, do you write their name smaller or larger?"

I don't get a flinch. I don't expect one. But the chandelier light over our table dims a fraction, like a cloud crossed a lamp that has never seen the sky.

"We do not," he says, and lets it hang like a picture frame with nothing inside.

A shadow detaches itself from a deeper shadow beyond the croupier's shoulder.

"Ms. Lane," Brad Wallace says, like we have a standing appointment and I'm very late.

The Pit Boss goes still, which is how I know he doesn't like being interrupted. The room tenses the way rooms do before something expensive breaks. Wallace steps into the lamplight as if the light owes him rent.

"Counsel," I say, because if I call him Brad or *Mr. Wallace* I'll spit. "I was just teaching your man about malice."

He takes in the table at a glance and then does the oddly human thing: his jaw tightens. "Spite and Malice," he says, and the S sounds like a cut. "How apt."

"House accepted the terms," I say. I'm not actually sure if the House ever has to accept anything, but I like the way the sentence tastes. "If you're here to scold, take a number."

Wallace doesn't look at me. He looks at the Pit Boss. It's a quiet look, the kind that happens between the person who signs the checks and the person who breaks the kneecaps. The Pit Boss's eyes do not move, but his shoulders tilt an eighth of an inch in a shape I recognize from court: the one bailiffs make when a judge speaks.

"Reset the board," Wallace says. Then he turns back to me and lowers his voice. "The stakes reset with it," he adds, a quiet annulment of the paper I offered. "We won't be finishing your game."

Neither of us stop.

"Afraid to lose?" I ask lightly, slapping a six onto the humming pile and discarding a ten to backstop one of my lanes. My stock's top shows a nine now. God bless cheap miracles.

"Afraid," he says, "that you have already cost us more attention than your lungs can survive. Children are not—" He stops, tongues the word back into a straight line and starts again. "Children attract eyes, Ms. Lane. Eyes attract ruptures in a very useful illusion. We prefer not to rupture."

And there it is—the humane face of self-preservation. It's not that a girl shouldn't live in a ledger. It's that a girl shouldn't be *seen* living in a ledger.

And then it hits me. The name. Valentine Little. A *legacy* name. But the elder Valentine's been dead since 1905, Marcel after her in 1919. I'd seen their records in Danielle's file—the deeds that never transferred, the probate never filed.

The clause in Victor's contract was "estate reclamation through lineage." The House worships precision but writes in nouns, not birthdates.

They hadn't meant to take the kid at all. They'd meant to collect on the grandmother. Same name, wrong century. And the House, so smug in its precision, tripped on its own wording.

For the first time all night, my grin is real. "That's your problem, isn't it?" I say, low enough that only Wallace hears. "You thought you were collecting on an estate. Elder Valentine Little, like a deed, not a person. Instead, you scooped up a fifteen-year-old because your research didn't go deeper. You don't just look like monsters—you look sloppy. And if I walk out of here with that story, your wallpaper peels down to the studs."

His pupils ripple, a flash of oil on water. He doesn't deny it. He's made of moving parts and PR calculus. And that's my in.

I press harder. "You want legitimacy? You don't get it by being the bogeyman in a missing-child headline. You can swallow adults every January and call it tradition, but you snatched the wrong Valentine Little, and now you've got a scandal with teeth."

The crowd stirs, the wolves and pearls and brass, restless. Even the Pit Boss shifts, as if the word *wrong* is a breach in their language. Wallace looks past me, to the hallway we came from, the one that smells like old oaths and new ink. He picks a word and discards it, then picks another. It looks like pain.

"Release the girl," I say, every syllable sharp, my fingers itching to open the stasis box. "Whole, unencumbered, now. Or tomorrow morning every name on those walls reads like an accessory after the fact."

The silence is absolute. Even the dice in the lobby stop rolling.

Wallace holds my gaze too long, too still. Then, finally, he flicks his hand toward the Pit Boss. A dismissal. An order. Both.

"You will take her," Wallace says to me, and the word *will* is gentler than it has any right to be, "and you will leave."

"Leave?" I echo. "Without finishing the game? What will the House *think*?"

"Let it think I'm protecting the floor," he says. "It prefers tidy narratives."

I let the queen drop gently into my discard lane and flatten my palm on my stock. "She walks, and she stays walked," I say. "No reassigning, no delayed considerations, no auxiliary liens filed by an affiliate foundation, no cute redefinitions of 'escrow' that translate to 'kidnapping with paperwork.'"

His mouth tightens again. "Do not lecture me on definitions."

"Then don't make me," I say, and I look deliberately at the crowd, then back to him. "Do you know what this room looks like to a reporter? To a judge? To a cop with a conscience? To Tash Ruiz or Danielle Greene?"

It's not the threat that lands. It's the names, I think—specificity is always scarier than abstract nouns.

He steps closer, lowering the volume so it doesn't carry. "You have made your point," he says. "A point I was, believe it or not, already making. The Covenant allows for many efficiencies. Children were never meant to be one."

I open my mouth to ask the next question—who bent the rules, who exploited the clause, who's on the hook when this goes wrong—and then swallow it, because it doesn't matter while Val is still in their web.

"Open it," I say.

Wallace doesn't hesitate. He slashes a hand and the sigils on the statis box unhook with a little sound like a violin string breaking. The glass that isn't glass becomes not there, and the air rushes in. Val slumps into the world, normal-sized, and falls into my arms. Warm. Breathing. A smear of blood down one cheek where the House's idea of preservation kissed her too close.

"Hey, kid," I whisper, because my mouth is going to do something dumb if I don't make it do anything. "Field trip's over."

The watchers murmur, as if a flock of cloaks remembered they had lungs. The Pit Boss's tie ripples the wrong way again, offended down to his brass.

"You will leave," Wallace repeats, softer.

"I will," I say. I should. I will. But I adjust Val against my shoulder, feel the stubborn, mortal weight of her—the thing they can't ledger—and the anger that has grown layers over the last week snaps into place like a well-cut suit.

"One more round," I say.

"Ms. Lane." The smile threatens to return. Then it dies before it wants to live. "Don't try my patience."

"I'm not." I nod at the walls like they're a jury and my client is the idea of daylight. "I'm still trying your legitimacy."

He stares. The crowd also stares, which is not how crowds usually behave. The Pit Boss doesn't blink, because movement is a liability.

"We finish the game," I say. "If I win, Victor's contract is renegotiated *and* Brian Fulton's candidacy ends tonight. If I lose, I still walk out with Val and my token—but I don't leave a match on your rug on the way. I go quietly and I give you time before I file anything."

The Pit Boss' head tilts, smaller than a nod. "Silence."

"Delay," I correct. After all, I'm on a fourteen-day restraint from using my license anyway. "You get time to tidy your house before the neighbors come knocking." I tip my chin toward the wallpaper. "You seem like tidy people."

"You bargain with air," the Pitt Boss growls.

"You run on air," I say lightly. "Air and paper. Let's not play coy."

"You're not asking," Wallace says.

"Do I look like I'm asking?" I should be gone. I should be sprinting for the funicular with an armful of teenager and a weeks-late prayer. Instead, I'm making Very Bad Career Choices without a career.

"I just watched a man who runs your contracts give me a child because optics scare you more than ethics," I say, and my voice shakes exactly once. "This isn't a request. This is me telling you what keeps your wallpaper intact. I walk out of here with Val. Victor's contract is renegotiated. In the morning, the candidate you've laundered through a century of paper announces he is withdrawing from the race for 'personal reasons.' You let the city keep believing in clean lines. Or I spend the next year of my life turning this place into the ugliest bipartisan scandal it has ever seen."

"You have no favor, no token," the Pit Boss says softly, meaning no other coin. No right. No teeth.

"I have a story with nouns in it," I say without looking at him. "Your man is in a century-old photo with my client in 1927, carbon dated, and yet he's running for mayor with cheekbones that don't understand the concept of time. Your candidate's compliance paperwork flows through a shell 'educational' fund—Solstice—whose counsel just filed my quasi-suspension and a TRO that took my accounts. The fund used to be Equinox, which used to fundraise under the same family of names, and in your private little museum is a letter from 1918 granting 'all rights and dignities of a citizen in perpetuity.' Perpetuity. I know what that word means. I can make a jury understand it, too."

Wallace stares at me. Too long. Then, slowly, he smiles—tight, brittle. "You argue like the bar never touched you."

"Bar's not what makes me dangerous," I shoot back. "Even benched, I still know what a press conference looks like. You think no one will connect your signatures to the filings that bought him a ballot line? That my ARDC record won't read like Exhibit A to a long, *loud* conspiracy? You think the city that forgave a bus fire won't foam at the mouth to eat a vampire mayor alive?"

"Not a vampire," Wallace says automatically, a reflex he can't help, and the way he says it tells me everything and nothing. "He's—"

"Anchor, handshake, perpetual, whatever. He's not who he says he is." My voice stays steady because this is the only thing about me that ever learned how. "Your poster boy is a perennial plant trying to pass as annuals, and your BAR member signature sits under his fertilizer. You like the legitimacy you bought? You like the January arrangement Peterson told me about? Then don't give Chicago a face to hate in daylight."

Silence is a living thing in this room. It moves. It stalks. It bares its pretty white teeth and waits to see which of us flinches first.

Wallace looks at the Pit Boss, and the Pit Boss very deliberately looks at nothing at all.

"Children attract eyes," Wallace repeats, voice low. "But faces attract cameras."

"Exactly." I set my jaw. "I'm revealing it regardless. The question is when. No matter what, the city meets your Covenant the way it always meets new taxes: pitchforks first, explanations later. This gives you a chance to play for a reprieve."

"If you shout in a closed room," he says, "it's still shouting."

"I don't have to shout," I say, letting the queen I'd parked in my far lane click against my thumb. "You've given me the microphones already. ARDC. Injunction. Compliance. Your signature under Solstice. You don't need me to tell the story. You wrote it down."

"You presume you have leverage," he says, but it sounds more rote than real.

"You just admitted you can't afford a scandal," I say. "And the thing about paper?" I look around at the walls and let my lawyer-rage smile. "Paper burns."

The contracts murmur like a bad conscience. The Pit Boss's jaw works: grind, grind. The croupier's hands skate over the deck as if they've been dismissed. Somewhere, roulette hits an edge and doesn't fall in.

Wallace looks at Val. It's the first time he's really looked, not just performed looking. Something flares and dies under the oil of his pupils. He flicks a hand at the Pit Boss—a dismissal, or an order to stand down, it's impossible to tell. The Pit Boss inclines his head by degrees and absorbs the insult like a black hole swallows light.

Then, Wallace steps back, smoothing his suit like he's folding away the panic. "Take the girl," he says at last. "Leave as you came. Quietly. Victor's contract will be reissued on revised terms. No collection this January. We'll negotiate the extension before the next window. And in the morning," he adds, "you will have something to read."

I let out a breath so slowly it's almost a prayer. "Make sure it includes a withdrawal."

He nods, sharp, angry. We stand there a second longer—me with a teenager's weight cutting a groove into my shoulder, him with a thousand years of bad ideas balanced in his jaw—and the Pit Boss with his wrong-shadow and carved-teeth learning how to lose.

"Then the game's over," I say, knocking over my discard pile as I step away from the table. I don't know why I do it. Maybe because I want to touch something that doesn't belong to them and make it mine for half a heartbeat.

Maybe because pettiness is a vitamin.

"Ms. Lane," Wallace says as I turn to go.

I meet his eyes. "Counsel."

"Do not come here again. Your account is not welcome under these terms."

"I didn't come here for the ambiance."

His smile does the thing that means to be amused and fails. "You came because you misunderstand us. We are not monsters with accounts. We are accounts with a monster for a guard dog." A glance at the Pit Boss, almost fond and completely false. "Go before the dog remembers he is hungry."

I shift Val higher—dead weight in the living sense, sweat and blood and breath—and look at the cards for exactly one second. My discard queen is sitting pretty and furious. I palm it as I turn. Souvenirs are a human right—and spite has sentimental value.

The crowd parts like money at a political fundraiser. I walk through it with Val against me and the House watching like a justice system that knows the verdict but can't decide whether it likes it. The wallpaper hums behind me, clauses fluttering like moths.

I don't run. Running is for prey.

We reach the door that isn't a door, the hallway that circles and straightens and kisses its own tail. We reach the oak with brass spades, the velvet lobby, and the funicular that pretends it's gravity. I don't look back.

I step into the car with a living girl and the worst enemy I've ever made and let the elevator lift me toward a city that still thinks law and paper are different things.

CHAPTER 24

Friday at Moonlit Haven usually means chandeliers on dim, citrus smoke in the air, and someone warming up to ruin 'Total Eclipse of the Heart.' Tonight, though, it's invitation only for Stardust and Ray's bonding. Half the crowd is dressed like extras from *Velvet Goldmine* and the other half like they wandered out of a coven council meeting by mistake.

I've claimed my booth early. Not *my* booth—not officially—but close enough. Danielle slides in across from me, badge already tucked away, hair pinned back with the frivolity of someone who doesn't want to think about work tonight. A moment later Megan drops into the seat beside me, slouching like she owns the place. She's technically my plus-one, but that undersells the fact that she practically saved my life yesterday.

"I still don't get it," Danielle says, cutting right in. "Wallace didn't show yesterday? Just—didn't show?"

Megan raises her glass in a mock toast, a vibrant teal that matches her nail polish. "Didn't show. Restraining order pulled, at least for now. Your license is still on the docket, but if opposing counsel can't bother to appear, it's not going anywhere fast."

"And for that," I say, sliding her my untouched water, "you're drinking free for the next decade."

She smirks, wagging her glasses at me. "Make it two."

Danielle doesn't share the smile. "Did Victor text you? He got a letter from the House today," she says flatly. "They want to renegotiate. Soon."

I lean back against the worn leather, forcing my pulse steady. Victor's contract had been reissued before I even made it back above ground—filed neat and clean as if the interruption never happened. I should be dreading it, but I'm looking forward to it. The House doesn't want to deal with me again, not if they can help it, but they have to.

"Good," I tell the table. "I can't wait to stroll back into Wallace's drama office and watch them twitch when I re-mind them what 'perpetuity' actually means."

Her stare could drill holes through oak. "You think this is funny?"

"No," I say, quiet. "I think it's leverage."

That earns me silence, not forgiveness.

I clear my throat. "And Val?"

"She's with her aunt," Danielle says, mustering up a grin. "The paperwork's still... complicated. But she's home. She and Victor are taking things... slow."

I nod, the word settling like a stone. "Home's better than escrow."

Danielle nods, but it still looks defeated.

"It's a long game, remember?" I tell her, and myself. We walked out of that place with the January burn still in place and the knowledge that it will keep coming.

Fulton vanished from the race almost as abruptly as he'd appeared. The morning after my jaunt to the House, a head-line declared him the inevitable next mayor; by afternoon, he was citing "personal reasons" and stepping aside with that screensaver smile. On paper it looked tidy. But I'd seen the scaffolding, and we know what was behind it. As promised, the House dropped him—quick, clean, surgical. But if they could discard their wannabe mayor that easily, it meant only one thing: Fulton had been a pawn, and they were already planning the next move.

"There's got to be an angle we're missing," Danielle mutters, echoing my thought. "Victor, Val, Fulton. They gave in easy."

"Easy?" My laugh scrapes. "It was like being cross-examined by a firing squad."

Megan arches a brow. "But they did give in."

I rub at my temple. "You're right on that count." I'm a good negotiator, but paranormal entities don't just fold. They calculated, and they decided it—and I—weren't worth the mess. I swallow the fizz from my champagne. "Victor's contract reissued, Val home, *and* Fulton out of the race by lunch. That's not charity. That's strategy."

Danielle tilts her head. "Sacrifice the pawn to clear the board."

"Maybe." I glance toward the bar, where Severin polishes glasses like they're weapons. "I don't know what the next move is. But pawns don't walk themselves off the board. The House didn't just... decide to tidy up out of kindness. They bought themselves breathing room, like I promised them."

"And you bought yourself time," Megan reminds me. "You've got ground to stand on while you figure it out."

"Ground is good," I say. "Until it shifts under you."

Sara passes by our table carrying a tray of champagne, doesn't stop, doesn't look at me. Lucian lingers at the bar, back turned, speaking low to Severin. His posture says everything—distance, disapproval, disappointment. Pattern reestablished.

But I don't blame them. And if Ray hadn't found the will and hidden it, it'd be so much worse.

The lights dip, and Stardust takes the stage in a riot of sequins and floodlight. Ray stands beside him, already grinning like a man who can't believe his luck.

The officiant raises her hands, calling for hush, and for once the room obliges. "Bonding is not lightly entered. It is not merely an oath. It is a tether—of joy, of pain, of permanence. Not for mortals. Not for immortals. For both."

Stardust seizes Ray's hands dramatically, cape flaring. "Darling, I've been rehearsing for this longer than Bowie rehearsed Ziggy."

"Not true," Ray mutters, but his ears are pink.

The vows unfold—part solemn, part absurd. Stardust swears to always let Ray pick the playlist in the mornings. Ray promises to stop hiding the good eyeliner on the top shelf. They both vow, with absolute seriousness, to never, ever play Spite and Malice against each other again. The crowd laughs, then cheers, then applauds when the officiant calls the bond sealed.

Magic shivers through the air—real, visible. A thread of silver arcs between them, settling over their shoulders like a mantle. Stardust bows his head as if he won an Oscar; Ray wipes at his cheeks with zero shame.

"Champagne," Severin grumbles, materializing beside our booth with a tray. He sets flutes in front of each of us, and a piece of plastic in front of me with particular finality.

"This goes on the back of the booth," he says.

I flip it over to see one of those placards that goes beside office doors, with 'Office of E. Lane' inscribed on it. My mouth pops open and I look back at Severin, sputtering.

"Lucian and Sara suggested it," he says, smoothing his cuff.

That restarts my brain. "*Recently*?"

"Wednesday."

Before my license hearing and after I did my self-sacrificial thing that I thought might ruin what I'd made of those friendships.

"I... I can't—" The words get stuck. "Thank you," I finally manage. "Does this mean I can put flyers in your window?"

His mouth twitches. "Don't push your luck."

Megan helps me center it on the wooden frame above the vinyl and stick it on with the attached tape. When I turn back towards the bar, Sara's got a hidden smile on her face, standing beside Lucian, who has his drink up in a toast. Not a cryptic one this time. One I think I understand.

I raise the glass in return. For Val, safe. For Victor, still breathing. For Fulton, gone from the race but not from the ledger. For my license, still in limbo.

But mostly—for this. For Ray crying openly while Stardust basks. For Megan laughing at Severin's glare. For Danielle staying, even mad. For Lucian, and Sara, and Matty. For the stubborn fact of chosen family, loud and fragile and alive.

For tonight, I let myself believe it's enough.

AUTHOR'S NOTE

Thank you for reading GHOULS AND GAMBITS, book 3 in my Emily Lane Paranormal Mysteries series.

If you're interested in more of my writing, check out my website (**kmalady.com**). You can find other fun information there about my other projects, like *The Ascend Trials* (a romantic YA portal fantasy all about subverting tropes), *Threads of Fate* (an NA romantic fantasy series adapted from greek myths), and more!

EMILY LANE WILL RETURN